D0383505

THE ICE BENEATH YOU

A NOVEL

Christian Bauman

SCRIBNER PAPERBACK FICTION
PUBLISHED BY SIMON & SCHUSTER
New York London Toronto Sydney Singapore

SCRIBNER PAPERBACK FICTION
Simon & Schuster, Inc.
Rockefeller Center
1230 Avenue of the Americas
New York, NY 10020

SCRIBNER PAPERBACK FICTION and design are trademarks of
Macmillan Library Reference USA, Inc., used under license by
Simon & Schuster, the publisher of this work.

For information regarding special discounts for bulk purchases,
please contact Simon & Schuster Special Sales at 1-800-456-6798 or
business@simonandschuster.com

Designed by Kyoko Watanabe

Manufactured in the United States of America

1 3 5 7 9 10 8 6 4 2

Library of Congress Cataloging-in-Publication Data
Bauman, Christian.
The ice beneath you : a novel / Christian Bauman.
p. cm.
1. Ameriacans—Somalia—Fiction. 2. Young men—Fiction.
3. Soldiers—Fiction. 4. Somalia—Fiction. I. Title.

PS3602.A96 I26 2002
813'.6—dc21   2002066837

ISBN 0-7432-2784-0

*This book is for
Nicholas DiGiovanni,
and Jon Colcord.*

And, for BLM.

CONTENTS

When the ice gives in beneath you
it changes how you dream.

—John Gorka
"Temporary Road"

PROLOGUE

Somalia—March 1993

More than two hundred miles south of Mogadishu—where children still have parents, where villages struggle to remain villages—a soldier sits on a rock. A modern soldier, a foreign soldier. Water laps gently around the rock, the tiny beach behind a scrabble of pebbles and coarse sand, wooden sailboats pulled up on it, resting above the tidemark. From the village that fronts the beach come sounds of confusion, people rushing around in the dark night; a woman crying, a man arguing with another man, none of this heard by the young soldier.

His knees bent, boots pushed into the stone, he sits and doesn't hear the world around him. Numb, yes, but actually deaf, too—sound just beginning to return to his ears in tiny, meaningless pings that are disorienting and make him feel dizzy. Best to just sit here until it passes.

He is white but very tan, small for a soldier. Three days without a shave—what would be a full beard on some is still just stubble on him, rough but sparse, and in the dark almost invisible. His uniform—his grandfather would have called them utilities, now BDUs—is the desert pattern the world got to know so well from watching CNN during the Gulf War. But this isn't the Gulf War, and the cameras of CNN are nowhere near this beach. Tans and browns, the uniform—although his ammo suspenders and his jungle boots are greens and blacks, like they would wear in the States, because there wasn't time before they left, no time to complete the uniform.

There is a brown T-shirt under his BDU top, and under that his dog tags; B-positive blood only, please—no religious preference, thanks. His dog tags hang on a chain that rests on bandages wrapped over his shoulders and neck. It was December when they got here, months ago, and in a rush to embrace the sun and shake off the cold of home they'd all taken their shirts off while they worked, and this soldier had gone swimming in the salt water after, ripping the dead skin off, then more time in the sun. Burns so bad he was told the scars would always be there. The doctor, a major, had slapped him on the lower back, laughing, *Ya got your war wounds, boy! I'll pin the Purple Heart to your ass!*

The soldier sits.

From his chest pocket, without looking, he pulls a cigarette and a Zippo, plants the smoke in the side of his mouth, flips the lid on the Zippo and lights it. He thinks idly he shouldn't be lighting a cigarette out in the open at night—light conservation and night vision and all those things he was trained to pay attention to. But, then, he shouldn't be sitting on a rock out in the open, his back to everything that could be wrong in the world, sitting like a target.

He doesn't feel like a target. He doesn't feel much of anything at all.

He draws in on the cigarette, holds it, breathes out. The smoke shoots in a stream from his mouth, out from his perch on the rock, over the water, gone into the dark.

The dark is where tonight's confusion came from. Sleep won't protect you from the dark, he'd learned. Eyes pop open, heart thumps once in chest, rifle stock to cheek—*too quick, too quick*. He doesn't really remember; memory must have been blasted out of his head with his hearing, he thinks. Just a flash of a face looking at him through a window—then gone. Too quick.

In the distance comes the sound of a helicopter, and this the soldier does hear. *That'll be the lieutenant,* he thinks to himself. He looks at his watch, glowing green in the dark. *Right on time.*

From the village behind him he hears someone call his name—faint, but there it is. They're calling for him, and for Trevor Alphabet, too. Trevor disappeared an hour ago. Just dropped his rifle and walked into the brush, straight and steady, as if he had somewhere to go. Just dropped his rifle. This soldier went to follow him, but all he found was this rock on the water's edge.

He doesn't turn around, he waits for them to call his name again. He knows they will.

But now his ears are open, and he can hear the confusion in the night. He looks out at the water, stars reflecting off the surface, and listens carefully to the wash of noise behind him, trying to untangle the sounds from the web of confusion into single, coherent strands. Everything sounds like an echo of itself, echo on echo on echo. He imagines this will pass, that his hearing will return to normal—but you can't expose your ears to such a loud noise in such a small place and expect to walk away unscathed. He knows that. It's okay.

Since he can't do anything but wait it out, he figures he will wait it out right here. On this rock. It's a nice rock, and it's a nice night, anyway. Warm breeze pushing gently on his face, the water lapping up toward his boots, cigarette smoke thick and soothing to him. He can wait here, wait for his ears to clear, while someone higher ranking than him deals with the confusion in the village. The villagers seem to have lost something, and the soldier thinks he might know where it is. It's almost close enough to touch, but like his hearing the knowledge is elusive, slippery. It will come, though, he thinks. And when it does I'll get off this rock and go tell them.

He flicks the butt of his smoke into the water, and as the red glow sizzles to black the knowledge comes to him, sudden and full, like a rude smack from a wave. His face goes white, his muscles limp, sliding off the rock into the water, and as his boots slam into the sand he says out loud, *oh God,* his voice leaving him in a startled gasp. He raises his head, yelling the name of his friend, Trevor, then turns and runs to the village, leaving the water and the stars behind.

PART ONE

PART ONE

The Ride West, *Part One*

Ohio—Early April 1993

Payphone, he's got a few minutes before the bus pulls out.

Two in the morning, sodium-arc lights turning the remnants of old black snow into yellow piles around the sides of the parking lot. Behind lines of Airstreams and idling semis the moon is trying to crawl its bloated self out of a frozen cornfield. Upturned collars and hands shoved deep in pockets for the rushed, half-sleeping walk from truckstop diner back to the Greyhound. The phone rings in Jones's ear, shivering cold plastic against his skin. Trevor Alphabet answers, from a barracks phone in Virginia. The army never sleeps.

"Where are you?" Trevor asks.

When the 710th shut down in Kismaayo—their southern Somalia home—Trevor went with the boats back to Kenya and Jones went with the lieutenant to Mogadishu. Trevor was supposed to get home to the States first, but it hadn't turned out that way. Jones beat him by almost three weeks, on a priority medical flight.

They were going to travel together, when they got home, got out of the army. That's what they'd said. That's why Jones was calling. That, and Trevor was his only way of getting in touch with Liz. That, and Jones was so lonely he didn't know what to do with himself.

"I'm in Ohio, on a bus," he said.

"On a bus?"

"In a parking lot. It's cold."

"What the fuck are you doing in Ohio?"

"Gone fishing."

"What?"

"I was gonna run off and be a rock star—you know." Jones laughs, nervous, a cloud of frozen breath escaping his lungs. "Changed my mind. I liked your idea better. So now I'm going fishing. Seattle, I think. You joining me?"

Silence from Trevor's end.

Then, "Jones, I reenlisted."

Silence from Jones's end.

"Did you hear me?"

"Yeah, I heard you."

"They offered me hard stripes."

Jones can picture Trevor's face as he hears this, how his friend looks when he makes a decision and then goes with it, as if there had never been any alternative course of action. Trevor's Polish eyebrows would set after a decision, just like they would set with a rifle sight to his cheek—sure and steady and confident.

"Good," Jones says. "There it is. Good."

Jones worries that the phone is going to spot-freeze to his cheek. His left foot is twitching, unnoticed. Hard stripes—good. Good.

"Jones—"

"Yeah?"

"Nothing."

"Yeah."

Silence.

Then, Jones: "Where's Liz? Where's my girl?"

"Still in Mogadishu. Until August. Maybe July. They held her back, said they needed her in the Harbormaster's office. She said she'd send you a letter."

Still in Mogadishu. This was news to Jones. He pressed his forehead against the cold glass of the phone booth, eyes closing by reflex, staring into depths of emptiness.

"I gotta go, man," he whispered into the phone.

"Jones, I—"

"I know, Trev. I know."

2

Two hours later the driver pulls the bus to the side of the Ohio Turnpike. Four in the morning, so cold outside, so cold, old black snow on the ground—isn't even winter anymore and that snow doesn't know to go away. The driver pulls the Greyhound to the side of the turnpike and opens the door, wind rushing in, Jones's body shakes, waking up, wondering *Where the hell did the heat go?*

The driver opens the door and three big men, all denim and flannel and boots, pull a little brown man by the collar, lifting him right out of his seat, legs kicking in surprise. They take him out the door to the side of the turnpike and beat the living shit out of him. It takes less than a minute. They go around and around with him, his face is such a mess. He's not making much noise, only a high-pitch almost-wail. Jones's face pressed sideways against the tinted glass of the bus window, so cold, he's sure he's still sleeping, his eyes open watching this right beneath him. They ditch the man head and chest forward into that old black snow, one guy driving his boot into the little man's side, a final good-bye, and they all get back on the bus, the driver closes the door, then pulls away.

3

The little brown man was Pakistani, Jones was pretty sure of that. There was a Pakistani infantry company in Somalia, living in a row of khaki tents in the far southern corner of the Mogadishu seaport—they'd been a friendly group, trading little tin plates of hot curried mutton for dog-eared copies of *Penthouse* and *Hustler*.

When Jones first got on the Greyhound, the day before, he'd been sitting forward in the bus, where the brown man would finally end up, next to a skinny, sickly woman who had three kids scattered around the bus, two boys and a girl. Her old man had put her and the kids on the Greyhound in Allentown; he'd meet up with them at her mom's house in Laramie sometime later in the year. Jones thought she was okay, a little slow, but she was putting a good face on things. The fella sitting across the aisle from them had brought on a case of warm Bud somehow stuffed in his overcoat, they'd been drinking it and offered her one. She said no, but later when her kids were sleeping she drank a few, and talked about her mom and her husband and her boys and her little girl and how much her little girl looked like her sister who had died in a car accident five years ago. She was putting a good face on things, and got a little silly with the beer in her, but it was good to finally see her smile. With the beer and the strangers and her responsibilities for the kids suspended as they slept, she smiled, big and wide, and it made Jones smile.

She woke up—she said this later—and thought she saw this guy, the one Jones thought was probably from Pakistan, put his hand on one of her boy's knees or thigh or something. Jones could imagine her, could see her in his head, waking up contorted like you do on a Greyhound, looking around half asleep through eyes that didn't see much better than Jones's had, pressed against the dark glass, but there was no glass, she was just looking around. She said he'd had his hand there, and she'd seen his hand move up and down and she screamed and it woke up these denim-and-flannel gentlemen sitting all around, half drunk, beat and tired and going home or going away but going somewhere they probably would rather not be—going where someone had said there might be a job or money, or promised something, Christ there must be *something* good, why the hell else would you be on a goddamn Greyhound bus in the ass end of winter—woke them up with her scared screaming, and the little brown man sitting there. They took him outside and they hurt him pretty bad. Jones sat and watched, his hands white-knuckled around the armrest, unable to move, unable to lift himself from his seat and help the poor son of a bitch getting the snot kicked out of him. *Buddy,* he thought desperately in his direction, through the cold, dark window, forcing his thoughts to him through the glass, *Buddy I'm with you, I'm here, hold on man, I'm here . . .*

But it's bullshit, and Jones knows it. He wasn't with him at all.

He couldn't get out of his seat.

4

Wayne is the name of the kid sitting behind Jones on the Greyhound, and he didn't wake up during this, same with the girl Jan, both directly behind

Jones, in the last seat. Slept through it, their arms around each other—found love. Craig, twenty with a cowboy hat and a world of annoying questions, sitting next to Jones, woke up and saw it but for once didn't say a thing. He watched over Jones's shoulder, pale and maybe scared, then just quiet and watchful as the men got back on the bus and took their seats. Later, twenty minutes later, back on the highway, the diesel low and pulsing under the floorboard, he chewed his gum and said, "Well, if I'da been up there I'd have done the same, y'know, that's *ALL* fucked up, fucking dot-head pervert, I'd have fucked him up good, too, I'd have *stomped* him."

Jones wants to slam him in the face with his open palm—what Trevor Alphabet would call a bitch slap—that's what he deserves. *But I don't have the right,* he thinks. *I don't have the right. I gave up all rights when I couldn't bring myself to get out of my seat and help that poor man on the side of the road.*

Jones looks at Craig quickly, without a word, then hurries into the little bathroom in the back of the bus, barely getting the door closed before he vomits into the blue sterile water in the steel bowl. He lights a cigarette and doesn't come out until the pack is gone. When he finally opens the door the sun is coming through the tinted windows and they were somewhere in Indiana.

JONES: One Sergeant

Ft. Knox, Kentucky—Winter 1991

1

I quit my job the day the Hundred Hour War started.

I remember sitting in the Holiday Inn's break room, in cook's whites and Timberlands, nursing my coffee, transfixed by what was happening on the TV screen in front of me.

The head chef walked in, walked back out, then walked back in. He looked at me, twisting the ends of his mustache. He said, "Jones, if you're not back at the salad station in one minute you can kiss your employment good-bye." Then he walked back out again.

I remember sitting there, still watching CNN. When a commercial finally came on I stood, lit a cigarette, dug my keys from my pocket, and went home.

I spent the next three days on the couch, not moving, just watching the live feeds from the Persian Gulf, watching it all unfold in front of me.

I enlisted three months later, about the time they started sending the troops home. The recruiter said my scores were high and I could pretty much have any job I wanted. When the options came across the computer screen he tapped his finger on the third one down. "Boats," he said. "Army's got boats. I seen 'em down in Virginia. Take that one. Slack life." I did, and he said I wouldn't regret it. He also said I wouldn't ship until October or November. I said that was unfortunate, but fine. I borrowed his pen and without looking up signed the contract for U.S. Army, E-1, 88L10, Waterborne. Private Benjamin F. Jones. I sat back, waiting to feel different, waiting to feel something. Nothing came. That was fine, too. I shook the recruiter's sweaty hand and walked home.

I didn't see the need to get another job to fill the intervening months. My three memories of that summer are the unchanging look of disgust on my wife's face, the unchanging scenes of smoke and destruction broadcast from Iraq, and the unchanging, nagging feeling that I was missing out on something. Something important, something necessary.

I turned twenty-one, and got two cards in the mail: one from my mother, instructing me to trust in Jesus, and one from my recruiter, instructing me to start doing push-ups.

I drank a lot of coffee, and took our baby Emma to the park every day, pushing her on the swings, smiling as she squealed. I watched CNN, Emma crawling around my feet, my eyes glued to the TV. I opened envelopes from collection agencies, read the letters carefully, then tore them up and stuffed them in the bottom of the garbage bag so my wife Katy wouldn't see them when she got home from work. Occasionally I fielded a call from a friend. Our friends were in college now, juniors and seniors most of them. They would sometimes call with invitations to this party or that, but we could never go and the phone calls stopped coming.

As the air turned colder I began running. It was hard; I was a heavy smoker. But I ran every day, farther and farther each day. Slow but relentless, coughing and wheezing my way through the New Jersey rain.

One Friday night I drove to my mother's house. She wasn't home. I left my Yamaha acoustic guitar in her basement, my record collection, and a box of my notebooks. The next morning the recruiter came to the door. He had a big, Southern smile on his face.

"You moving and motivated, Private Jones?"

"Moving and motivated," I mumbled, grabbing my shaving kit, closing the door tight behind me.

2

Drill Sergeant Rose. Sergeant First Class Daniel Rose. Senior drill sergeant of our basic-training platoon.

Forget any jokes about a drill sergeant named for a flower—after the first twenty-four hours with him the thought never again crossed our minds.

There were five other drills under Rose in 2nd Platoon, Delta Company, and they all looked how a drill sergeant should look: scary, tough, built like tanks. Most tankers are indeed built like tanks, and since this was Ft. Knox most of the drills were tankers, not grunts like Rose.

Rose looked like none of them.

Drill Sergeant Rose stood at a slight five foot seven inches. Not a steroid-looking boy like the tankers, just a lean and strong grunt. He wore his hair in an extreme high-and-tight, like the recruits. His choice of footwear was green jungle boot, even in the winter mud of Kentucky. His skin was olive, with no tattoos. And his eyes—arctic blue, hard, dismissing you through round steel frames.

In the whipping winter wind of 5 A.M., first formation of the day, shivering so hard your muscles turn to rock from the strength of the vibration, praying that today the drills would let us wear the geeky but oh-so-warm army winter face mask, Rose would stand at the front of formation in not even a field jacket. Not once in eight weeks did I see the man wear his coat, or a pair of gloves. He was impervious. Army regs wouldn't let him force us to strip down to this, but his face—his *eyes*—let us know what he thought of soldiers who needed to bundle up so, soldiers who obviously shivered, soldiers who *allowed* themselves to feel the cold.

Enlisted don't salute enlisted. Even in basic training, the army doesn't play pretend like the Marines do, spending eight weeks calling the drill "sir" and treating him like an officer. In the army, it's real-deal from day one, something you learn on the first day when some slob, thinking he's got it going on, calls a drill "sir."

"*Sir?*"

"Sir! Yes, sir!"

"What did you fucking call me?"

"Sir! Sir."

"You *worthless* fucking piece of—" Etc.

The proper form of address is "Drill Sergeant," they don't get saluted—they work for a living—God help the man who forgets.

Except in formation.

In formation, a whole different protocol takes effect. In that case, the squad leaders (those on the end of a line) *do* salute whoever is in front of the formation, officer or enlisted, as they report the whereabouts of their squad members.

"Squad One, present and accounted for," the only acceptable report—where else would anyone be?—a sharp salute, returned crisply by Rose.

And here is the only place, the only place I can remember, when Rose would truly break with his ironclad reading of regs and follow his own rules. Because Rose couldn't stand a man who would salute with gloves on. Doesn't matter the regs don't have a problem with this, doesn't matter the regs actually order you to put some gloves on when the temperature drops below zero, and continue using your hands just like you would without gloves.

Rose had decided he would let us wear the gloves, if that's what had to happen, but he'd be goddamned if you'd salute him while wearing them. Problem is, in formation—the only time you would ever salute a drill sergeant—everyone has to be dressed exactly the same way. *Exactly.* This little problem took us a few days to figure out. Like most problems, Rose made you figure it out on your own, suffering the consequences when you got it wrong, safe in the knowledge of success not from praise but simply the absence of an ass-kicking.

Day One: The squad leaders make their report, saluting with gloves on. The whole platoon, except them, gets dropped for push-ups and leg-lifts to encourage them never to do this again. The logic here is if the entire platoon but you is punished for your error you're not likely to make that error again.

Day Two: The squad leaders make their report, saluting with gloves off. The whole platoon, except them, gets dropped for push-ups and leg-lifts because of the obvious problem that the squad leaders were out-of-uniform for having no gloves when everyone else did.

Day Three: The squad leaders make their report, saluting with gloves off, because no one in the platoon is wearing gloves, ergo no one is out-of-uniform. This time, the squad leaders get dropped for push-ups and leg-lifts while we watch because it turns out that *everyone* is out-of-uniform: regs require a platoon to wear gloves when the weather is below freezing.

Day Four and every day after: The platoon forms up with gloves on. As the squad leaders prepare to make their reports, the entire platoon removes their gloves, shoving them in their pockets. The squad leaders report, salute, and then the entire platoon puts their gloves back on.

No problem.

"About fucking time, Privates. About fucking time."

Basic training with Drill Sergeant Rose was a puzzle, and if you kept your head together, sooner or later you'd figure it out. Rose would lay out the clues; it was up to you to put them together, and in the right order. Our platoon of almost-soldiers, trainees, slugs, none of us ever destined to be infantry like Rose or even tankers like our other drills—we were future combat medics, mostly, plus four Waterborne like me—we learned slowly but surely how to fit the pieces of Rose's puzzles together.

Every drill has their "thing." This is the thing they believe is most important to making a good soldier, the thing they work on hardest. Drill Sergeant Cecil—the only other drill who, like Rose, was a grunt—was a runner. He was tall and skinny and could run for days. So if Cecil was the main drill that day, you could expect to do a lot of running. Likewise, Drill Sergeant Johnson was a bodybuilder. The army doesn't supply weights in boot camp, but if Johnson had the duty that day you could guarantee you'd be spending a lot of time hanging ridiculously from a pull-up bar.

But Rose was the senior drill, so his philosophy pervaded the platoon, even when he wasn't there. And Sergeant Rose did not believe in sleeping.

"Privates," he would say, his voice loud and thick and lower than you would expect from a man of his slim build, "half—*half!*—of the casualties in war come from sleeping. Either some sorry fuck who was sleeping when he shouldn't have been, or a whole goddamn platoon or company wiped out because they were napping when the enemy wasn't. He who sleeps— dies."

We would be standing in the bay for one of these lectures, toeing the line literally, in rows next to our bunks, Rose moving up and down the bay, always the same tone of voice with him: a sneer, a put-down; the man could tell you it was snowing out and have it sound like it was almost certainly your fault—the fact that some soldier had died in France fifty years ago because his buddy fell asleep was probably your fault, too. His BDU shirt would be off for the evening, just a brown T-shirt tucked into his BDU pants. We were the same size almost—I'm sure he wore the same size uniform I did—but where my arms hung loose out of the sleeves of my brown T-shirt, with a lot of room to spare, his arms would be tight against the fabric, veins lined on his muscles. He was not a built man, but he was ripped.

"So, *Privates,* there is a solution to this little problem."

Yes, of course there was. And I had a good idea what it might be.

"You *don't fucking sleep.*"

No, no, of course you don't.

"Privates, most of the world's fuckups over the years, military or civilian, have happened because some sorry pussy was *tired,* too tired to go on, too tired to think, too tired to *kill.* We will not have this problem. *You* will not have this problem. If I do nothing else, I will do this for you: train you to teach your body to stop fucking whining, shut up, and drive on."

If Drill Sergeant Rose was nothing else, he was honest.

In eight weeks, none of us ever slept more than four hours a night. And never, *never,* was more than half the platoon asleep at once. Not just a single house mouse or fire guard awake through the night like the other platoons in the company. No, no. We *accomplished* things at night. Halls were buffed, uniforms pressed, manuals studied, boots shined, latrines scrubbed.

There was no coffee to help you through this, no caffeine of any sort. No nicotine, either. I entered the army a young man who would drink two full pots of coffee a day, with a minimum one pack of Marlboros to break it up. This is why I don't remember the first two weeks of boot camp particularly well: it was a haze, a dream, something happening to someone else, someone else's body, while I endured withdrawal.

I do remember something toward the end of our second week. We were getting ready to qualify at the rifle range for the first time. I remember Rose meeting our formation at 5 A.M., and he was with us all day without a break. He was there for chow that night, and in the barracks after. At lights out, when half the platoon went down for their brief nap, he was still there, pulling the awake privates into his office one by one to have them go over the parts of the M16 with him. He was there all night, working individually with the idiots, as the rest of us worked and cleaned and napped. There was never a moment, not even a moment, in the whole night when someone from the platoon didn't see him. At five the next morning he was there for formation, then chow, then drawing-of-weapons, and he personally marched us to the range. He was with us all day, through the range, through the march home, through chow again, rifle cleaning, and weapons-return. Finally, at ten that second night he walked out the door. Through the window I saw him, two floors below, get into his white topless Jeep with Florida plates and drive away.

Forty-one hours he was with us, wide awake.

I never saw him yawn.

We hated him.

Oh my God, we hated him.

For the most part you could tell the drill sergeants held the attitude that this was a job to do, like any other job in the army, and they were just trying to do it. They were there because they were squared-away, and the army had noticed, and sent them here. I didn't have a single drill in boot camp who had volunteered for this duty—the only personal piece of information any of them would share with us.

They could joke, too. Drill Sergeant Johnson, especially. He was young, just a few years older than me—at twenty-one, I was one of the old men among the recruits. He played Metallica tapes in the drill office when he had night duty, he bitched openly about not being allowed to smoke around the recruits. After chow, when we usually did something or another in the barracks bay—clean rifles, shine boots, get a lecture on first aid, whatever—Johnson would go up and down the line, hanging out with some of the privates he liked the most, talking to them about their home, giving them shit about their girlfriends or their moms. He was the one who taught us what real army life would be like; that this torturous shit wouldn't last forever. He was the one Rose put in charge of our graduation ceremony, teaching us close-order drills and marches. Instilling discipline, but with a sense of humor: although our drill ceremony was exactly precise and by regs, at one point in the ceremony, when the platoon was in block formation, he had us re-create the scene from Bill Murray's *Stripes* (filmed at Ft. Knox, and treasured by all GIs) by yelling out once in cadence "That's a Fact! Jack!"

Most of them were like that, in one way or another, in their own ways.

Not Sergeant Rose.

I didn't understand this at the time, but later, in the real army, and almost two years later in Somalia, I met men like him, and I better came to understand what he was. Rose, who had a college degree, was someone who had spent most of his army career in small units—units given wide latitude and autonomy from the army because of who they were and what they could do, and coming to expect it. This was someone who had no time for bullshit, and no time for anyone or anything that wasn't as high-speed as he was. Someone who would give more respect to a PFC or corporal in his unit—because he wouldn't be there if he couldn't hang—than he would to a colonel or a general from the Pentagon.

I try to imagine the look on his face when he opened the envelope telling him he was on orders for drill sergeant duty. Jesus H. Christ. It was the early 1990s, the army was smaller, good talent was hard to come by, and sometimes being good had its penalties. This was one such penalty. Duty as a drill sergeant, especially at Ft. Knox—*tanks,* for Christ's sake!— would be akin to having a leg amputated.

Us being worms wasn't an act with Rose.

I remember Drill Sergeant Adams—an older guy, with almost fifteen years in—saying once, and he was being honest, almost sad, "Fellas, I been in the army a long time, and quite frankly, anyone not wearing army green is an asshole in my book." He turned his head and spit on the parade ground at this point. "Civilians, they're fuckers. They'll send you off to die, send you off to protect their sorry asses, then fuck you over when you come home, treat you like dirt, and shit on you first chance they get."

Rose took this even further: It wasn't just civilians he considered subhuman, it was anyone not wearing a red beret.

As for a bunch of recruits who couldn't even wear the uniform correctly?

He hated us, and we hated him.

But did that stop us from trying to impress him?

Of course not.

It doesn't work like that—*men* don't work like that. One of the first conversations I ever had with Liz, she said this: Spit on a woman and she'll smack your face and walk away. Spit on a man and he'll probably punch you, but he'll follow that up with hours and hours of trying any way possible to prove he shouldn't have been spit on in the first place—that he didn't *deserve* it.

On a day when something big was going to happen—rifle qualifications, a major PT test, a command inspection with the brigade colonel—it was Rose we secretly wanted to be there with us. To fuck up during such a time, especially with him there, would be worse than horrible; it would have been inconceivable. But you didn't plan on fucking up, you planned on success, and if you were going to succeed, there was no drill we wanted there more to witness it than Sergeant Rose. One tiny softening around the eyes, one grunt of acknowledgment, getting marched back to the barracks *around* the huge hill the drills called Agony—the easy way—rather than *over* it—a sure sign of punishment—was worth ten times any other drill sergeant actually saying congratulations or well done.

I was not the best in my platoon, and I was not the worst. I found I had strengths, and I used them. We all did. The lines the drills would dish out about relying on one another turned out to be true: like it or not, the only way to successfully complete basic training was to do it together. This was hard for someone like me; hard, but I learned not impossible. Not when you wanted to succeed. Not when you had to succeed. You learned. Learned to rely on others.

I was a master of bed-making. I could make a bed like a motherfucker. Don't laugh: it isn't easy. And your life will become hell if you don't get this task down right. But my corners were perfect, my creases aligned. Fuck bouncing a quarter, you could bounce a helmet on a bed I'd made. My bunkmate, a pale, stocky kid from Michigan named Trevor we all called Alphabet, could polish boots with the same level of insane quality. I couldn't polish a boot to save my life. And he couldn't make a bed. Once we figured this out, after the first week or so, I never polished another boot and he never made another bed. Simple.

I was brought up in the New Jersey suburbs, I had never fired a gun in my life. Our first day at the range with an M16 rifle—*how hard can it be?*—was a lesson in sheer humiliation, so completely not able to do this one small thing that makes an American male real, this thing so many can do so easily: to shoot, to shoot straight, to hit what you're shooting at. I left the range in disgrace, one of a small group of only four taking the brunt end of Rose's wrath that night. But Trevor guided me, molded me, taught me, quietly at night, mock rifles in our hands, learning to breathe, learning to sight, steadying a shiny dime on the flash suppressor while I slowly squeezed the trigger.

Trevor Alphabet from Michigan, my new and immediate best friend, was a big boy—not fat, but thick. He would literally scream on the grass during morning PT (he wasn't the only one), trying to do one more sit-up; unable, simply unable to force his body to bend one more time over his belly. So every night before chow, or in the latrine waiting for the shower, or right after lights-out, sneaking from our bunks, we hit the ground: doing sit-ups together, me slowing when he did, but never stopping, never allowing him to stop, tears popping out of his eyes, unable to fail in front of me, forcing his stomach into shape by sheer force of my presence on the floor with him.

I did finally learn to shoot, I qualified, but it would be another year in the army before I earned my Expert badge, and even then I would hold it only a few months before dropping back to the second tier of Sharp-shooter.

When you arrive at Ft. Knox as a recruit, riding in on the bus from the Louisville airport under a big sign that says WELCOME TO THE U.S. ARMY AND THE START OF YOUR LIFE, you spend a few days in a place they call Reception. Fill out forms, get your head shaved, get your shots. (I remember the apron-clad PFC who bent over to stick a needle in my ass had a bumper sticker plastered to the wall behind his little desk that said "To err is human, to forgive is divine. Neither is U.S. Army policy." Judging by his lack of accuracy and mercy with the needle, I could see he had taken this to heart.) Then you get to "meet" your drills for the first time, and they march you off to your new barracks; one duffel full of uniforms strapped to your back, another full of equipment strapped to your front, trying to march precisely with all this heavy shit making you wobble and weave, drills screaming in your ear the whole two-mile march, trying to make someone fall out—eventually succeeding.

My first meeting with Drill Sergeant Rose was me on the ground, him looming over, swearing and cursing while I trembled and shook.

The first thing you have to do for your new drill sergeants when you get to the barracks area is a minimum number of push-ups and sit-ups. If you can't do them, they won't let you into basic. They send you instead to the fat-boy farm—land of pussies and other lesser men—to get to the minimum standard. Once you attain it, usually a few weeks later, the next platoon starting up takes you. There is nothing worse than this. Going in to the army I had a good idea that I would soon attain a whole new definition of humiliating—and in the frame of mind I was in at the time that didn't seem so bad. But I didn't want to start *this* way. I at least wanted the dignity to begin my army life with a regular bunch of guys.

The minimum was then, and is now, staggering to me. Thirteen push-ups, twenty-five sit-ups. In a row, no break.

Why staggering now? To graduate from basic, eight weeks later, you had to do *fifty-five* push-ups in less than two minutes. When they called two minutes time for me the day before graduation I was approaching seventy perfectly executed push-ups and had barely broken a sweat.

Why staggering then? I knew I couldn't do the thirteen. Knew it. Had tried it. Could barely do ten with my skinny arms. Never more than eleven. And I knew there would be no mercy, no "almost" allowed—twelve push-ups or less and you were off to the fat-boy farm.

We stood in a line, the air just turning cold in Kentucky, late afternoon, what had to have been the hardest day of my life more than half over, but the trauma I feared most was still to come and I knew it. I watched as this man, this small, strong monster in immaculate BDUs, made his way down the line, dropping each private individually, counting and watching, making notes with a pencil on a clipboard. Most of the recruits, if they had a problem, had it with the sit-ups. Big boys most of them, high-school football players like Trevor, who just couldn't make their bodies move that way. But the push-ups? No problem, for almost all of them. Once Rose actually had to stop some show-off private with bulging biceps who thought he should keep going after thirteen. Rose paid off this kid's enthusiasm by making him continue until his arms gave out from muscle failure.

I was a wreck, beyond frightened. After fifteen guys in a row, not one of them had failed. Not only would I fail, fail in front of all these guys, I would be the first to do it.

Rose stepped in front of me with an impossibly sharp and perfectly executed left-face, my first good look at this man.

It is impossible to describe to someone who hasn't been a military recruit just how close another human being can come to your face, just how much of your personal space they can invade. It is beyond intimidating.

His eyes were not exactly level with mine, I was one maybe two inches taller. He was perfectly shaved, but I was so close to him I could see where the stubble would come out, given the chance, could see a few pores on his forehead, could smell coffee on his breath. His face was perfect, and, had he been in any other line of work, what someone might call beautiful. His cheekbones were high, sculpted, lips thin, teeth white and aligned.

And then he exploded.

I was prepared for it, knew it was coming, but never in all of my life have I ever been so shaken by one man who wasn't even hitting me. The force of his words, the full weight of his utter contempt for me, came screaming from his mouth at a hundred miles an hour, and it only had to travel one inch. His disgust slammed into me like a whack in the face from a two-by-four.

I did my sit-ups first. No problems there, I was skinny. Alone in a cheap motel room in Jersey City the night before the recruiter put me on a plane to Kentucky I had executed sixty perfect sit-ups in a row and stopped only because I was bored. Sit-ups would not be my problem. Unfortunately, my arms were as skinny as my midsection.

"Drill Sergeant!" I screamed from the ground, trying to do the right thing. "Private Jones requests permission to roll over and execute thirteen perfect push-ups, Drill Sergeant!"

His face again in mine, ripping off his campaign hat and throwing himself to the ground next to me, his face now touching mine, screaming in my ear:

"Why are you fucking talking to me, Private! When did I tell you to fucking talk! Do your fucking push-ups, Private! NOW!"

He had yelled at the last guy in line for beginning his push-ups without asking for permission, now he was yelling at me for asking. I immediately saw how this next eight weeks were going to go.

If I would even get the opportunity to start my eight weeks.

I rolled over, assuming the push-up position. My hands were too close together, and he screamed again, putting his hands around my wrists and dragging my palms across the gravel to their proper position. I thought I was going to pass out, and when I stood some minutes later I saw that my palms were bloody.

I began.

I know, I *know,* to this day, that my thirteenth—if not my twelfth and thirteenth—push-up was not correct. My arms were wobbling, my back was swaying, my head down. And you weren't just supposed to do thirteen, you were supposed to do them *perfectly.*

I had failed.

But when I looked up, Rose was gone, standing, as if he had never been next to me, now with the next private in line, repeating this game.

I got to my feet and went to attention, wanting to weep, assuming I would be called out when this was done, to take my place among the assholes and subhumans.

But three guys down the line, as I watched out of the corner of my eye, a boy failed. And there was no question about it. The humiliation wasn't even mine and still I could taste it from where I stood, hot and sharp, five feet away, as this poor, poor kid—too tall, too fat, too weak—fell to the ground sobbing in pain and horror after only his fifth push-up.

And if getting yelled at for doing the opposite of what the last guy had done to get yelled at was my first lesson in Drill Sergeant Rose, this was my second: Rose didn't say a word to the kid. He didn't yell, he didn't scream, he didn't talk. Rose watched, hawkeyed, intent, as the kid struggled through his five, but when his chest hit the ground Rose didn't even so much as flinch. He signaled with his fingers to a soft-capped non-drill NCO standing on the parade ground, and that sergeant came over, helped the kid up, and walked him away.

He wasn't worth the breath to yell at.

This was the lesson I carried—we *all* carried—through the next two months: the real fear should start when Rose gets silent, when Rose ignores you. If Rose ignores you, then you as a person have ceased to exist.

I knew then I'd made it, and I sort of swooned, the blood rushing to my head, too miserable to be happy—that would have been ridiculous—but more relieved than I had ever been in my life.

I was fooling myself, of course. If I could have foreseen the agony that awaited me in the future as Rose built up my chest and arms I would have quit right there. No question about it, I would have.

But, what you don't know can't hurt you. Not yet, anyway.

Four other guys failed right there on the parade ground, led away by the same NCO, like the first unfortunate fat boy. But it was small consolation, because I was the only member of the surviving platoon who had passed with the bare minimum of push-ups. And so my life for the next eight weeks was to become one big push-up, at the hands of Drill Sergeant Rose. While the other guys were more frequently dropped for leg-lifts (Rose was a big fan of the gut-wrenching leg-lift) I would almost always be dropped for push-ups, and not just when I had done something wrong.

Oh, we hated that motherfucker.

No doubt, the other platoons had it bad, too. There is no getting through basic training without it being bad. I remember reading once, some months before I joined the army, that if you've successfully completed boot camp you never have to prove anything to anyone ever again, and I believe it. But as bad as it must have been for those other platoons in our company, they got rewards. When things went right for them, when they performed like good little privates, there were days off, phone privileges, extra chow. Once I even saw a drill buy a pack of smokes for the smokers in his platoon after they had all qualified with high scores at the range; smoking has been outlawed in basic training since 1987. So it was hard, but at least they had something, something tangible, to work toward.

Not 2nd Platoon. The harder we worked to please Rose, the harder he pushed us. We had the best scores at the rifle range, the best scores on PT tests, the highest marks on written exams; but our only rewards were lectures, given to us as we grunted in the snow through push-ups and leg-lifts, on how we were a second-rate, sorry bunch he would refuse to call "soldiers," and only addressed us as "privates" because army regs said he had to.

By the second month we could tell the other drills didn't always agree with him. There were exceptions, but generally the better and better we got, and the closer we came to graduation, the easier the other drills were on us. Not Rose. Once I saw Johnson and Cecil whispering to each other on the other side of the parade ground, shaking their heads, as Rose explained calmly to our formation—a formation that was flat on its collective back, sweating through leg-lifts—why we wouldn't have phone privileges that weekend like the rest of the company, why we had *let him down* again.

And, silly as it sounds now, the worst thing, the thing that really pissed us off the most the closer and closer we unknowingly came to evolving into soldiers: he kept our guidon cased for almost the entire eight weeks. The guidon is the platoon flag, the physical symbol of the platoon, carried ahead of the formation in marches and runs. Rose said we didn't deserve to show our colors, that we were an embarrassment to all the men who had previously sweated and served in 2nd Platoon, and that our guidon would remain rolled up on its staff until we could prove otherwise. So there we would be, in company formations, with platoons we were better than, had scored better than, with their flags flying proudly, and ours rolled up like a dirty secret.

But it didn't matter. Rose wasn't psycho, he wasn't out of hand. He was just hard, and he was the senior drill, so what he said was the gospel, and the other drills certainly weren't going to get in his way over a bunch of lousy privates.

He wasn't a machine, of course. There were times, quick moments, when you got something from him.

Rose believed, for obvious reasons, that the perfect soldier wasn't the Hollywood stereotype: the perfect soldier wasn't huge, Rambo-like, grunting biceps and calves, carrying rocket launchers on his back. Rose believed the perfect soldier was strong, yes, but lithe, able to easily move quietly and quickly; and smart, too. He was always talking about education, how smarts were what made us stronger than Marines—Rose defined Marines as walking bullet catchers. And if you passed by his office late at night when he was in there alone you would always see him: not drinking coffee, not watching the TV, not doing the things the other drills did; he would be reading. Manuals, regs, yes—but novels, too. And history texts.

Rose liked it when you figured him out, when you deduced on your own—collectively, of course—what he was after. Just like nothing could bring his rage on more than having to spell something out for you, conversely nothing pleased him more than the platoon reading his mind. Like the gloves in formation, or us figuring out how to really clean our rifles: Regs said you couldn't *completely* disassemble an M16 rifle—for instance, you weren't allowed to use a wrench and unscrew the flash suppressor—

but it was clear you couldn't completely clean one without doing so. He told us this, read us the regulation from the manual, then left the room for an hour, dropping an open-ended wrench on Romig's bunk on his way out the door—we figured it out. No comment was made by Rose that night after we all successfully returned our weapons to the armorer—the only platoon to get them all past his eagle eye—but when we marched to the range the next morning we marched blessedly slower than normal, and Rose himself took the platoon, singing cadences that from his mouth weren't just time keepers, but history lessons.

In our platoon, we learned about the army, army life, Vietnam, the Gulf, World War II, and brotherhood not from textbooks, but from the cadence calls of Drill Sergeant Rose. Like everything else, Rose took cadence seriously. If he was singing it personally, not handing it off to another drill, it was clear he was pleased with something the platoon had done that day. And in those cadences—unlike any of the other drills' standard cadences, no simple Jody calls for Drill Sergeant Rose—we found the real Rose. This was the only way he was ever going to share these parts of himself, his soldier-self, with such unworthies as us, and on those few occasions when he did sing we felt strong, proud; like we had a view at the keyhole of the secret home of a mighty warrior. On those nights, marching back to the barracks from the range or the field, the sky already dark and dotted with stars, the air so cold you could cut it, even with our guidon rolled up I'd have sworn our thirty voices sang out so loud and so full of pride of what we were accomplishing, of what we were becoming, that certainly lights must be going on at the general's house four miles away, wondering what in the hell the racket was, who were these incredibly loud *soldiers*?

Second Platoon, sir. Delta Company, 2nd Brigade, 46th Infantry. Rose's men.

3

Zero-dark-early, the platoon bay door crashes open, sleeping privates instantly rolling from bunk to floor then on their feet to toe the line, the already-awake cleaning detail snapping to attention where they stand—

better to be at attention and in the wrong place than stumbling toward your destination as the drill sergeant passes. Trevor Alphabet falls on top of me as he drops from the upper bunk, smashing my chin into the cold tile floor. But we're both on the line—in boxers and T-shirt—seconds before the lights switch on. "Fucking Rose," Trevor whispers as I quickly check my chin and face for blood.

But it's not Rose. It's Johnson. The young buck sergeant, muscles so huge they strain the fabric of his BDUs. He's through the door like a crazed elephant, halfway down the bay before the door swings closed behind him, head back to gain every inch of power from his windpipe and lungs.

"*Front-fucking-leaning-rest!*" he bellows, giving the command for the push-up position. We drop, palms flat, legs back, feet spread, desperately terrified of both whatever we did wrong and whatever our punishment will be.

"*In cadence!*"

We answer: "*In cadence!*"

Then he stops.

All the way down at the far end of the bay now, he stops, turns. The next command, one we're anticipating, is "*Exercise!*" This followed by the count as we number our push-ups. But he doesn't give the command. He turns instead, looking down the line, his troop of privates with arms bulging, waiting for the command, the order, to start our push-ups.

We wait.

Johnson walks slowly back toward the center of the bay, stopping almost directly in front of me. I can see a flash of reflection from my pale skin in his glossy black jump boots. My arms tremble from the sudden stop of not completing my first push-up.

"Privates," he says, "Freddie Mercury just died."

Johnson's arms go behind his back, in a kind of parade rest. He walks slowly down the line.

"Freddie Mercury was a dirty faggot," he barks, "and he died of AIDS, which is how all faggots are sure to go."

He stops near the door, turns, and faces us.

"But I *liked* Freddie Mercury. The motherfucker rocked. Queen rocked. Freddie Mercury was a genius, and he rocked."

Johnson removes his campaign hat, holding it over his heart.

"Privates, a moment of silence for Freddie Mercury."

Hat back on, Johnson brings himself to attention, holds it, then spins a perfect about-face and leaves the bay, door swinging shut behind him. We hear his footsteps trail off down the hall, then silence. I watch a bead of sweat fall from my nose and splash the tile.

Less than ninety seconds before, I'd been sound asleep.

Someone down the line, Fogel I think, whispers, "Are you fucking kidding me?" From the other end of the bay Romig half-sings, "Fat-bottomed girls, you make my rocking world go round." There's a few chuckles, and a few groans.

Across from where Trevor and I hold our position, a skinny Italian guy named Leo slowly brings himself to his feet, glancing nervously toward the bay door. Trevor growls, "Someone give you the order to stand, Private?"

Leo drops back down to the push-up position without a word and waits. We all wait.

For an hour.

Within minutes I've drifted back into a half-sleep, a warm and tortured dream of my face in someone's boot. But I don't move. None of us moves. Holding the front leaning rest, forever if necessary.

At 0500 the bay door slams open again, and Rose storms in. Without so much as a blink of surprise at our condition, he picks up where Johnson left off an hour before.

"In cadence!"

"In cadence!"

"Exercise!"

"ONE! Drill Sergeant. TWO! Drill Sergeant. THREE! Drill Sergeant . . ."

4

The final week of basic training, what was the easiest week for the other three platoons, was the worst week of our lives.

We spent the week in the field, and it rained and snowed then rained again for five days, the temperature never rising above thirty-five at best. The last two days of this week were supposed to be a mock battle between the platoons, but Rose took his platoon into the field three days early.

While the rest of the company got measured for dress greens for graduation, shined up low quarters, and in some cases got orders for permanent party, we slogged through the mud and the woods, sleeping in shelter-halves that offered no protection from the freezing cold and the wet.

At ten on the fourth night we saw the lights of the trucks that brought the other platoons to the field exercise site. The closest platoon, 3rd, was camped just a half mile from us through a stand of forest. The battle would begin the next day. As we saw the lights and heard the trucks bringing in these fresh and well-rested privates, Rose and Cecil handed our MILES gear to us. MILES gear is a strap around your waist with a light and a buzzer, and a sensor to snap onto your rifle. If you "shoot" with the M16, the MILES of the soldier you're shooting at goes off if you register a hit. That soldier is then "dead," and out of the game. We would play the game the next morning. The winning platoon would be Honor Platoon at graduation.

We were beyond exhausted. Rose had worked us like he had never worked us before, lectures in the rain by day on signals and tactics, exercises by squad at night, tripping over roots in the forest, bumping into one another, trying to put what he had taught us to some practical use, failing to figure out how. There were only twenty-five of us left, from a platoon that had started as forty. This was an incredible attrition rate: the other platoons had thirty-five or more left. I never came closer to quitting, in the whole eight weeks, as I did in the field there. So worthless, so pointless, so miserable. My impressions of Rose as a hard but educated, reasonable man had dried up: he had lost it, he was psycho, and we were suffering. Someone had to stop him. And if they couldn't, then maybe there wasn't too much shame in just saying, "You know what? This sucks, and I don't need it." That's all it would take. I had seen others do it: just drop their M16s, and start walking back toward the barracks. Rose never said a word to them, just processed their discharge and within twenty-four hours they were gone, back to whatever life they had come from.

God, how easy that would be—and how much sense it made now.

I thought of the privates in 3rd Platoon across the hill, so clean, so happy to be close to graduation; probably they'd all had hot chow tonight, and probably they looked forward to tomorrow as a game. But it wasn't a game for us, there was no excitement. We were done.

At 11 p.m., after we all had our MILES gear on and had learned how

to use it, Rose did something he had never done before: he told us to go to sleep. All of us. At once.

"Privates," he said softly, standing there with no coat, rain pouring down his face, his BDUs black from the wet, "go to your tents. I will stand the watch while you rest."

What a fucking hero.

Stand the watch against what?

But, truth is, we were relieved. So relieved it didn't register how out of character this was for him. All we could do was stumble to our shelter-halves, hoping this wasn't some kind of cruel trick, and fall instantly asleep.

At 2 A.M. I woke to a hand firmly over my mouth, and jolted up so hard I almost toppled the shelter-half. It was Rose, kneeling in the puddle between me and Trevor Alphabet, one hand over each of our mouths.

"*Quiet!*" he hissed through his teeth, then slowly let us both go.

"Drill Sergeant!" Trevor whispered.

"Get up, get your gear on, then wake those in the next tent the same way I did to you. Total silence, and no lights, *stress that,* and make sure the others understand. Have them pass it down the line. I want the whole platoon gathered in five minutes."

Then he was gone.

"What the fuck?" Trevor whispered.

"He's lost it, man," I said. "Just fucking lost it. FUBAR. Stone gooney."

"Whatever. Let's go, Jonesy."

When the whole platoon had gathered, he had us strike camp, removing any evidence of our existence. Then he led us into the woods, about twenty paces. He stopped at the base of a huge tree, and turned to face us. Even those almost on top of him could barely see; the night was black and thick, the rain so hard it pushed through the forest canopy, the wind pushing limbs across your face and path.

"Gather round," he whispered, and he flicked on a red light as we circled him, then sat at his feet as he motioned to us with his hands. He stood over us, red light clipped to his lapel glowing on his face, like some god or demon rose from the depths into civilization to take revenge, whatever that revenge might be.

And then he started talking.

I can't even begin to duplicate his speech here. What was real, what was not, what was really said, and what we just thought we remembered as we talked about it later; who knows what is true and what isn't. He talked quietly and he talked slowly, for almost an hour, that much I do remember. He talked about soldiers, about the honor of that, the esprit de corps. About politicians who control soldiers, but never own them. He talked about dark forests, and dark nights. He rattled off foreign names—Belleau Wood, Normandy, Cahm Rahn Bay, Nicaragua, Panama City, Riyadh—as if he'd been there, as if he'd been silent witness to the bloodletting and planning. He talked about how a soldier, a *real* soldier, has more in common with his enemy across the line than he does with those he is called on to protect, and he must always remember that, and respect that—but at the same time not let it get in the way of his duty. He talked about battles, wars, skirmishes; how they turned out, why they went the way they did. Mistakes made, good men lost for stupid reasons. And then he started talking about us, not individually, but as a group. He recounted every major incident of our eight weeks, he had remembered them all, in the finest of detail. He talked about our losses, our failures, and then he talked about our victories—what *we* knew had been our victories but didn't know that *he* knew—why we had succeeded those times, what we had done to accomplish it. Never did he say what *he* had done to teach us, but what *we* had done to win. And then he pointed over the hill, through the trees, and talked about the other platoons. He told us their scores, their numbers, their failures, and their victories. Knowledge, he said, knowledge is key, and now you know how it is with them. And how it is with you. And what you do with that knowledge will make you or break you here. Tonight.

Tonight?

Tonight.

There it was.

Now we understood why we were all awake, awake and alert and learning, four hours before the battle was supposed to begin.

There it was.

He clicked off the red light and his face was gone. We were alone in the woods, in the rain, in the dark. Then he said this:

"Privates, I am a soldier. That may mean nothing to some of you, and I don't care. Some of you think I'm an asshole—I know that, I don't care. I also don't care that most of you will never really be soldiers. It's out of my hands. But someday, some of you, maybe even just one of you, will look in the mirror and say to yourself, 'I am a soldier, a man with honor, and it is an honor I have *earned*.'"

At that moment I understood why the Allies won at Normandy, why men were willing to fling themselves into bullets and die without question. It didn't have much to do with politics or geography or who was right or who was wrong. It was about people, individual men. And this thought was simultaneously exhilarating and repulsive to me, and to what I thought I believed in. Because here, here in Kentucky, a few thousand miles from the closest war, we were faced with a man we loathed, feared, and hated, but at that moment, if he had asked, we would have followed that man to the ends of the earth, into death itself, without a question.

We would have.

I would have.

No doubt about it.

In the pitch black, the silence, the absence of voice, was awesome.

Slowly, slowly, our eyes recovered from the spots left by Rose's extinguished red light. He let us gather ourselves, and quietly we all remembered where we were, who we were, and why we were here.

The rain poured down. I remember shivering, and feeling guilty about it.

Finally, he spoke again, and I realized that sometime during all of this the other drills had made their way quietly into our ranks, were standing among us, watching him as closely as we were.

"Privates," he said finally, "now it's time for *our* war. And the biggest lesson about war I can teach you is it doesn't run on schedule. It makes its own schedule, sets its own timetable, and the secret to being a soldier is to read those fluctuations and follow them. If you try to force it to your will, you will fail. Countless generals and politicians have learned this the hard way. But the smart foot soldier knows that if you listen to it, to the pulse of the battle, you will learn when it's time to sit, and when it's time to act."

He crouched down with us.

"And, now, *right now,* is the time to act."

He paused, one second, then stood again.

"We will start with Third Platoon, because they are the strongest, and they are the closest. They're asleep in their tents in the middle of a clearing with no trees—smart, for a situation like this, when they know we are on foot with small arms and have no artillery. They have guards posted in a ring around the tents, and there is no way you can approach those tents without them seeing you."

And here, I swear, he smiled.

"Unless you're very, very good."

Standing, he moved through our ranks and quickly touched six of us on the shoulder—seemingly at random, obviously not—motioning for us to move to the front. Looking at them, these five and myself, I didn't see what I had expected: we weren't the best in the platoon, and we weren't the worst.

But, we were all small.

"Privates," he said, addressing the whole platoon, "I have watched you on the ranges, watched you make your way through the obstacle courses, watched you cross the barbed-wire fields. On your bellies you did this, like I taught you, and you think you're so small, so close to the ground."

He paused.

"You're not."

Now he made his way through the six of us, pulling off our helmets, forming a pile on the ground.

"Even here, even in this situation, in U.S. Army basic training, a man will try to retain some *shred* of civility, some *shred* of respect. I've watched you crawl through the mud, but did you really? How close were you? Did you eat it?"

Now he was in front of me, my helmet in his hand, staring me straight in the eye. Or maybe I just thought he was.

"A man, even at this level, will not allow himself to totally give up, give in, and *immerse* himself in misery. And because of that, he will fail. Because of that he will die."

He dropped my helmet on the pile, but stayed in front of me.

"Tonight, these six men will have their lives, and all of your lives, in their hands. It's a personal decision they will have to make, as they crawl on their bellies. 'Am I really just crawling on my stomach, or am I *one with the mud*?' What they do with that decision will decide the evening for you. They have to pass guards in the wide open. But it's raining, it's dark. And those men, those guards, are like most of you: they're not totally, not *totally* capable of immersing themselves in misery. And a man who cannot comprehend himself doing that cannot really comprehend another man doing that, and so their eyes will be up, and forward, they will be tired and bored, and you will pass right beneath them."

Rose turned, as if to move down the line, then stopped, and swung back toward me, his fingertip poking into my chest.

"And Private Jones will lead."

I had never, in eight weeks never, been singled out by Rose before. I don't think he'd ever uttered my name. I had made it a point to be small, to not talk, to not be singled out. I had nothing to prove by being here, in the army, no personal agenda; I wanted to do it, get it done, and be left alone. I had a daughter to support, a paycheck to collect; beyond that, I didn't care. And as he poked me on the chest, I knew that he knew this, and that I was the only one left in the platoon who had yet to be singled out.

"When you are done, when the guards are down and the officers and radio neutralized, you will signal with the red light and we will come in and clean up."

With that, he stopped talking, stepped back, and looked at me. Out of nothing but fear of him, I directed my five squad members to remove their ponchos and coats and gear, replacing only the MILES straps over our BDU shirts. Without anyone having to say anything, we all scooched down as one on our heels, dug into the icy wet ground with our fists, and layered our faces and hands with cold mud, leaving not a spot of skin to show through. One kid, Sharps, was black; even he layered on the mud, growing blacker and darker.

Rose pulled out a map, and gathered the six of us around it. Using the red light, he showed us where we were and where they were, and oriented us with his compass.

And then, with a final tug to tighten the M16 slung over my back, we were gone.

As I made the first step, it occurred to me I hadn't felt the cold or the rain in the last twenty minutes. Even now with no poncho, no coat.

The night was so dark we didn't see 3rd Platoon's camp until we had almost, but not quite, stumbled out of the woods and onto it.

Wouldn't that be a fine ending to all this, I thought to myself. *Running right into the arms of their guards.*

I motioned to the other five privates and they gathered up around me, two or three trees in from the edge of the clearing. I spoke quietly, but wasn't worried about being heard; the rain drowned out everything, an advantage for us.

"Are we in this?" I asked.

I thought at that moment I had never said anything so stupid sounding in my life—but it was right, and I felt it.

Everyone knew what I meant, and nodded.

I lowered my head, closing my eyes.

"I want to do this. I really want to do this," I whispered. "It's got nothing to do with him . . . it's me. *Us*. If it's just going to suck for you, there's no shame. Hang here, hang back, wait for the main party, and join them. I'll never tell a soul, I'll never tell Rose. But—" and I looked up now, overcoming my fear of stupidity, making myself understood, "I want this, and if you want this too, then let's go."

Every one of them stayed with me.

We dropped and ate mud.

Rose was right. Crawling—no, *slithering*—through the mud, I could see the guards, five of them, standing wide out in the open, and I panicked for a second, no way they won't see us, six guys crawling through the mud with rifles on our backs. But they didn't. With the rain, the dark, their discomfort, boredom, and—in the end—lack of belief that someone could get by them, they didn't see a single one of us move through the mud by their feet. I passed one guard so close I literally could have reached out and untied his bootlace.

Incredible.

Past the guards, we regrouped and quickly saw the antennae sticking up from beside the largest tent. Sharps unscrewed it from the housing, then disassembled it, putting all the pieces in his cargo pocket. We looked at each other, unslung our M16s, clicked the safety, held our breaths, and crawled into the tent. Two privates, sleeping peacefully on cots—*cots!*—acting the roles of the company officers. We shot them both, their MILES lights going off, grabbing both of them around the face and the mouth to keep them silent as they woke. We explained that they were dead, and would have to stay quiet. We knew they'd do it, and they did.

Out of the tent, the rest of our group came together: all the "officers" were dead, the radio worthless, and we split up into two teams to quietly take out the guards from their rear. Had the bullets been real, they never would have known they had died.

Within five minutes of having crawled by the guards I was standing in the open, raising my red light in hand, flicking it on and off.

The main body would appear in seconds, to wipe out the rest of this platoon while they slept in their tents, but the battle was already over.

He who sleeps, dies.

Say it again, Private: He who sleeps—*dies.*

We hadn't slept in eight weeks.

In the next ten minutes, every single member of their platoon, right down to their pissed-off drill sergeant, was killed. We lost only one man, a kid named Todd, slipping on the mud as he tried to enter a tent, the clatter waking the occupants, killing him just seconds before they met their own MILES-blinking fate.

After the silent all-clear had been signaled, Rose inspected the camp, shaking his head at our own single casualty. When he was done, he came and stood in front of me, handing me my helmet. He locked eyes with me, just once, then looked away, never saying a word.

I didn't expect him to.

I opened my mouth to say something to him—I'm not sure what—but never got the chance. Drill Sergeant Cecil walked out of the wood line toward us, our rolled-up platoon guidon in his grip. He handed it to Rose. He held it briefly, looking at it, then Rose untied the strings, letting the flag wave. He hefted the staff in his arms, and slammed the point down into the mud.

The Ride West, *Part Two*

Utah—Early April 1993

1

Jones wakes with a muffled yell, face pressed into the glass of the dark bus window, jumping back quick in his seat—

—but no one is looking at him, no turning heads, the seat next to him empty, everyone asleep. Everyone sleeping. He decides he didn't scream out loud, couldn't have, it was in the dream—but it's hard to believe.

This dream doesn't come often—only once since he got back Stateside, only three times total. In general, he doesn't dream much at all.

But when it does come, this particular dream, it packs a punch. No nightmares of a Somali clansman, which might make sense, or even of long-ago but never-forgotten Drill Sergeant Rose. Instead, the walking remains of a dead Belgian soldier who seems to have something he wants to say—

(—*a flash of a face at a window, looking in—TOO QUICK!*)

Jones closes his eyes tight, holds it, then opens them. The vision scares him into a cold sweat, and he always wakes from it trembling and pale and anxious. He's never been able to remember why. All he ever remembers is the shape of the Belgian soldier, and he doesn't understand why that would scare him, why a soldier, a friend, would scare him.

Whatever, he thinks. Rolling his shoulders, closing his eyes again, he tries to clear his mind.

He pictures Jan sitting behind him, sleeping, resting easy in Wayne's arms. Jan was married to a Marine for a year. Jan thinks Jones is AWOL.

Jan is sure of it. He considered pulling his DD214 from his pocket to show her, to prove the point. But why? What does he care what Jan thinks? And, a DD214, gazed at too long, raises more questions than it answers. He'd learned that. He had to show it to an MP at Ft. Eustis before they'd release the box of clothes and CDs he'd stored with the provost marshal before he went to Somalia. The fat fuck of a staff sergeant had let his eyes linger on the page longer than he'd needed to—*Purple Heart? You're a regular hero, ain't ya, buddy? You don't look too broke to me.* Yeah, whatever. Just give me my shit.

Jan could think what she wanted. In a way, she was absolutely right: Jones *felt* AWOL.

Jan was cute, and Jan's sense of humor reminded him of Liz, and now he's thinking about Liz, and what the hell do you do with that?

Liz, keeper of his secret. Liz was in Mogadishu, being a soldier. Jones was—where?—just over the Utah border, he thought. Half a day away from a city where he has no friends, half a day away from dealing with his complete lack of money. Liz is in Mogadishu, and Jones has gone fishing.

He rests his brow against the window. *No more sleep tonight,* he decides, *but I can rest.* Rest and doze.

In his head, he recites the only mantra he knows.

I am a soldier, an American fighting man, a protector of the greatest nation on earth. I am loyal to those whom I serve. I will never disgrace my unit, my uniform, or my country. I will not disgrace the soldiers' arms, nor abandon the comrade at my side. Whether alone or many I will fight to defend things sacred and profane . . .

And he falls asleep.

2

Hmmm.

The bus makes a good sound, a dead sound. You can dive into that sound, let it take you where it will—away from dreams. Stick to memories. Memories aren't any easier than dreams, but at least you can control them. Just by virtue of the fact that it's over, you have control.

Hmmm.

3

Katy made Greek salad the night Jones came home from basic training. Later she tried to make cheese balls in the skillet. They came out terrible, sticky and burned, but they laughed.

The kitchen was cold, even for this time of year, wind creeping through cracks around the door and windows. He said all the places they'd had together had been cold in the winter, and now here alone she had done it again. She smiled, yes, but mostly they had been nice homes all the same, and here the living room was warm for Emma to play in, and she sipped her tea.

He hated tea.

They talked of nothing—long and slow and tentative, conversation moving around edges and corners. She laughed at his shaved head, and he tried to tell her about basic training but it was impossible to tell this and she didn't want to hear it so finally he shut up. She had not kissed him when he arrived and he brought this up—trying to make it into a joke, failing. She said she was tired and don't be ridiculous and would he please reach over and get her a napkin from the shelf.

Their eyes moved as the conversation did, darting always and settling on nothing.

She watched as he got up to get her more tea. He moved differently, and it was enough for her to notice. He moved slower than he ever had, slower and with thought, as if the act of pouring a cup of tea required some decision to be made, some important decision. And his face she couldn't figure. *Maybe he's lost weight,* she thought. And she followed that with, *of course he has, don't be stupid—he's in the army.* There was a change, and she felt it, but she couldn't figure it.

She hated him.

Maybe not right now, maybe not right this instant, but there it was, right there, she knew it, he knew it, and this was all just window dressing.

Turning around, her steaming tea cup in his hand, he caught her looking up at him, and he smiled.

She would have liked to have seen that smile six months ago.

It didn't change anything.

He didn't look away, just stood there in the middle of the kitchen, tea in hand, and when she finally raised her eyes again she was smiling too. They stayed like that for a while.

"Maybe," she said, "maybe, in the end, it doesn't matter."

"No. No, I don't think it does."

He wasn't sure what she had meant by that, but it seemed right—it seemed necessary—to agree.

He smiled at her again, and then she was out of the chair and they kissed, warm, tongues and teeth exploring gently, as if they had never kissed each other, as if they were each with someone new. She laughed and backed up then, pushing her long hair out of her face.

"Help me with the dishes?"

"Yes."

Side by side they stood, hands in hot water. An asparagus fern in a wicker container hung from a chain in front of the window over the sink, its soft, green leaves drooping heavily over the sides, beads of water collecting on the tops from rising steam. He had bought the fern for her two years ago, had stopped one day on the way home from work. The wicker container was new, though, and she waited for him to ask about it—like he seemed to need to ask about everything in her new place he didn't recognize or didn't remember touching with his own hands once—but he didn't.

He dried the dishes with a hand towel while she went to the bathroom. He had to yell through the door asking questions because he did not know where she kept things in this house. She laughed from the bathroom, and he laughed back. His knuckles went white around the glass he was holding and he quickly set it down before it cracked.

They thought they were in love. Their connection had been there for a long time in their short lives, and their need of that connection remained, great and terrible and heavy, and they hated each other for it. But he didn't know this yet, and because of who he was he'd been unable to leave her, and he resented that now, and she hated him for it.

When they were finally together that night—this was inevitable, they both knew it—it was different from what they remembered and not what they expected, each bringing something from their new life. It was good, and they breathed together and held tight to each other, moving from room to room, legs and hands and lips and hair, soft satisfied sounds from the carpet. They were as quiet as the dead, skin smooth and white in the cold, dark house.

They fell asleep entwined, like they hadn't since they were sixteen. They woke the same way, but sore and awkward. He made his coffee and put butter on their toast while she dressed and picked up the house. He got an outfit from the baby's dresser to change her into when he picked her up from the sitter to bring her to preschool. Katy kissed him on the cheek when she left for work, and he promised to call sometime the next week, after he got settled in Virginia. And then Jones was alone and wanted to smoke and he remembered to take it outside on the porch because she didn't smoke and this wasn't his house.

4

A hand on Jones's shoulder, big and warm and brown, gently pushing his body.

"Son?" the quiet voice asks. "Where y'all going? Frisco?"

Jones turns his head, eyes still closed, and says, "Katy?"

He says Katy, but it's Liz's face in his head.

"Son?" the voice asks again.

Then he's awake. It's dark on the bus, dark and completely quiet. Just Jones and the driver.

"Berkeley," he finally answers. "Yeah. San Francisco."

"We're here. Best collect y'things."

The man backs up, standing straight between the seats, tall and thick, tight haircut peppered with gray, small pebbles of black freckles around his eyes. His sweater smells like a cigar.

He smiles. "We're here."

"Thanks," Jones says. "Thanks."

Africa

Kismaayo, Somalia and Mombasa, Kenya—December 31, 1992

1

PFC Benjamin Jones had heard about but never seen phosphorescence in the ocean. It was spellbinding. Even now, three hours after he'd noticed their tiny army Mike Boat was leaving a glowing, yellow trail in the dark nighttime ocean, he sat and stared at it, mesmerized.

Called a Mike Boat by the soldiers, it was an LCM, seventy-two-foot gray steel landing craft, like the one Jones's grandfather rode in to hit the beach at Guadalcanal, but bigger, slightly faster, and with more electronics in the wheelhouse than would have been necessary for a suicide beach landing. And it didn't belong to the navy. The army kept two companies of Mike Boats in active service; even fully loaded they only drew a couple of feet of water and, although their flat bottoms made for torturous open-sea sailing like tonight, they had proved useful in Vietnam and then Panama for running up rivers and into shallow ports. The forward three-quarters of the vessel was all open welldeck, for carrying troops or supplies, fronted by a ramp that, hopefully, dropped when you needed it to. The aft quarter of the boat was a raised deck, with a small enclosed wheelhouse in the center, two fifty-cal machine guns mounted pointing out, and hatches dropping into the tiny engine room and even tinier storage lazarette. Jones sat with his back to the wheelhouse, staring at the eerie glowing ocean behind them.

They were near the equator—relative to the whole world, right on top of it—and he pictured in his head the illustrated copy of *Doctor Dolittle* his mom read to him when he was a kid: when the good doctor approached the equator in his boat, he'd seen it laid before him as a red ribbon cutting across the ocean, with a sign sticking up that said EQUATOR. This was the closest Jones could come to compare to the trail they were leaving in the sea. He tried to explain this to Trevor Alphabet—the *Doctor Dolittle phenomenon* he called it—but Trevor was sleeping, his back against a steel ammo box, hands crossed on his lap, and had told Jones to fuck off and leave him alone.

Some people, Jones thought, had no appreciation for literature—or magic.

To add to the effect, to the magic—tiny, lonely boat, no land in sight, cutting through the Indian Ocean up the coast of Africa, leaving a glowing trail—there was no sound. That took some getting used to.

An army Mike Boat is usually noisy. Two V-12 Detroit Diesel engines, nothing but a thin steel deckplate between you and them, usually running full-out at max RPMs. You got used to yelling everything you had to say, to straining at all times to hear if someone was calling on the radio. It wasn't natural, being this quiet. Their first hour onboard tonight Jones realized they *were* yelling at each other, out of habit. Funny.

No noise tonight. They were being towed. Engines off. If Jones had stood and looked forward, past the wheelhouse, past the welldeck, past the ramp, he would have seen through the mist three tiny lights some five hundred yards ahead of them, rising and falling in the swells. An army LCU-2000 class—pregnant Mike Boat they called them, shaped similar, but triple their size—pulling them through the ocean from Kenya to Somalia. Mombasa to Kismaayo.

So the ride was silent. Silent, dark, wet, chilly, and the painted glow of their yellow trail to point out where they'd been.

Where they'd been was Mombasa, the oldest pirate port in Kenya, a day's sail south of the Somali border. A neutral city for a company of American troops to sit in for a month and gear up and await orders to move north. Mostly all they'd done was drink—the Florida Club had been their usual spot, a three-level bar in the center of town that welcomed them with open arms. It had all been fun, mostly, except for the tension with Liz—unresolved before they'd left the States—and one bad night that had ended in a fight between Trevor and a local pimp, somehow Jones waking up the next morning and realizing his wallet was gone.

He thought about that now, and did automatically what he'd been doing a few times every day for almost a week: pass his hand over his empty pocket, feeling for something that wasn't there. *Where's my wallet? Where is my fucking wallet?*

The Mike Boat rose on a large swell, and Jones pushed his palms down against the deck to steady himself for the sharp drop that would follow.

Things were calm now, but picking up. Conditions had been terrible before: the first ten hours out of Mombasa had been the worst seas Jones had ever witnessed from the deck of a Mike Boat—and the deck of a Mike Boat, flat-bottomed vessel that it is, is not a place you want to experience any kind of bad seas. The current and the swells had calmed a few hours ago, as the LCU finally made the brilliant decision to drag them out to deeper waters, but they were going back in now, Kismaayo just five hours distant, and the ocean would be rising again; Jones could feel it starting.

Trevor slept next to him on the aft quarterdeck. Bob had crawled into the lazarette hours before; he could sleep anywhere, through anything. Sid was in the wheelhouse, sitting hunched over on the duckboard, scribbling in the coxswain's log.

They were a funny kind of squad, not making any military sense: two privates—Jones and Trevor—and two sergeants—Bob and Sid. But they had been a boat crew, and then friends, for a year before Bob and Sid got their stripes. There had been no time to make adjustments to the crew in the hurried hours before they'd deployed, and Sid—who by birthday alone outranked Bob—had done nothing to raise the issue with their lieutenant. Sid didn't trust anyone but Bob to be his second coxswain—mostly because Bob was better than Sid. So the crew didn't follow the organizational structure as it should; Sid had kept his mouth shut—it was the crew he'd had for almost a year, it was the crew he wanted in Africa.

Jones yawned, closing his eyes, then opening them. He was tired, very tired. The ride was exhausting. Once you got over seasickness, the ocean put you to sleep. It was axiomatic. But he kept thinking he didn't want to miss anything—he didn't want to miss this. Floating silent in the Indian Ocean, yellow trail in their wake, the Southern Cross rising majestically. No, he didn't want to miss this. He thought about grabbing his notebook from his ruck, getting some of this down. But no—he wouldn't get it right. How could you get this right? Sometimes it was time to write, and sometimes it was time to watch.

He sat; he watched.

They'd left Mombasa, Kenya, not onboard their towed Mike Boat but in the LCU that was doing the towing—a more comfortable ride. Waterborne was Waterborne, they all knew each other even though they were from different units—the Mike Boat squad was welcomed onboard and treated kindly by the LCU crew, fresh coffee poured in the tiny mess, *Star Trek* reruns playing on the VCR. Less than an hour out of the Mombasa channel, though, Mr. Rintel—the warrant officer who skippered the LCU—had stuck his head into the mess, pointing at Sid.

"Ya wanna come with me, Sarge?"

They'd all gotten up and followed Mr. Rintel to the aft deck of the LCU. In the sunset light they could see their towed Mike Boat; it wasn't following course straight like it should, but was yawing all over the water, port to starboard and back, the tow cable tensing and relaxing across the distance.

"Someone forget to tie the helm, Sarge?"

Someone had, indeed. The helm was supposed to be tied tight so the Mike Boat's rudder would be dead-straight. The rudder was obviously floating free, though, sending the Mike Boat into a see-saw dance.

Sid rubbed his temples, closing his eyes.

"Yes, sir. Seems that way." He shot a look of death at the other three. No one could remember who had been responsible for the helm, though, and in the end everything on the boat was Sid's responsibility. He wasn't mad, he just sighed.

"Gonna be a problem, Skipper?" he asked.

Rintel laughed.

"Yeah, bit of a problem. It's throwing me off course. And the seas the way they are, it's going to become an even bigger problem. We'll probably snap the towline."

Sid rubbed at his temples again.

Jones looked past the dancing Mike Boat. They were already miles from the Kenyan coast. In the sunset it was almost impossible to make out land anymore. He looked to his right and his eye caught the LCU's bright orange Zodiac workboat, lashed off the port quarter.

"Hey, Skip," he said, getting Rintel's attention. "Can one of your boys take us to our Mike in that thing?"

Rintel looked at the Zodiac, looked at the sea, then looked at Jones. He smiled.

"Yeah, that's the only solution, really. If we want to keep going. And we have to keep going—got a deadline. Ain't gonna be pretty, though. It's rough out there."

They could see that. Besides the side-to-side dance the Mike Boat was doing, it was also riding up and down violently, cresting then falling with a clap on each successive swell and wave.

"So much for *Star Trek*," said Trevor.

Rintel clapped Sid on the back, looking at Jones and Trevor. "You fellas ready to earn your water-wings?"

A corporal named Smith was called down from the bridge and prepped the workboat. He and Jones and Trevor hopped in, and Bob and Sid and Rintel's ACE lowered the craft into the ocean.

"How bad is this gonna suck?" Jones yelled to Smith right before the bottom of the Zodiac hit the dark waves.

"Real bad, Jonesy, real bad."

He was right.

They hit with a smack, instantly drenched from a swamping wave, Jones and Trevor quickly slipping free the cables that had lowered them from the LCU, Smith firing off the outboard motor and pointing them out and away from the larger vessel.

Smith guided the Zodiac back to the Mike Boat, spun around, then spent five minutes or so carefully pacing it, all of them eyeing the frequency and timing of the swells, trying to find a pattern and a safe opening for them to board their boat. Finally, Smith yelled, "Okay, now or never, guys. Skipper wants me to get Bob and Sid on board too before it gets dark."

Trevor nodded.

Smith brought the Zodiac right next to the Mike Boat, a torrent of seawater shooting up and over them as the two crafts bumped. The quarterdeck of the Mike was about four feet over their heads. Trevor threw a looped line over the aft bit of the Mike, pulling it tight to make sure it was seated. He waited for the next swell to rise, cutting the climbing distance by a foot or two, then gripped the line and heaved himself up onto the Mike's deck. He rolled quickly, coming to a stop just aft of the wheelhouse.

"Fuck," Jones whispered softly, taking the line into his hands. He waited for a swell, tensed, lost his nerve, then waited for the next. This time he took it, jumping up and in, bracing his boots on the side of the Mike, then flinging himself over the lip of the deck. As he finished his roll he could hear Smith yell a war whoop in the distance, then the Zodiac was gone, Smith going back to pick up the two buck sergeants.

Jones rolled over onto his back, staring straight up at the sky, adrenaline shooting through his limbs, tingling. Trevor was sitting now, next to him, wiping water from his eyes and ears, laughing out loud. "Waterborne!" he yelled, slamming his open palm down onto Jones's chest.

"Waterborne, my ass," Jones growled, getting to his knees and crawling over and into the wheelhouse to tie the helm into place. By the time he was done Sid and Bob were climbing on board. Trevor dropped into the lazarette to dig through their duffel bags and retrieve dry uniforms for them all.

"Did anyone think to bring something to eat?" Bob asked, leaning with hands on hips against the aft stanchion line. Bob was big as a bear—as big and bulky as Sid was small and skinny—and he ate constantly.

"Fuck," Sid said, and started rubbing at his temples again. "Fuck."

"Gonna be a long night," Bob said. "Happy fucking New Year."

"I am an American fighting man," Trevor recited dryly, his arm around Bob's shoulders. "I will fight to defend things sacred and profane, and I will do it on an empty belly because my dumb ass forgot to bring chow."

Once they were dry and settled, though, it was okay. They all finished puking—with the rough seas, they wouldn't have been able to eat, even if they had brought food—then they got as comfortable as possible, and as the sun finally sank into the waves Jones noticed the phosphorescence for the first time.

And now, middle of the night, radio quietly static, boat silently rising and falling, they slipped through the Indian Ocean. This made it all worth it, Jones thought, stretching his legs out on the deck, turning his nose into the breeze, Trevor snoring quietly next to him. This is a thing you don't want to miss. This is why you're here. His skin was tacky and sticky from sea salt, and it made him smile.

Jones sighed, brought himself to his feet, taking in a last look at the yellow, glowing trail behind them. He lowered his head and slipped into the wheelhouse, nodding to Sid sitting on the duckboard. Jones reached up and switched on their shortwave receiver. They'd been listening to a lot of shortwave recently; Voice of America was silent on the subject of Somalia, but the BBC was giving regular updates. Jones sat next to Sid, and they listened for a while to a British sports show, news on cricket and horse racing mostly. Then the news came on. For the first time they heard mention of the actual city they were en route to: Kismaayo. Plenty of jokes on that name, of course, between them—"Kiss my *what?*"

The clipped British accent on the shortwave reported a death the previous day, a French relief worker, shot in the head at a food and medicine distribution point, just inside Kismaayo proper. Assailants unknown, trying to steal the food stores. They listened wordlessly to the rest of the news, then Jones switched the radio off. They sat there next to each other, on the duckboard.

"What do you think, Sid?"

"I don't know."

Jones nodded, resting his chin on his fists.

Sid closed the log, slipped the book onto the shelf under the radios. He lightly touched his thin mustache, then asked, "Did you see Liz before we left?"

"Briefly. Hard, you know. Getting ready to leave. Not much time. Complicated."

Sid nodded, then said, "You could do worse, Jones."

Jones closed his eyes. "I know," he said.

They sat silent for a while, the boat rocking under them. There was no question to him, not anymore, how he felt about Liz. Not quite lovers, but only by inches, only by strict definition. She fascinated him, captivated him, this woman in a soldier's uniform; her drive, her determination, just as strong as Jones's, her reasons just as dark and unexplored. This was only half the picture, though—her anger, her temper, deserved or not, driving him to stupid actions, spiteful deeds.

And somehow, whenever he opened his mouth to tell her, tell her what she already knew but needed to hear, the words choked stupid in his throat, and they never came out.

"I'm gonna go catch some sleep in the laz," Sid said finally, Jones nodding. Sid stood and stretched. "Happy New Year, Jonesy," he said and ducked out of the wheelhouse.

Alone, Jones stood, then switched the radio on again, not really listening. He held to the edge of the helm console for support against the rocking of the boat, peered out the aft window, into the dark, watching the yellow trail again, trying to imagine this place they were going to, not able to picture it. He was thinking of the French relief worker, head blown off.

These things happen, he thought. *These things happen. Gotta watch yourself. Gotta keep it all together.*

Then: *I am an American fighting man. I will pass out bags of food and try not to get shot . . .* and then he smiled, turning the radio off, wishing now for sleep.

He passed his hand over his empty pocket, thinking silently: *I wish I knew where my wallet was.*

2

PFC Liz Ross sat, legs hanging off the edge of the pier, watching as the small, gray army boats steamed out of Mombasa harbor, into the shipping channel, then disappeared. Nothing left but twinkling reflections off the setting sun. She was smoking a cigarette and humming "Auld Lang Syne" under her breath. *Happy New Year,* she thought.

She was in civilians—all American soldiers in Kenya dressed in civilians, it was part of the arrangement—shorts and sneakers and an Ohio State T-shirt. Her arms and legs were tan after three weeks of African sun. The hotel they put her in had a pool and sundeck; she took full advantage of both. She'd been assigned to HQ, to the Harbormaster, but she didn't have a job yet. Mostly she just tried to stay out of the way, spending her days either sunbathing or exploring Mombasa, looking for cheap gems to bring back to her grandmother to make jewelry, going out at night drinking with the boys.

But the boys were gone now. Just the HQ and Harbormaster detachments left behind in Kenya, another week here then a plane ride up to Somalia, to Mogadishu.

She'd come down here to port today to say good-bye to Jones. He was going to Kismaayo, it wasn't likely they'd see each other again before this was all over, whenever that might be. She'd come down to say good-bye, but they'd been busy—most of the troops on the Mike Boats and LCUs dressed in desert BDUs for the first time, looking like soldiers instead of college kids on spring break, scurrying around, setting tow cables and sealing hatches against ocean swells, piling up cases of MREs and water bottles and counting ammunition and packing rifles and pistols tightly into waterproofed cases for the ride. Jones's head had popped up out of the engine room hatch on his Mike Boat and he'd seen her standing there quietly on the edge of the pier. He'd climbed out and walked over to her, wiping greasy hands on khaki coveralls, sweat pouring off him, reaching into his pocket for a cigarette.

"Soon?" she'd asked.

"About an hour, I think," he said, squinting against the smoke.

"How long up?"

"A full twenty-four hours, they say. At least. We'll ride it on the LCU, though. Mister Rintel's boat. Comfortable, at least."

He was distracted, and not doing a good job of hiding it. When it was time to soldier, nothing else mattered. He was also mad at her, mad for rejecting his apologies weeks before, mostly mad at himself for being mad. Oh, she knew this guy's head, all right; but nothing could be done about it now. Timing had never been good in their relationship.

Is that what we have? she thought. *A relationship?*

Jones smoked, glancing back to the boat, watching Trevor Alphabet and Bob drop boxes into the lazarette.

She reached out and grabbed his hand.

"Careful, right?"

He looked at her directly now, squeezed back once, smiling weakly, then dropped her hand. "Always," he said. "Born careful."

Jones smoked his cigarette and walked back to the boat.

Liz had watched him walk away, down the pier. She shivered, took one step forward, then stopped. She would not follow any man—even this man—down a pier.

Liz sighed now, swinging her legs in front of her over the water, watching as the last LCU rounded the channel bend and went out of sight.

Fuck him, she thought to herself.

But she didn't really mean it.

Jones wasn't really an asshole, even when he acted like one. And maybe this was as much her fault as his. Maybe it was nobody's fault. She adored him, loved him—but she had very set ideas about things, and would not fling her heart indiscriminately. Life was too difficult, the army too difficult, to bear that kind of pain.

It was a back-and-forth thing with them—juvenile, she was quite aware—for almost two years now, since they'd met as newbie privates in AIT school at Ft. Eustis. He'd push, and she'd pull away in the opposite direction. That's how it started, with young Jones newly separated from his young wife, a wild private, a whore like all the other young and shaved soldier-whores at the NCO club on a Saturday night. She liked this guy Jones, this walking contradiction, was drawn to his conversations and laugh, to his acoustic guitar hidden in his wall locker, to his drive and determination to outsoldier anything and anybody that crossed his path. But she wasn't interested in falling for a cute soldier-whore. Jones pushed in her direction, but she refused to go there. Not trusting his words, but happy with his friendship. After they graduated from AIT and moved on to their respective companies she dated some of their mutual friends, easy and quick and uncumbersome relationships, and Jones laughed and always bought a pitcher for her and whoever her date was that night.

In different corners, with different dates, closing in on midnight at the Gasthaus, she remembers looking up every few minutes to see if he was looking and every time without fail he was. She squeezed out from her group, around the corner, down the hall, and there was Jones, good old Jones, standing outside the ladies' room door.

"You must make a lousy date, Ben," she laughed at him, slapping her open palm down on his chest. "Have you said a single word to her tonight?"

He shook his head, putting his hand around hers, holding it against him. "She hasn't noticed," he said, smiling. "Besides, I never talk to civilians."

"You only fuck them?" she asked, raising her eyebrows.

"You said it, Lizzie, not me."

Keeping her eyes on his she pushed past him into the bathroom, crowded with nineteen- and twenty-year-old girls laughing and teasing in deep Southern accents, primping at the mirror, comparing rank and income level of their respective boyfriends. *Groupies,* Jones called them—when he was being gracious. He was with one of these girls tonight. When

Liz pushed back out into the hall he wasn't there. In the bar her group was drunk and laughing by their dartboard, and the booth where Jones had been sitting with the civilian girl was empty. He came up behind her.

"Dance?" he asked.

Liz looked at him, then nodded, without saying anything. He held her, and they turned slowly to Marvin Gaye. In all this time, in all their nights at this and every other bar, they had never danced together. She expected him to be awkward and uncomfortable and laughing and apologetic, but he slipped around her perfectly and moved quietly and she tightened her arms around his waist in relief and looked very hard at his face. When he noticed her looking he smiled sadly, lowering his head. "Do you know why I like you, Liz?" he whispered into her ear. She shook her head. "Because you get the joke," he said simply, then kissed her.

Later she explained the reasons for needing to leave with the friends she came with, and she apologized and she meant it, and he knew it and said so. He said, "You know where I live," and as she squeezed his hand and turned to go he pulled her back quickly and asked, "You do know where I live, right?"

She thought on it, dreamed on it, all the bad in falling for a friend, especially this friend. Jones knew too much about her, and that bothered her now. Things she'd said, just venting with a friend, none of them things she would want known to a lover, a man, in a relationship. But Liz did know where Jones lived, and finally she closed her eyes and jumped.

It was the week his final divorce papers came in the mail. The legal black-and-white that made him less of a father, less of a man, half-souled and a hollow failure. A repeat of his parents. Jones looking up at Liz from his fourth-hand barracks couch, wide-eyed and hurting, not saying anything. He didn't just pull back from her, he recoiled.

It stung and she tried not to take it personally—she understood—and walking back to her room that night up the wet alley between the barracks all she could think was *How could you be so fucking stupid?*

Then Jones was back, and Liz took him in. A different Jones, but there he was, slowly, slowly, over the next months, neither of them pushing, as if in silent agreement, two wounded and recovering monks. Sober and alone and away from the army they quietly spent time together, driving in Jones's little red Mazda up to Washington to see the White House and the

Smithsonian, driving down to the Outer Banks in the winter to see the snow on the beach, watching the flakes pile softly on the sand and drown in the ocean, just watching and feeling it like two adults might, two friends, red cheeked and smiling. He took a week's leave to go play guitar with friends in New York and she and Trevor Alphabet had gone with him, Alphabet keeping quiet in the backseat, giving space—*a smart one, that Alphabet,* she thought now.

When Jones was there, he made her laugh and he made her warm. When he was gone she missed him, missed his fingers, even missed his silent gaze. And over simple thoughts like that come dawning realizations of things deeper, something going on, emotion catching in the back of the throat, something sliding heavily in the heart.

And then Jones, in her barracks room, just a month ago, all the lights out, David Letterman yabbering away on the tiny TV, sitting on the bed together. He was pushing a brush through her long hair, slowly combing it out, and he'd reached around her and put his fingertips on her chin and turned her head back toward him and kissed her gently. She'd turned her whole body then, reaching back for him, sliding her arms around him, her lips and tongue finding his throat and cheeks and mouth and—

And then he was gone, dropping the hairbrush, mumbling—something, *what?*—a flash of light from the hall as he'd opened the door, slipped out, and was gone.

She was mad, so fucking mad, madder than she'd ever been in her life. *What the hell is this?* she'd thought.

He'd been back the next day, showing up at her door in the morning, sweaty from running, apologizing as if his life depended on it, babbling about fear and not wanting to hurt her, and for the first time coming out and saying what she'd waited so long to hear, those three words—she'd refused to talk to him. The next day as well. And then the next day after that, her hand trembling with decision and forgiveness, she'd called the CQ phone at his barracks at 1098th and asked for him and the private who answered said no one could talk they were all locked-in for deployment and when she'd thrown on a robe and gone down to her own dayroom the company was forming and her platoon sergeant saw her and said she'd better get into uniform because we'll be traveling soon, we're all going to Africa.

Liz stood, stretched, then began the long walk back up the hill from the Mombasa port to the city and her hotel.

Fuck it, she thought, making no decisions. Fuck it.

She always fell for musicians. Liz had told him this once, early on, and Jones had laughed and quoted from something she couldn't remember anymore, saying *Careful, Liz—musicians lead complicated lives.* He'd smiled then and put his arm around her, the way a friend puts an arm around another friend, driving slowly through traffic toward Norfolk and a blues bar they had found on the waterfront there. After a moment he added, *So do soldiers, so I'm two for two.* He laughed again, looking straight ahead through the windshield, and said *Good thing you're not in love with me, Liz.*

Yeah, good thing, Jones, she thought now, walking slowly up the hill. *Good fucking thing.*

JONES:
Thirty Days in San Francisco, *Part One*

California—May 1993

1

Three weeks out of Somalia, one week out of the army, most of the way to Seattle. San Francisco is colder than expected, and I'm not well prepared. I'm staying in an attic, it's unheated, and in the mornings I can see my breath circle around my head like smoke as I pull my body from under the thin comforter on the bare mattress. I've always wanted to see San Francisco, and now I'm here because I have no money to go any farther. Seattle beckons, but Seattle will have to wait.

The only reason I have a bed at all is Dave Yunger. Sitting in a corner of Dave's Brooklyn apartment last week, the night before I got on the westbound Greyhound, sucking cheap red wine. Dave's apartment had been my second home back when I thought I knew how to play guitar, before I learned to execute a perfect left-face. I didn't want to come here now—had not planned on it, did not want to see anyone—but I needed a place in New York to crash before the bus departure, and it occurred to me that Dave used to live in the Bay Area.

He asks what I'm up to—making conversation as we drink.

What I'm up to is leaving. I say I'll be taking a bus to San Francisco. I've never been. Gonna regroup my head there, build up some cash, then head to Seattle maybe.

"A little vacation? After the war?" He smiles.

Not vacation, because I have no plan to come back.

"Are you and Katy splitting up?" he asks, nicely.

Pause.

"Dave, we've been divorced for almost two years."

But Dave doesn't know—couldn't know. I've been gone a long time. No one in Brooklyn knows what to make of me, no one in Jersey. I sure as hell don't know what to make of me.

But Dave lived in San Francisco—he's got this friend, Cliff, a guitar player he was in a band with. Cliff's mom left him this big old house right on Asbury Avenue in Berkeley.

"I'll give him a buzz. He'll put you up. He's got more room than he can deal with."

Truth is, Cliff doesn't have much room. He got married, had a kid. Then he needed money, so he turned the place into a quasi commune and rented out the empty rooms to various folks. But, he does agree to put me up. Way up. In the attic.

But that's nice enough as it is, a very friendly thing for him to do considering he knows me not at all and hasn't seen or heard from his friend Dave in almost a decade.

2

It's an attic.

The top floor of a Victorian, unfinished, bare wood floor and cross beams. It's clean, though, and there is a corner set up for living. Cliff rents the space to a woman, a writer. She spends most of the year in Arizona, using this space when she's in town for a month or two. She'll be back in June, so Cliff says I'll have to be gone by then. He hasn't told her I'm using her bed.

It's cold, and it's quiet, and the light in the morning is a dark red, the sun coming through the windows and melting into the large colored tapestries she's hung to cover the naked walls. I spend my mornings sitting at her desk with a mug of cold instant coffee, trying very hard to write something. Anything. A song, a story, a poem, a letter. And, on every morning I try this, nothing comes to be written. I put a picture of Liz in front of me on the desk, her in green BDUs, smiling and strong. But her smile looks hard to me, questioning—*Jones, where are you? What are you doing?* I am embarrassed, ashamed, and I turn the picture over and get back to my not-writing.

I give up after an hour or so, and turn on the clock radio, tuned to Pacifica. I listen as I go through this writer's stuff. She's got boxes of manuscripts, poems, journals. She has three published books, and I read them all. Her writing feels close to me, nearby. I'm surprised to find I like it. I imagine this woman writing here, in this very chair I'm sitting in, at this very desk, words flowing from her effortlessly, getting the feel, the nuance she's after, stories just coming—maybe from the depth of the red glow that fills the space here in the morning. I read of her mother, and of her daughter, who is my age. I find a picture in a frame under a box, and realize it must be this woman, this writer. She's a big gal, not fat, but grand. She's in a bright dress with a wide Bella Abzug hat falling over her shoulder.

I put her picture on the desk until it too makes me uncomfortable, then I put it back.

The radio blabs on and on, saying not much at all about the horror this particular reporter feels about the ongoing American imperialist mission to Somalia. Pacifica Radio hasn't had this much to bitch about in twenty years—this is even more fun than the Gulf War. I turn the radio off, suddenly inspired, lift my pen, and . . .

My pen floats there in my hand, floats, then comes to rest finally on the table next to my head, my head now sideways, resting on the table. I put the radio back on, and now I push back the red tapestry and look out the window. It's far enough along in the day to go outside with the light clothes I have. It's warmed, and I really should be going out now.

3

Cliff is skinny, thirty or so, a friendly guy with black, curly hair. He's on the porch, smoking a toothpick joint. His wife is gone, as is everyone else in the house. Besides the warmth factor, another reason I wait so long to leave in the mornings is an attempt to avoid the others. This really is a commune, not just a rental deal, and I think the others are pissed that Cliff let me move in without asking them their opinion on it. I don't think they trust me. I don't think they trust anyone from east of Sacramento. I try to avoid them, and I certainly never share with any of them that I'm just out of the army. I think of telling them Jan's story: that I'm AWOL. I'm sure they would rally behind that. When I see them in the evening, though, picking through lentils in the kitchen, sliding down the hall toward the toilet, I find I don't want to speak to anyone, especially to gain a questionable acceptance.

But Cliff is okay. I like him, and I can tell he likes me—Dave clued him in on my deal, and Cliff is fine with it. He's strumming an old Alvarez acoustic, the roach tucked into the corner of his mouth. He says he hasn't played in years, but my being here inspired him to pull out the ol' ax and pound around for a while. He's pretty good, too. I pull a root beer barrel from my pocket and fiddle with the wrapper while I listen to him.

We sit and talk, him strumming as our words flow, and an hour slips by. He's easy to talk to, an easy person. He'll be going to Sacramento tonight with his wife for a Dead show, and asks if I'd like to come along. He doesn't have a ticket for me, but it's a nice ride, and the parking-lot parties are always fun. But I tell him no, tonight is an open blues at the Freight & Salvage, and I really should be over there, I owe it to myself to play after being away from music for so long. I have no intention of going to the Freight & Salvage, I don't even know if they have an open blues night, but that's what slips out of my mouth when he asks. Truth is, I can't imagine myself wandering through a parking lot filled with whirling teenagers in hippy clothes. I imagine my fifteen-year-old self twirling happily, stoned and stupidly blissful, bumping into my current self at a Dead show. I think my fifteen-year-old self would be revolted. I thank Cliff for the invitation.

Time flows, and it's time for Cliff to get to work. He does something at the university—I never did quite figure out what—and he goes in at noon.

I think, and I can't fathom, these people, all of these people, with their jobs, and how did they get them? They've got these jobs and it all seems like a given; they don't seem to think about it much, and they go in at noon.

It's noon now, and Cliff is walking up the sidewalk to work. The day, like all my days now, is sliding, sliding along.

4

The walk to the station to catch the BART train into the city is almost a mile, neighborhoods changing along the way, from old and rich to old and middle-class to old and poor. BART itself is shiny and quiet and clean and makes me very nervous. San Francisco in microcosm, the BART. Too polite. Walking to the station isn't bad, it's all downhill. Going back up the hill to Cliff's house is another matter.

When I first got to town on the Greyhound at the beginning of the month I followed Cliff's directions and took BART out here and walked up the hill. Me, my backpack, my duffel bag, my guitar case, and the big hat I bought at a truck stop in Wyoming. The handle fell off the guitar case about halfway up the hill, the case hitting the ground with a thud, a dull musical echo from inside, my heart falling from my chest as I sat on the ground, giving up. Giving up; I think it happened right there at that moment, as my guitar hit the sidewalk, and I realized my whole problem was that I should have given up months ago—years ago. I took off my big hat and sat on my backpack in the middle of the sidewalk, letting the foot traffic flow around me, and I was quietly miserable for a while.

Don't mind me, sitting here on the sidewalk with all my shit around—just in town, dead flat broke, halfway walking to someone's house, someone I didn't know, who was expecting me.

Don't mind me—I'm a soldier, an American fighting man, doesn't that explain it?

No, of course it doesn't. No one knows what that means anymore. Not even me.

5

Berkeley is clean longhaired kids in new BMWs, perfectly manicured lawns, crowded coffeehouses, smart-looking fuckers walking around with hands in pockets, women in suits smoking cigars, and lots of gorgeous little parks filled with an unbelievable number of homeless people in stinking rags. The only thing I can figure about the homeless is that, like me, they thought it might be warmer in northern California than it is, and all headed this way. I've spent large chunks of my life in Philadelphia and New York and I've never seen so many homeless in one place. It scares me.

6

I desperately need to make some money.

Besides the impending return of Grand-Writer-in-Abzug-Hat to her attic room, and my probably joining the ranks of the Berkeley homeless, I have to send cash home, cash for the baby, money for my little Emma. Having decided I don't like making a living with a gun, and with the woman I'm in love with somewhere overseas, I'm on my way to Seattle, to work the fishing boats, and maybe even get in touch with my generation, my people, my clan. Can you dig it? *Time* magazine says while I was gone in the army all my people moved to Seattle. Dig it. Who am I to argue with *Time*?

I think so, anyway. The destination was Trevor's idea, carefully explained to me one night in the barracks—months before Somalia—after he'd been watching too much MTV. He said it's the only city to perfectly combine our personalities. He did the research, though, and he used to say there's a lot of money to be made in Washington on fishing boats for those who don't mind being uncomfortable for long periods of time.

I have a need to both make a lot of money and be uncomfortable for a long period of time.

But I don't have enough money for the last part of the trip, which is why I'm stuck here. Here and broke. And wondering about vows. And worrying about a little girl in New Jersey, and a strong woman in Mogadishu. And starting to feel just a bit like an asshole.

There are no jobs in San Francisco, not for twenty-three-year-old ex-soldiers with no college and no real experience in anything. Go figure. I go to the VA to check into job placement, they say it will be three weeks until my paperwork catches up with me from back East. I don't have three weeks. I'm starving.

I answered an ad in the paper for cook at a vegetarian joint in Oakland. I dropped by, interviewed, and the woman, Grace, told me to come by again the next day. Grace was amazingly tall and even more amazingly thin, a dirty-white apron hanging off her pale and scrawny neck, over a long dress that looked like a burlap sack. She was a nervous woman, tapping her fingers on the counter the entire time we talked, sipping on a never-ending supply of what I guess was tea but smelled like cow shit. She glanced over my handwritten application, said she'd take me on for a day, see how it went, and then we could talk more.

So I came the next day. She seemed surprised to see me. But I worked the day. It felt good to be working, good to move. As the dinner rush, such as it was, got under way she started asking me about other places I had worked, what could I contribute to their menu. I was thinking seafood, I don't know why. Dreaming of Seattle, maybe. I started telling her about a scallop pasta thing I learned to make on Easton Avenue in New Brunswick.

She dropped her knife.

"Scallops?"

What I wanted to say was, "No! I said *scallions* . . ."

But that wasn't it, and she knew it and I knew it and less than five minutes later I was out the door.

Once a flesh cooker always a flesh cooker, I guess.

San Francisco. Jesus wept.

7

The next day, in Chinatown, I pulled a flyer off a phone pole and shoved it in my pocket. The flyer said "Wanted: Strong Men, Great Pay. Military a Plus." It gave an address ten blocks east.

I found the address, looked around, then looked up. I looked back down, and shook my head. The sign said xxxTASY.

Jesus wept.

I looked around again, wiped at my mouth, then opened the door.

Kismaayo, *Part One*

Kismaayo, Somalia—January 1, 1993

1

The seaport of Kismaayo, Somalia, lies on the tip of a peninsula—half a mile wide at the thickest, only one hundred feet in some spots, a big and rocky hill in the middle—that curves out in a crescent from the city proper then parallels it two miles down the coast. Stand on the western shore of the port and you're looking at the city of Kismaayo, a mile or less across the bay; stand on the eastern side of the port and you're straddling the equator, with the Indian Ocean stretched out forever, nothing but water until Indonesia.

The docks, built by the Italians during the colonial era, had been all but destroyed in the war with Ethiopia a decade before; the tops of sunken Soviet-built gunboats sticking out of the water in the shallower sections of the bay stood like a ghost fleet, silent and dead—like a warning. Because there were no docks, the few vessels in port had to tie-up directly to the concrete quay wall. With the tide rising and falling as much as ten feet some days, life seemed to consist of nothing but the never-ending task of letting-out or tightening-up lines; those failing ended up with either a boat still tied but floating twenty-some feet from the wall, or a boat lost at sea because the lines snapped overnight. You could walk on a vessel at noon, one flat step from quay wall to deck, and come up from down below four hours later to find that you need to climb the quay wall to get yourself back on land.

Their first night in this port, exhausted and drained from the forty-eight-hour run up the coast from Kenya, Trevor Alphabet and Jones sat on the quay wall and watched something few Americans in a hundred years had seen: the absolute disappearance of an entire city. They knew there was no electricity in Kismaayo, there hadn't been any public utilities in Somalia for well over a year—most places well over a decade—but it's one thing to know that, something else entirely to appreciate it. Sitting on the quay wall, pasty white and still too seasick to eat anything but a cracker, they had the length of a minor African city laid out in their view across the bay. But as the sun dropped, the shadows lengthened, the dark of the water rose to meet the dark of the sky and intertwine, and slowly but surely the entire city was swallowed by the dark. Not a light, not a sign of a building, nothing.

The LCU that towed them from Mombasa had dropped the tow cable five miles out from Kismaayo—Mr. Rintel saluting a farewell from the bridge wing—then steamed on north toward Mogadishu, leaving the Mike Boat to motor in here alone. The other two Mike Boats making up 2nd Platoon of the 710th Provisional Boat Company would be towed in the next day, along with their Transportation Corps lieutenant, a mostly harmless Jesus freak named Klover. Sid and Bob, the two sergeants, had gone to find someone in charge to report their arrival, so Jones and Trevor sat and took this sight in alone, as awestruck as their seasickness would allow.

A corporal, wearing the shoulder patch of the 10th Mountain from Ft. Drum, New York, walked up from behind them, M16 slung across his back. He stamped out a smoke under his boot on the concrete of the quay wall.

"Quite a sight, yeah?" he asked, more than a bit of Alabama creeping through his voice. "It don't get more fucking *gone* than that, boys."

He shifted his rifle, then turned to face back to wherever it was he had come from.

"It'll light up soon enough, though," he said, turning back and reaching into his pocket for a Tic Tac. "You give her an hour or two, you'll see some fucking light."

Trevor looked up at him, raising one of his huge Polish eyebrows in a question.

"Y'know, tracers," the corporal drawled. "Tracers, mortar tracks, that kind of shit. Fireworks. The moolies all come out of hiding around ten or so and start shooting the bejesus out of each other. Hell, you can pretty much set your watch by it. I been here from the start, two three weeks now, and they ain't let me down yet. You watch, you'll see."

Trevor raised the other eyebrow in response, creating one thick line over his eyes, brushing cracker crumbs from his lap.

"Do they come over here?" he asked.

"Who? The moolies?"

Alphabet shook his head. "No, the tracers. Do you guys ever get hit here? Do they shoot at us?"

"Nah," said the corporal, pocketing his Tic Tacs. "You see 'em go back and forth but I ain't never seen one come this way. Ev'r now and then you'll see a flash make for the water, but she won't ever get no farther than say halfway 'crost. I don't think they got anything powerful enough to send this way."

He stopped, then smiled. "Hope not, anyway!"

Jones looked over at Trevor, who was silently eyeing the distance from the edge of Kismaayo to the deck of their boat.

"Well, though, now that I think on it, you fellas might want to not sleep right quite out in the open tonight, though. Gonna be a *BIG* fuckin' show tonight I think, so you never know. You guys wouldn't have seen it, just comin' in and all, but the Belgians are gearing up right behind the gate to the port, couple-a platoons of 'em, in them fucked-up white Volvos they call trucks. Some rumor going around that Adid is down from Mogadishu—" (he pronounced this *Maahg-aa-dee-scheew*) "—and I think they're gonna go light a fire under his ass."

The U.N. operation in Kismaayo was still mostly the Belgian army. 10th Mountain Division had a force slowly building here, but it was still just commo and support and MPs. Otherwise, the only other Americans in port were a dive detachment and a small group of army utility boats (three tugs and a crane barge) sent to raise and clear the sunken gunships from the shallows—all these from Ft. Eustis, like Trevor and Jones—and a Special Forces ODA that spent most of their time in the desert and coastal villages south of the city. The Belgians had a regiment's worth of infantry camped out here, and it sounded like they would be making themselves known tonight.

The corporal eyed their Mike Boat, tied to the wall fifteen feet away.

"I thought y'all was the navy when ya pulled in," he said, pushing his helmet back on his head, wiping some sweat. "I was actually comin' down here to raz ya a bit. Didn't know the army *had* boats."

Jones nodded, smiled weakly, and forced another cracker into his mouth, still fighting nausea. Sometimes it was worse after you got back to dry land.

"My name's Dale, by the way, Dale Scruggs," the corporal said, sticking out his hand to Jones, who shook it in return. "You guys get to do any fishing off that thing?" Dale asked, pointing to the Mike Boat, coming to the sudden realization that he might have found a new diversion from his boring duties, and quickly and silently counting how many cartons of cigarettes he had stashed in his duffel that he might trade for a spin out of the bay.

Before Jones could answer the corporal's question, a desert-tan American deuce-and-a-half truck sped behind them down the dock, screeching rubber as it braked hard in front of a large tent with a faded red cross painted on the top. A strangled howl came from the back of the truck, making Jones's skin crawl and pushing Trevor up on his feet. Four soldiers, 10th Mountain MPs, jumped out of the back and started pulling off two stretchers with bodies on them. A nurse in BDUs came running from the tent.

"What the hell is that?" Jones asked the corporal, who—after looking over at the truck—seemed perturbed his question about fishing had been forgotten. Another cry came from the one stretcher, the body on it writhing. His companion lay motionless on the second one.

"Ah, that ain't nothing but moolies," the corporal said, glancing over. "No sooner than we get here two weeks ago and secure the port, the moolies started trying to find ways in. Y'know, to see what they could take that wasn't pinned down and such. A few of 'em got in one night, snuck through the salt flats over by the gate, and stole an M16 out of some tent. Idiot fucking private sleeping right there on his cot, left the rifle laying on the ground beside him, moolies snagged it and made off. Same damn thing happened to a lieutenant in Mogadishu. I know 'cause replacement requisitions gotta come through me."

The corporal was facing them again, no interest in the action on the back of the truck. "Anyway, the next night, here, and ever since, the Belgians been sending a sniper team into the flats after dark. Them boys is *fucked!* Stone-cold badass. Y'know, I guess they're just supposed to scare 'em off or something, but the moolies wasn't getting the hint, so a few nights ago them Belgians started shooting for keeps. 'Cept they don't aim for the head or chest. They wait until the fuckers are facing the other way, then aim for their assholes. That way, when the bullet hits, it goes through and tears their jimmies off'n the other side."

Jones turned from the tent and looked back at the corporal, hoping to see some sign that this guy was making this up, or even exaggerating. Seasick again, he wondered if he should go over and help the troops from the truck, but both stretchers were in the tent now. A third, and last, scream came from inside.

"Sick, huh?" the corporal said, gleefully. "Well, y'know, us Americans being the pussies that we are, the colonels and the generals get all fucked up, like they don't want to leave these fuckers bleeding in the flats. So every night around sundown you'll hear a couple-a pops from in there, and when the Belgians come out, they send our guys in to pick 'em up. Mopping up the moolies, I call it. Some fucked-up war, huh? Ya shoot 'em, then ya gotta go drag 'em out and fix 'em. What's the fucking point?"

Jones saw Sid and Bob come walking around the tent, from the other side, oblivious to what just happened. They were joking with each other about something.

Trevor was still staring at the first-aid tent, like he was waiting for another scream. The corporal saw the two sergeants walking toward them and, in the time-honored tradition of corporals about to be approached by ranking soldiers they don't know, decided to play it safe and leave.

"Gotta go, y'all," he said, raising a hand to Trevor and Jones. "Maybe we can talk about that fishing tomorrow?"

Jones nodded at him absently, running his eyes back and forth in a line between the departing corporal, the first-aid tent, and Bob and Sid. "Yeah," he mumbled. "Yeah, thanks. Stop by tomorrow if we're here."

The corporal grinned.

"Don'tch'all forget what I said about tonight," he yelled back over his shoulder. "Ten o'clock light show. Set yer watch by it!" Then he was gone.

The corporal was right. About an hour later, the four of them playing poker on the quarterdeck by the glow of the port running-light, tape player in the wheelhouse turned down low to Ozzy Ozbourne, a green army canteen filled with cheap vodka set down next to the cards between them, Jones turned his head in the direction of the city and saw five red streaks go blazing south along the far coastline. He looked down at his digital watch; 2154—six minutes to ten. They put their cards down and turned to watch the show.

Within fifteen minutes it had heated into what had to be a blazing firefight over there; but from the port it looked simply like a pretty fireworks show, albeit one that ran horizontally rather than vertically. The illusion was made complete by the wind and noise from the water completely erasing whatever sound must be accompanying the shots and explosions occurring just a mile across the bay from them. None of them had ever seen anything like this before.

"Jesus please-us," Bob whispered quietly.

"You think we should get in the welldeck, or move behind one of the warehouses?" Sid asked, to no one in particular. He outranked them all. No one answered, so they stayed put. Jones looked over and saw Sid, probably unconsciously, reach out his hand and pull his Kevlar helmet, resting on the deck about a foot from him, over to where it was touching his leg.

They stayed glued to the show ("It's like MTV," Trevor said at one point, "just a little more dangerous") for almost two hours. The firefight would wax and wane, building in intensity, then stopping altogether for as long as twenty minutes. It drifted in a very determined line, from the southern portion of the city, up the only hill visible, then straight into what had looked in the day to be the center of town. "Someone's got a plan," Bob said, observing this. "Someone's got an objective." At one point what seemed to be a whole second battle opened up just to the north of the main fight, a series of bright explosions (these they could hear, finally, causing Sid to take his helmet from the deck and actually put it on his head), followed by the largest grouping of tracers they had seen yet, these headed south and into the main fight. "Gentlemen," Jones whispered, "I give you our next guest, the Belgian airborne." And, indeed, it did seem like a superior force had thrown its hand in, maybe overwhelming the two sides that had originally been fighting. After a heated ten-minute exchange, the biggest yet, most of it coming from the north, the whole thing seemed to simmer down.

"Jesus," said Trevor, "it really is like fireworks, right down to the big finish."

Another hour passed, and they sat there, not saying much, still staring at where the city should have been if they could have seen it. A few occasional tracers crossed ("Mopping up," Bob said, not unkindly, but it made Jones think of the corporal's heartless comment), but for the most part the fight seemed to be done.

"That kid said they do this almost every night," Trevor said. "It's a wonder there's anyone left in the city to kill."

A Belgian officer, they couldn't figure his rank, came running up to their boat, motioning wildly with his hands, trying to say something in stilted and accented English. Jones finally figured out he wanted them to turn their running-lights off.

"Fuck," Sid mumbled to himself as he reached into the wheelhouse to flip the switch. "What the fuck was I thinking?" Sid took his new sergeant stripes very seriously, and was easily embarrassed when he made some kind of "military mistake." Bob, just as new to his stripes, seemed not to give a shit. Even though they were pinned the same day, Sid was a year older, which gave him the ranking position. Bob, who really hadn't sought after the stripes, figured that was reason enough for him not to be concerned with anything approaching responsibility. The Belgian officer hurried off, cursing at them under his breath.

Bob and Trevor already had their sleeping pads laid out on the deck, Bob sitting on his, taking off his boots, Trevor on his back, staring straight up into the sky. Jones reached down into the lazarette for his pad, while Sid did what he always did when mad at himself for a breach of NCO responsibility: he crawled into the wheelhouse and scribbled furiously into the logbook, hoping to make up for his error of leaving the lights on at night by keeping the ever-important log up to date.

2

Jones didn't realize he had fallen asleep until Sid woke him—thirty minutes later, and Sid had his soft cap on, shaking him violently with one hand while his other hand was shaking Bob. Trevor, Jones saw as he looked up, was standing on the quay wall, waiting for them.

"What the fuck?" Jones whispered loudly. "Are they shooting at us?"

"No. Get up, man, *get up!*" Sid crossed the quarterdeck in two steps and joined Trevor on the wall, and the two of them broke into a sprint, making for the first-aid tent.

Bob shoved his feet down into his boots, shirt still off, his chest the size of a tank. As he and Jones rounded the wheelhouse to step from the deck onto the wall five white Volvo trucks with Belgian colors on the door pulled up to a screeching halt in front of the aid station. There were at least thirty troops scattered around the trucks, all of them with some kind of weapon in their hand, all of them in some kind of motion. Jones and Bob saw Sid and Trevor reach the first truck and jump up on the back where a Belgian soldier, his rifle slung across his back, was hanging off the rail, waving at them for help. As Jones stepped up onto the wall from the boat, he saw Sid look down into the back of the truck, then yell something he couldn't hear. Sid's whole body shook in one big wave, and Trevor grabbed him by the belt to steady him. By then two other American soldiers had gotten there, MPs with stretchers, and were motioning for Trevor and Sid to grab whatever was in the truck and lower it down to them.

Jones jumped up onto the truck and looked in. It didn't make any sense to him. Some part of his brain recognized he was looking at flesh, human flesh, but he couldn't grasp the big picture. He knew it was flesh, but the *shape* of it didn't make any sense. *Is this guy rolled into a ball?* he thought. *What the hell happened out there to scare him so much that he rolled himself up in a ball?*

Trevor, in the back of the truck now, reached with both arms and picked it up. *How did he do that? He picked up that whole guy, rolled in a ball . . .*

And then Trevor lunged and passed it to him, and Jones saw that it wasn't a guy rolled in a ball, so that all you could see of him was the back of his torso. It was very simply just the back of a man's torso. He held it close in his arms, looking down, recognizing it now, feeling its heft, a small scream building itself up in the back of his throat. He bit down fiercely on his lip and whipped his head to the side, looking in anguish at Bob, still on the ground, then back at the mass of flesh in his hands. What he saw now was unmistakably a tattoo, a serpent curled around something, but you couldn't see the serpent's head because where the head should have been the body ceased to be. The sound overpowered his clenched teeth and he let out a cry, turning and throwing this thing, this fucking disgusting thing, onto the stretcher, falling then off the back of the truck, landing so hard on his ass he bit his tongue. His hands were covered in the blood of the dead Belgian soldier.

Off to his right, coming around the side of the truck, an American officer, an MP major, was screaming into a walkie-talkie, but all Jones caught were bits:

"... *helicopter now!! ... don't fucking tell me ... Yes, the whole goddamn squad, they were all in the truck ... mined, bombed, I don't fucking know!!! ... went back and got them from the city ... I don't speak French, Jesus Christ there's only three alive ...*"

As the major passed, Jones saw Sid, sitting on his hands, ten feet away, mumbling something under his breath, his eyes two pieces of blank coal.

Looking back up, Jones almost screamed again: Leaning out of the back of the truck above him, both Trevor and Bob were furiously lifting bodies from the truck bed, passing them to the stretchers below, but Bob hadn't put his shirt on, and when he turned back toward the front of the truck the light hit him just right and Jones saw his entire chest, and half his face, was awash in blood.

Jones got up, furiously wiping his bloody hands on his BDU pants, and stumbled over to the door of the aid tent. The inside was brightly lit, and nothing but movement: soldiers running back and forth and, more than once, into each other. People screaming in French and English, nobody understanding one another. Two stretchers had been laid out on top of a pile of boxes, a swarm of men in white seemed to be doing something to the bodies on them. He heard a nurse, crying hysterically, and caught "... aren't we here to help?!? Why are they killing us?"

A soldier with a stethoscope around his neck—Jones assumed he was a doctor—grabbed him by the arm. "What's your blood type?" he yelled in his ear.

"What?"

Blood type? Killing us?

Where's my fucking wallet?

The doctor grabbed at Jones's dog tags, dangling loose around his neck, studied them quickly then said, "B-positive. Your lucky day." The man threw him back into a folding chair in the corner, as another soldier walked up and rammed a needle into his arm. Jones looked up at him, then at the needle hanging from his own flesh, two steps behind what was being done to him.

"Just in time, fella," the doctor said, and walked away. The second soldier sat down to collect Jones's blood in a bag, not saying a word, his fingertips tapping nervously against his thigh. For a second, Jones almost said to him: *Hey, my buddy Bob out there has got all the blood you guys need on his chest . . .*

He closed his eyes and tried to let his brain flat-line. It didn't work. Over and over in his head, like a mantra: *my buddy Bob has got the blood, if only I could find my fucking wallet . . . the pimp's got my wallet, and if we could find it you'd have all the blood you need from Bob . . .*

He was in the tent thirty minutes, and when they released him he was wobbling on his feet. "Go to the mess and get a banana," the bloodsucking soldier said to him, then was gone behind a curtain.

He pulled the tent flap back and stepped into the night. The trucks were gone, like they'd never been there at all. There were still soldiers around, mostly Belgian, but not as many. Over by the closest warehouse he could see an American colonel, head down, listening to a Belgian NCO who seemed to be crying, his hands gesturing wildly as he explained something. A squad of Belgian enlisted were behind them, standing guard over what looked to be a group of three Somali men lying facedown on the ground, hands tied behind their backs.

He found Trevor, standing alone at the side of the quay wall, looking across the bay toward Kismaayo. His soft cap was in his hands, and he was twisting it.

"Where'dya go?" Trevor asked—three sharp, pounding syllables.

Jones held out his arm, pointing to the bandage. "They needed blood."

Trevor nodded.

Jones pulled out his Marlboros then his lighter, dropping them both the first time, then getting it to work.

"Jonesy, they . . ." Trevor started, then stopped himself short. He paused, then turned and faced Jones. His eyes were wide, like a kid's. There was a streak of blood on his cheek.

"Another Belgian truck pulled up right after we got the last body off. They pulled these three guys, local guys, outta the back, cuffed and blindfolded. They pulled 'em off the truck, and threw 'em against this wall." Trevor sucked in quick, coughed, then grabbed Jones's arm. "I saw this colonel, I think he was a colonel, American, running toward them, he was yelling at them to stop, and I didn't know what the fuck he was screaming at. I'm watching him run over, and as I'm watching him—Boom!— I hit the floor of the truck, I'm like 'Shit, one of 'em had a fucking gun.' And when I stick my head up, I see this colonel, he stopped running, he's just standing there, staring, shaking his head. I look over, and they shot them, Jonesy. I think they lined these three sorry fucks up against the wall and shot them."

Jones looked down at the cigarette between his fingers, shaking violently, then back up into Trevor's eyes.

Where's my fucking wallet? he thought. *Where in the FUCK is my motherfucking wallet?*

Without a word, he walked back to the boat, leaving Trevor alone on the quay wall.

JONES:
Thirty Days in San Francisco, *Part Two*

California—May 1993

1

It's dark and it's cool as the doors of XXXTASY swing shut behind me. My eyes have trouble making the quick switch. It smells of disinfectant in here. Disinfectant and armpits.

I'm in a foyer, I guess, and there are three doors leading farther into the building. The one on the left standing open into the book and video store; it's bright in there, four or five men pulling magazines and videos off the shelves and examining them. The door on my right is closed and has a sign over it, LIVE WOMEN ALL ACTION $1 PEEPS. And directly in front of me the door says BOYS ON PARADE.

The fat black guy behind the counter is named Gunther, and he wants to know which job I'm here for and how much did I want to make? I tell him I have a feeling I don't want to make too much. He asks, so why am I here, then? I've got no answer for that.

He tells me to come around behind the counter, and he lifts my shirt up. He stares at my chest, and the spray of little purple scars across it. Then he turns me around and stares at my back.

"Army?" he asks, tapping his fingertips on my tattoos.

"Yes."

"That'll be good for business," he says.

The front door swings open, blinding me with bright sun, and out of the light walk two girls, passing me and going into the Live Action door. Action Ladies, I guess. Live and All Active, these chicks. The one on the right has a pimple in the middle of her forehead, and she turns to stare as she walks by, staring at me getting stared at by Big Black Gunther. She giggles, but her friend just keeps walking. That one is cute, she's in a Nike warm-up suit, her hair tied back, and she's got a knapsack slung over her shoulder. They swish through the curtain and they're gone.

Gunther lets my T-shirt drop and tells me in his own, distinctive, Gunther-way that now it's time for me to drop my pants.

Gunther and I are getting to be close friends.

The door swings open, and the sunlight rushes in again.

2

The booth is three by three and maybe eight feet high. The door is shut behind me. I was spared the sight of my fellow laborers on my way in, so I feel completely alone, locked in my little, smelly box. It's red, a different red than the red in Cliff's attic in the morning. This is plastic red, Formica red. The speaker over my head crackles "Dancing Queen" at an ear-busting volume.

They don't come more naked than me. I've got combat boots and socks on, but it's not quite the quality of cover I'm wishing for. The patrons pay a dollar to get the solid partition to rise for a few minutes, leaving nothing but Plexiglas between us, then they're supposed to stick a few bucks through the slot to me. Gunther, always informative, has let me in on the fact that there are some booths farther down the line where, when the partition rises, there's no Plexiglas between the two sides of the booth. Gunther says that's where the big money is. I tell Gunther I wouldn't know what to do with that kind of money. Gunther and I are old pals, now. Gunther says I've got big money written all over me. Looking down at myself, here in the booth, I'm having a hard time imagining anyone getting excited.

I smoke three entire cigarettes before I hear the other door open. A few seconds go by, then the partition creaks up. Gunther says the women's booths, on the other side of the building, where I saw the two girls go before, only have one-by-one-foot openings, either glassed or open depending on your financial commitment. But here in the Parade of Boys the partition raises to uncover a life-sized window. And there I am, the size of life.

For one brief second, as the partition rises and before I can see who will be watching me, I have a quick thought—remembering a night in our dark barracks room, a chubby girl so trusting of Trevor, so unaware of me watching from the dark.

What goes around comes around, buddy, I mumble to myself.

3

Miguel is twenty, about five foot five, Puerto Rican and ripped. He's got a towel tight around his waist, drinking a Pepsi. Choice of the nude generation. I'm drinking a Pepsi, too, but I don't have a towel so I'm in my boxers and boots. The room is dark and small and limited to the Pepsi machine, a picnic table, and one rickety bench.

"You're cute," he says, looking at me just slightly less carefully than Gunther did. "I like your hair, sweetie." He laughs around his Pepsi, swiping at my high-and-tight. "Everyone loves an army boy, Pancho."

Miguel is from Oakland, and has worked here for three months. "It's all right, sweets. I shake my ass, I make a hundred bucks. My ass is worth a hundred bucks, so why not?"

Why not indeed?

"You don't look too comfortable, sweetie," he croons in his velvet accent. "It's just pervs. Pervs gonna look at you on the street anyway, making up shit in their head about what they gonna do to your buns. Fuck 'em, if they gonna dream, make 'em pay to dream 'bout you. Shake it and stroke it and smile nice. Fuck, they can't touch you, so who fucking cares?"

I ask Miguel about the booths at the end of the line, the ones that open full size with no Plexiglas.

"Fucking needles, man! Who else could do that? That's AIDS time, Pancho. Walk in there, drop your drawers, and get the instant AIDS injection. Wit' a quickness. They don't even make much for it. They're so fucking stoned and strung out. I bet most of them pervs that do 'em, they walk outta there, never even paid the boy and he don't even fucking know it. They're walking death, sweetie. You ever seen death walking around?"

I nod my head once. Turns out, I have seen death walking around.

Miguel, who has no idea, and couldn't care less, nods back. "You watch one of them boys open their booth at the end of the day. That's black fucking death walking out of there."

He lights a smoke, then he lights one for me. His hair is black and short and greased. It shines in the fluorescent light as he hands the smoke up to me. His arm muscles are tight, and I can see the vein that crosses his bicep twitch as he flips his wrist back.

"Y'know, I think about it. Sometimes, man, you're just broke, y'know? Fuck. It happens. It's easy cash, right? It's like, 'Well, so I get this guy off and now I'm not broke so what's the problem?' Right? Ya gotta think about it."

He shakes his head and rubs at his shoulder.

"But nah, sweets. Nah. Word is bond. This is all right, this don't bother me, what we're doing here. If my mama found out it wouldn't kill me. But no more, ya can't do no more. Fuck, it's dangerous, anyway. You wanna be locked alone in a booth with some fucking guy? This honey, this honey we called him Smoothie on accounta his back ain't got no ass, y'know? He ain't got not an *ounce* of ass on him. It's just smooth, right down his back to his legs. Well, this Smoothie . . . *fuck*. He was a back-booth boy. He was like seventeen, I think, and tracks all up and down his fucking arms, sweets. All *up* and *down*. So one night, late, y'know, he's in his booth and this guy in there with him just fucking *loses* it. Just fucking *beats* him senseless. He's in there, and it don't take much I guess 'cause Smoothie ain't got no fucking muscle, and he's strung anyway, so fuck, he can't even think to put two words together. He just gets his fucking ass *beat* by this guy, and the guy leaves, like, he's just gone, got his rocks and he's gone. Well it's late, and there's all these fucking weirdos in here, man. I can't work here late anymore, I won't fucking do it, I don't give a shit what that Gunther says, man. I give not a *shit,* sweets. So this dude, he leaves, and Smoothie's all fucking beat to shit and sprawled in his booth, and it's a back booth, y'know? Ain't no fucking window. That's how he got beat in the first place. Well, all these guys have lined up, and they go in and they all take him, one by one. This guy, man, he's passed fucking out! He's got no idea. He's fucking bleeding like a stuck-fucking-pig, man, he's out, cold stone out, and these four five guys, all in fuckin' suits, fuckin' brokers y'know, and straight, all come in and each of them does him, passed out, they're fucking him all the same."

I ask what happened to Smoothie.

"Ah, *fuck*. They took him outta here in a cab, wouldn't call no ambulance, y'know. Took him in a cab somewhere, I guess. Maybe Gunther took him home, I don't know. Gunther's a good guy, really, ya get to know him, he's just a workin' hog like us. But Smoothie was back in here just a week later. No other way for him to make cash, sweets. None that he know of, anyway."

Miguel stubs his smoke and stands, pulling off his towel. His body is completely shaved.

"But I tell ya, what I don't understand so much ain't the boys here, man, the boys working. It's the fucking *guys* that come in and *fuck* 'em. Some old bags, they come in here, wanna suck off a boy. Suits, too, like I said. And who the fuck you think is gonna wanna put some piece of shit like Smoothie in their mouth? But they do, man. They do."

He stretches, reaches for the ceiling. His armpits are shaved, too. He looks like a little boy. A little Puerto Rican boy, but full sized.

"They come in here, throw a few bucks looking at a cute boy—like me," he laughs, "or *you*, y'know? They watch and watch, and then when they're so horny they don't fucking care, *then* they go to the back booths and get some poor fuck like Smoothie to finish it for 'em.

"Nah, man. Just shake your ass. Keep that window in the booth. You be all right." He tosses me another cigarette. Maybe he thinks I don't have any.

"You're cute, sweets," he winks. "You dance? We'll go dance some night, sweets."

And then he's gone.

4

Five hours later. My workday finished, I've dressed and walked upstairs to the straight section of this little house of fun.

"I'll be right back," she said.

Her name is Kelly, and I watched through the little window as she walked, naked, across the ratty, dark, shag carpet to an open window directly across from me. This place is all windows and booths and naked people. And it *all* smells of disinfectant and armpits. I could barely make out the outline of a chubby, white male face through the literal hole in the wall she was headed for. Three other girls were in the room with her, all of them in various stages of undress, none of them over twenty, all of them with their midsections pressed to an open window. Hands—mostly with wedding bands, mostly white—groped out and grabbed at breasts and stomachs and asses. The pimple-headed girl that had giggled at me—how long ago? forever I think, but it was five hours ago—had her ass pressed into one of the openings, while she stared distractedly at her fingernails, occasionally chewing one. Her rear grinded absently through the hole. Her cute friend who hadn't looked up as they passed by my inspection was Kelly. She had jammed a textbook, *Fundamentals of Abnormal Psychology*, into the window I was at, keeping the partition up. Across the way, as Kelly reached her new customer, the partition grinded down pushing Pimple-Girl's ass back into the room, a pale hand quickly extending, trying to grab at it, then whipping back before it got caught.

I had stayed—naked of course—in *my* little booth in the basement for hours, working my way through two packs of cigarettes. I had made almost two hundred bucks in tips without moving a muscle. All afternoon they came through, some in suits worth more then a car, some in greasy khakis, some in bad tie-pant combinations, some in sweats. They came, and it all pretty much went the same way. I stood there in my boots, pale and skinny, cock limp against my thigh, balls tight and crawled up in the beginning, then hanging as it got warmer, chain-smoking. They'd look at me from the other side of the glass, shove some bills through the slot, then quickly drop their pants. I got to watch as they jerked-off. I figured they'd get mad that I wasn't dancing or jerking-off myself, that I was just standing there, smoking, but most didn't seem to care or even notice. They'd stare down at my cock with a dead, blank look, like a fish, as they pulled themselves out of their pants and tug and tug. Most used spit on their palms, and most didn't take very long. Tug, tug, *spurt*. Some guys managed to splash the window, some barely cleared their pants. I couldn't imagine the mess on the floor over there. Some guys, the partition would start coming down between us before they finished. Some, in a panic, would grab for money to get it back up again. Most didn't, though. I guess they finished up alone over there. Some guys talked to me as they worked. I couldn't really hear them through the glass, though, and I didn't pay attention. One guy, this one in a suit and a bad hairpiece, stood there with pants to his ankles, limp and spent dick hanging, and professed his love to me. He'd paid to have the thing open for twice as long as usual, and had started off by slipping a twenty to me through the slot. He leaned against the glass now and started whispering. I made out like I couldn't hear him, which was pretty much true. So he stands there, undressed and dripping, while he takes a pen and paper out of his suit jacket pocket, writes a note, and slips it through the tip slot. It hit the floor as the partition went down. I picked it up. "$200," it said. "Claridge hotel - 1 block south - rm 721."

Jesus wept.

Gunther opened the back door of my booth at 5:30. "Go home," he said. "You got a home?"

I nodded as I gathered up my clothes from atop the stool in the corner. The partition was up, a banker/lawyer/doctor with shiny white teeth on the other side of the glass, watching us, his dick deflating in his hand. Gunther stared at him like a bug. I shrugged, and left.

There was no one in the foyer at the top of the stairs when, dressed now, I got there. I stepped into the women's section, slipped into one of the doors, and paid my buck to open the window.

Kelly was eighteen, a student. Some community college I'd never heard of. Her knapsack was open on the floor against the back wall of the chamber, and she'd shoved her textbook into the window when she, surprisingly, recognized me. This was the third time she'd been called away in the ten minutes or so we'd been talking. She had said she'd be right back, and this time she was. The guy in the booth hadn't wanted to touch her, he'd wanted her to watch as he jerked-off. She didn't like that. "Go downstairs for that," I heard her say, not entirely unkindly, as she turned away.

She was as pale as me, maybe whiter. Her hair was long and brown, still tied back, her breasts full, with tiny pink nipples. Her pubic hair was a shock of thick black against her skin. She was back, kneeling on something I couldn't see, her face close to mine through the opening.

"So, don't ask me anything stupid, okay?" she whispered.

I knew what she meant. I was beyond stupid questions, beyond any kind of question, really. I hadn't even asked her her name. She had offered that, and the college stuff, on her own. Frankly, I didn't even know why I was here.

"Have you been here this whole time?" she asked.

I nodded. "I guess I passed the test. I've been downstairs." I smiled.

She shrugged a bit, again not unkindly. "Front or back?" she asked.

I didn't know what she meant.

"Front line of booths, or back?"

"Front. First one, actually. Next to Miguel."

"I don't know him. I don't know any of them, really. Not the boys. One or two, I guess. Some are fun. I went dancing with a few one night. Gay boys are the best dancers. Most of them downstairs are scary, though."

I had only met Miguel, and only seen one or two others. I thought of Smoothie, and wondered if she'd met him, or knew about what had happened to him. I figured that probably fell in the realm of a stupid question, though, so I didn't ask.

She lived in an apartment with a bunch of the other girls, and this was how she was paying for community college. She took the train into the city three times a week and did her five hours at the window. Today she was staying later, because things had been slow and she hadn't made enough yet. She smiled at me, and wrote down my name in her notebook I don't know why. Naked, in the window, bent over her textbook, scribbling on the paper. She was left-handed, her nipple caressing the page right above her pencil.

"Do *you* want to touch me, too?" she whispered, leaning in the window toward me. I couldn't tell if she was kidding or serious.

And if she was serious, I didn't know what I wanted to do.

"I'm lonely," I said quickly, not knowing where these words were coming from, not making even the slightest move in her direction. *That's me all year*, I thought, *not making any moves in any direction*. I was lonely, though—it just hadn't occurred to me until I said the words. I wanted to take them back immediately.

She looked at me for a second, smiled, then blew me a kiss off her fingertips. When she pulled back she took her textbook with her, the partition fell shut, and I was alone in the dark booth.

Kismaayo, *Part Two*

Kismaayo, Somalia—Late January 1993

1

Most of January they lived on the peninsula's hill, days spent squinting into the sun through sledgehammer heat, waiting for word of a mission to come across the radio, nights at a bonfire in a little hollow of boulders fifty feet above the ocean, drinking and watching as the twigs they'd piled in a circle of stones crackled and spit then burned away into gray-white ash that blew out over the surf.

Trevor Alphabet, his back against a rock, bonfire glow in his eyes, bottle of hooch in hand, takes a deep pull, then—wiping his mouth with the back of his hand, in his best John Wayne—drawls out, "Yes sir, there I was . . ."

Pause.

"Africa."

Pause.

"Winter of ninety-two. Or was it ninety-three?" Takes another pull off the bottle. "I don't rightly remember."

Passes the bottle to Bob.

"But yes sir, there we was. Africa. The sand was hot. So was the liquor."

Jones, sitting against his own rock, staring up at the stars, thinks *Yes, sir, here we are: Africa.*

Dirty and unshaven, a week from their next shower, not one of them farther than two quick steps from his M16—suddenly not an object anymore, a thing to clean and carry; now it's a needed thing, a thing you don't lose track of—in a country with a name you can't easily shorten-up or funny-up.

It occurs to Jones they're officially considered veterans now, and he mentions this to Trevor, across the bonfire.

"Yes, sir," Trevor answers, close to crossing the line into serious inebriation. "Yes, sir, there we was. Veterans, we was. Entitled to all that we survey."

"What do we survey, Alphabet?"

"Cheap beer at the VFW and a government funeral with a cheap-ass headstone and a squad of ignorant privates to see us off."

Bob blinked twice, then mumbled, "I regret I have but one liver to give my country."

2

The night of this bonfire on the hill overlooking the port they'd been in Kismaayo for three weeks. Jones and Trevor and Bob and Sid arriving first, with the other two Mike Boats and Lieutenant Klover pulling in the next day. Then three weeks of sitting, sweating, waiting for an order. Finally, one came, but it wasn't what they expected. Sergeant Morgan's boat, with Norm and Schaeffer, Burr and Jimmy Two-Balls, was ordered to Mogadishu, to pull port security. The rest would stay in Kismaayo for the duration, however long that might be.

The first single boat in Kismaayo had gotten a quick taste of what life was like in Somalia. A truck carrying a Belgian patrol was ambushed deep in the city, a mine detonated by radio as the truck passed over it. Three of the fresh Americans had to give blood, and no one had gotten any sleep.

Lieutenant Klover asked Sid about the incident, an hour or so after the second and third boats arrived the next day. Klover had heard a rumor, something about executions, but he didn't want to come out and ask directly, because that's the kind of man he was. Sid didn't like the lieutenant. Veins popped on his forehead and his fists curled when talking to him, even if just about the weather.

"Well, L.T.," he said finally, unable to tell this man what happened, knowing he already knew anyway, not willing to *make conversation* out of this, "I think we all just better brush up on our basic soldiering skills."

A good sergeant's answer. Brush up on soldiering skills.

It was apparent—probably even to the lieutenant—that Sid meant just *him,* not anyone else. Certainly not Sid.

"Well," replied the lieutenant. "Well." He coughed. "I guess we can all use some good training." A standard lieutenant's answer. He wiped his brow, then laughed. "Nothing like good army training! Right, Sergeant Mason?" He slapped Sid on the back, and Jones thought for a moment that little, skinny Sid was going to haul off and hit him. But he just grimaced and walked away, smoothing his thin mustache and clenching his fists.

Lieutenant Klover had graduated from West Point in June, arrived in the company in September, and took command of the detachment platoon in November. He seemed a nice enough guy to Jones. He played piano, he liked The Beatles. A nice enough guy. Jones mentioned this to Sid once, the very day Sid and Bob were pinned their sergeant stripes back in Virginia, right after they'd met the lieutenant for the first time—right after they found out they were going to Africa. Sid took a big swallow from his celebratory can of beer and said simply, "Nice guys die first, Jonesy."

Bob, from over Sid's shoulder, stumbling drunk, said, "Nope, nope, that's not it at all . . ."

He grabbed at Sid's arm for support.

"Nice guys let *other* guys die first."

He belched, loud and explosive.

"*Fuck* that lieutenant, anyway. We get shot at on the boat in that fucked-up African country—what the fuck is it called?—I'm shoving him down into the engine room. He tries to come up, I'm gonna fucking pop him."

Jones listened to the two of them, enjoying his beer and the cool air of the Virginia afternoon and the thought of two of his friends *(friends! remember them?! good to have friends . . .)* now being sergeants. It was fun to listen to, but none of it meant anything to him.

Of course you shoot the lieutenant, that's what they do in all the Nam movies . . .

It was definitely something ol' Drill Sergeant Rose would have done: pop the ignorant lieutenant. No doubt about it.

Sid and Bob had been in the Gulf War together, as privates. Neither of them had seen direct combat, but Jones was pretty sure they had seen something. Something . . . something disturbing.

Jones decided he had no idea what *disturbing* was.

But he liked them both. Trusted them both. Enjoyed their company—him and Trevor quickly hooking up to form this quartet. Jones thought that although he would probably *never* know what "disturbing" was, maybe by knowing them, by being their friend, he could at least understand it better. By seeing their level of disturbing, maybe, just maybe, his would not seem so large. He couldn't count his own little life problems—kids born to kids, marriages made from circumstances, fucked-up families—as disturbing. He knew better.

People living in a time made safe for them by others, by other generations even, have difficulty in understanding how close we all are, what a thin line it is, to suffering. To *disturbing*.

3

Those first few days in Kismaayo—and later, after January, for most of the rest of the deployment—they lived on their Mike Boats. That's what they did in the field in the States, that's how they liked it. It smelled and was uncomfortable, but it was theirs, and they understood it, and liked it that way. It made them different from other soldiers, gave them an identity.

The first boat got there on a Monday. The others on Tuesday. On Friday afternoon, Lieutenant Klover climbed down from the pier to the quarterdeck of Sid's boat, where they were playing cards. They'd been playing cards for days. Chess, too, but still mostly cards then. What had happened on Monday night had shaken them up, and they weren't doing much talking, or interacting with the other boat crews. The other guys weren't talking either, because they had heard about Monday night—about the Belgians and how they'd looked as they were peeled from the Volvo trucks, about three tiny black men facedown on the pier with blood pooling around their bodies—and it scared them even more because they *hadn't* seen it—fear of the unknown. The worst fear.

The lieutenant stepped onto the deck of the boat where they sat playing cards, pulled up an ammo box and sat down, watching them play for almost ten minutes without a word. Finally, Trevor looked over at him.

"Can we deal you in here, sir?"

The lieutenant shook his head and laughed that laugh of his. "Oh no, fellas! Thanks, though. I think you'd just clean my clock." He slapped Bob on the back, looking for a smile. Bob didn't move.

"Well," said Trevor, "probably, sir. Probably."

Another few minutes went by. Sid was getting agitated, just by the man's silent presence. Working as a squad detachment, a unit for hire, Sid had a degree of autonomy most buck sergeants never see. Lieutenant Klover was his commander, but the officer didn't sail, they seldom saw him, and when they did he was generally ignored—an army Transportation Corps lieutenant might as well have a big IGNORE ME sign pasted to his chest; even one from West Point.

Finally, Klover spoke.

"Ah, listen, fellas. I was just up in the HQ building."

He coughed his nervous, bad news cough.

"There's a colonel up there? Yes. From 10th Mountain Division." He paused, coughed again. No one was looking at him. Sid threw a poker chip to the pile.

"Well, guys, seems he's noticed you out of his window. And he—well, he's got some concerns."

Sid looked up now. "Concerns, sir?"

"Well, yes, Sergeant Mason. Some concerns, y'know . . ."

Jones lit a cigarette. He knew where this was going.

"Well, guys, he just mentioned to me that it didn't look real sanitary down here. Y'know, all of you living here on the boat, sleeping on the quarterdeck."

"Is that right, sir?" Sid put down his cards.

"Um." The lieutenant coughed again. "Well, guys, it's just that we've got all these GP tents we brought over, and everyone else here is living over on the hill, in their tents, and well it did make some sense to me, like maybe the boat squads should billet there when you're not sailing."

"Oh," said Sid. "I see. Sir."

Bob started shaking his head, slowly. Trevor looked out over the water.

"Well sir," Sid said, looking him right in the eye, "I'm sure you squared him away, right sir? Told him how it is with us, how we need to be close to our stuff, how if we weren't living on the boat someone would have to guard it anyway, how by being here we can roll at a moment's notice—how we're used to this? You squared him away, right, sir?"

"Um, well . . ."

"Because, sir, I gotta tell you: we're not leaving. This is where we belong, and this is where we're gonna stay. That's just best. Sir."

The lieutenant stood up, hands in pockets.

"Well, Sergeant Mason . . . fellas. Um, no. Fact is, we're gonna have to take you and the other guys up the hill. I, uh, I listened to the colonel, and I thought about it long and hard, and this is best, and we'll all just have to make do. And that's my decision."

Sid lowered his eyes to the deck. "Would that be an order, sir?"

The lieutenant didn't say anything for a minute, his face twitching over the left eye, sweat popping on his brow.

Jones sighed. He sided with Sid, agreed with him—he didn't want to leave the boats. But he felt a sort of pity for the lieutenant; he played the piano. It was painful to watch this.

Just as Jones decided the officer would back down, the lieutenant stood and said, "Yes, Sergeant. Yes, I've decided. So . . . So, yes, that's an order. I'll just show you where I've got my stuff up on the hill, and we'll set up those GPs, and we'll have you fellas all square by tonight."

Within the hour ten of them were with Lieutenant Klover, on the hillside. It was four in the afternoon, ninety-eight degrees. As the crow flies they were only a quarter mile from the main port and the boats, but it was a long, hot, hard walk up the rocky hill.

The lieutenant's pup tent was set up alone on a small flat area on the west side of the hill. "Once we get these GPs set up," he said, "I'll move my stuff in with some of you."

Sid and Bob didn't go up the hill. They said they'd follow later, and help put up the tents. Fat chance, Jones thought; there are benefits to those stripes.

Lieutenant Klover took his cap off, and turned to face the water.

"What a view, eh?" he said, gesturing out with his arm. It was quite a view. The port was below them, a little south, and from there lay the expanse of Kismaayo bay, water twinkling in the sunlight. Across the bay sat the city of Kismaayo, ancient beyond understanding, then the brown and golden desert behind it. A light breeze blew up the hill, a smell that would always mean Africa to Jones: the smell of hot, the smell of dry, mixed with traces of shit and diesel. Not unpleasant, just distinctive.

"Who could ask for a better place to live?" the lieutenant laughed to himself. No one was listening. Privates and specialists scurried behind and around him, already laying out the tarps and setting stakes in the ground to support the big GP tents. Jones took a swig from a water bottle. He had stopped watching the lieutenant. He was watching Norm, the engineer of the Mogadishu-bound Mike Boat.

Norm was looking around, scratching his head in an exaggerated way. Jones liked Norm. Ol' Norm who, if you didn't know him, could look so stupid—so *Norm*-like—and then come out with the damndest things.

"Hey, L.T.!" Norm hollered, waving his arm wildly, the lieutenant turning to look at him. Jones wiped the sweat from his eyes, watching.

"Listen, I got a question."

The lieutenant nodded.

"No disrespect or nothing, sir . . . I think you've got a *great* plan here." Norm smiled, huge.

The lieutenant nodded again.

"Um, you know," he continued, "this *is* a great view. Great, great view. Why, we got the whole damn city in view!" Norm laughed, the L.T. now laughing with him.

"But here's what I'm thinking, sir. *Strategically,* y'know. If we can see *them,* well, then . . ."

The lieutenant wasn't getting it. Jones smiled, wishing Trevor was watching this.

"Well, what I mean to say, sir, is that perhaps we should go to the *other* side of the hill, facing the ocean, sir?"

Klover still wasn't getting it.

"Um, I just mean, sir, perhaps we don't want to throw big tents up right in range of where the skinnies can see us—and shoot at us?"

If the lieutenant got it at this point, he didn't let on. And they set up the tents right where he wanted them, right on the flat, even ground he liked so much. Facing the city. *Here we are!* Jones thought, shaking his head. *Yes Sir, there we were, and here we are. I regret I have but one liver to give my country . . .*

Sid and Bob came up the hill later with their gear slung over their shoulders, rifles in their hands. Sid took one look at the lieutenant's glorious view, then turned and walked on, cresting the hill, going down the other side. Jones followed, finding the two NCOs spreading out their sleeping bags in a tiny hollow of rocks right below the crest of the hill, the Indian Ocean spreading out in front to the east.

4

The bonfire was burning bright on the other side of the mountain. It was a good-bye to Norm and the other guys leaving the next day for Mogadishu. By midnight they were good and drunk on the hooch and weed they'd brought from Kenya, laughing at their own stupid jokes, spitting into the fire.

"Yes sir," mumbled Trevor, eyes almost closed, "there I fucking was. Africa. Winter of ninety-two. Or three. Fuck, who can keep it all straight?"

Bob threw a boot at him, hitting him in the chest. Trevor didn't notice. Bob reached down and pressed play on the tape player. Jim Morrison came out of the speaker, droning on and on . . .

> *Out here in the perimeter there are no stars.*
> *Out here, we is stoned.*
> *Immaculate.*

"IMMACULATE!" Jones yelled, surprising himself, laughing.

"Shut up, Jim!" Trevor yelled at the tape player from behind closed eyes. "Shut up with that shit!" This got Bob's other boot thrown at him. Again, he didn't seem to notice. "Fucking Jim Morrison. Shut up with that shit . . ."

Jim kept his rant up. Trevor opened his eyes.

"*Heeeeeeey* Norm!" he yelled. "Ya got mail for us?"

Norm passed out the mail, cigarette hanging from his mouth, his helmet on, backward. He was pissed he had been assigned to Mogadishu, but—as always—he laughed it off.

Dom, a tall, skinny Latino, the sergeant on the second boat staying in Kismaayo, fired up a joint. He was trying to talk to Jones about the two things they had in common: New Jersey, and divorce. He was always trying to talk about them. Jones tried to be polite. He liked Dom.

Dom was all ready now to settle down with someone else, a new wife. He was Catholic, he said. It was unnatural for a Catholic not to be married. Jones, reaching for an MRE bag, searching hard for a BBQ-and-rice, said it was unnatural for a Catholic to get divorced in the first place. Dom didn't like that.

"What about you, man?" Dom asked. "You, too, you know. It's right, for a man. To have someone to come home to. You got to get on that." He gazed at his joint, balanced between his fingers.

"What about being alone for a while?" Jones asked. "Can I do that? Wouldn't that be smart? Can't I just be alone?"

"I dunno," Dom said. "Sounds of it, you been alone all along. Maybe you need someone, someone good, to take care of ya."

Bob pulled himself up from his stupor, looking over the boulder he had been lying against.

"Liz!" he shouted. "That's for you, Jones! Lizzie. She likes you."

His arm slipped, and he disappeared behind the boulder, his voice coming a second later: "I can tell, man. She likes you."

Jones looked up, expecting a comment from Trevor, but Trevor was engrossed in the letter in front of him, reading by the light of the bonfire.

Liz was now the Queen of Africa. In Mombasa, Kenya, two days before they sailed north, two days before their strained good-bye, she showed up in port, a big bag in her arms. In the bag was a limp chicken she'd found at a bazaar in town and convinced a hotel cook to prepare for the Seadogs on the Mike Boats. "Christmas feast!" she'd called, climbing over the stanchion, almost dropping her present. "Oh my God!" Trevor had yelled, sticking his head out the wheelhouse window. "The Queen of Africa! Come to deliver goodies!" Jones had been in town during this, and when Trevor told him later he'd just missed her Jones crawled down into the engine room with his wrench roll and didn't come out for two hours.

"Lizzie loves Jonesy!" Norm cried gleefully, dropping the empty mail bag to the ground and grabbing the bottle of hooch from between Trevor's feet. His helmet was sideways now, a cheerfully stoned Gomer Pyle. "Queen of Africa wants her king! King Jones!"

"Not right now she doesn't," Jones said quietly. "Not anymore."

He shifted his bottom around, pebbles digging into his spine.

Jones had noticed a thing about women in the army, women in uniform: guys either loved them or hated them—not much in-between. Liz was one they loved.

Trevor, who had been so engrossed in his mail, started cursing loudly. "Sonofa*bitch!* Fucking Millet!" he yelled.

Before Jones had moved in with him, Trevor's roommate back in the States had been a corporal named Millet. Millet hadn't deployed with them to Somalia, and no one talked about him: earlier, last summer, Bob had come home early to his apartment to find Millet in his living room, talking with Bob's wife. That's all he was doing, talking, but it was too much for Bob. He could smell it, he said, smell what had gone on. Millet left the apartment in an ambulance, and Bob—after a brief discussion with the MPs—had moved back into the barracks. After a few months things calmed down, and Bob was ready to get back together with his wife, but then they deployed. She'd gone home to Ohio for the duration, and they planned to move back in together when Bob got back from Somalia.

Trevor stayed removed from all of this. He respected Bob's opinion, but Millet had been his roommate, his friend, and they'd always gotten along.

The letter Trevor now held in his hand was from his mother, in Michigan. She was getting his bills while he was gone, and had sent along his calling-card bill with a note saying she'd had it deactivated. The bill was for a few hundred dollars.

"That sonofabitch," Trevor said again.

Millet, left to care for all of Trevor's worldly possessions, had apparently been having fun with them. Including the calling card.

"I'll talk to the lieutenant," Sid said quietly from behind a rock. Jones had thought he was asleep. "I'll call back to the States and have him arrested. Don't sweat it. You won't have to pay the charges." Sid stuck his head up, rubbing his eyes. "You sure it was him?"

Trevor, ignoring Sid, was whipping the pages back and forth, trying to figure something out.

"Where the hell is he from, anyway?" he said finally.

"Who?" Jones asked.

"Millet."

"Don't even say that fucker's name," Bob growled, from behind his boulder.

"Arkansas, I think," Dom said, and Sid nodded his head.

"Arkansas?" Trevor motioned for Norm to bring him the hooch, and he took a swig. Over the ocean the moon shone brilliantly, shimmering on the water, a quarter mile below them. Quiet, peaceful, endless black water.

"There ain't a single fucking call here to Arkansas," Trevor said, looking again at the bill in front of him. "They're all to Ohio."

"What's the exchange?" Bob yelled, his head coming up now, interested. "I can tell you what city, anyway. Maybe he's got a girlfriend there."

Trevor told him, the three digits rolling smooth off his tongue.

Bob's eyebrows raised, and he got a funny look on his face. "What's the actual number?"

Trevor looked down at the papers, but Bob was already over the boulder, and ripped the phone bill out of Trevor's hands. His eyes searched around. Then he dropped the paper, and just stood there, looking at the ocean.

"Oh you fuck," he whispered slowly.

Trevor picked up the phone bill, looking up at Bob.

"That's my wife's mom. That's where she is. With the boys. That's it."

Dom laughed out loud, sitting up. "Wait! Kidding, right? Millet fucking stole Trevor's phone card, ran up a hundred-dollar bill, and did it calling *your* wife in Ohio?" He laughed again.

Bob took a quick step toward him, fist raised, then stopped. His face said it all. Dom looked down fast, shutting up.

"Oh, man. I'm sorry. I didn't mean . . ."

And then Bob was gone, down the hill—not toward the port, but the ocean. They heard pebbles sliding as he made his way, then he was gone from view.

No one said anything for a long time.

"Wow," Norm said, breaking the silence. "That's a buzz kill."

5

Wives. Girlfriends.

Jones, lying back against his boulder with eyes closed, remembers lying awake in the dark, the top bunk in the Virginia barracks room he shared with Trevor—maybe three months before Somalia? Maybe two.

Too drunk to sleep. He had lain then as he lay now, faceup, eyes open then closed then open.

Too much in his head, too much to take in. He'd had a phone call from Katy earlier in the afternoon, an earful of how her new man—*Rich? that's one click away from Dick, Katy*—had been expanding her horizons.

Sid and Alphabet walking down the hall as he hung up the payphone. "Bar?" Yes, by God. To the bar.

Bucks Grill. Quarter drafts on Wednesday night. Bad country music. Close enough to Ft. Eustis—walking distance from the gates—that obvious army haircuts won't get you hassled. Close enough to stumble home on foot if it's Breathalyzer night at the MP vehicle checkpoint.

Drink, by God. Surely, that's the answer. Beer.

At ten Jones left them there, Sid and Trevor chatting up two girls, and he walked—*stumbled*—next door to the titty bar just so he can fulfill the soldier-pig stereotype Katy has of him. Reaches into his pocket to pay the cover. Nothing comes but lint.

Eyes the Ft. Eustis gate across the street—cars backed up, Breathalyzer night. Jones started walking.

A phone booth right inside the gates, and Jones has the number memorized. Leigh, her name is; doesn't know how young, doesn't even remember how he met her or how long it's been since he's seen her, but he knows her number. She'll pick me up. She'll take me home. Liz never met her, so she won't recognize her car in the barracks parking lot tomorrow morning. Not that he should care. *It's not like me and Liz are sleeping together, right?* Jones thinks. It's not like she hasn't had *boyfriends,* right? Right.

But, he cares anyway.

Leigh it is.

Ring, ring—anyone fucking home? It's cold out here.

A click, then a low male voice, "Hello?"

Her father, Jones thinks. Must be.

And then: *What the fuck am I doing calling anyone who lives with her parents?*

As if in answer, a blue Geo pulls through the gate, driving past him. Liz. Through her windshield he sees her, still in uniform for some reason, driving with one hand, looking down and fiddling with the radio with her other hand. She doesn't see him, but now it's too late anyway.

"Hello? Who is this?"

Jones mumbles a sorry, slams the phone down. Starts walking. *Fucking cold, fucking drunk, fucking sorry for myself.*

He cuts through the woods toward the barracks. There's an occasional rustle of leaves and bushes, and he wonders if he's startled a few soldiers engaged in acts that would surely get them kicked out. He doesn't see anyone, certainly it's the wind, but he wonders. His friend Todd went through boot camp with him and Trevor, a veteran of madman Rose and the nighttime raid on 3rd Platoon. Todd is gay. He hasn't shared this with Trevor—good idea—but has felt okay sharing this information with Jones.

Why do you trust me, Todd? went unasked.

Todd once told Jones this stand of woods is where he goes with friends he meets—too dangerous in the barracks, even behind closed doors—and since then Jones has made it a point to walk through here at night—he's not sure why, there's a voyeur in everyone he guesses. A sick fascination with breaking the rules.

He's drunker than he thought, doesn't remember walking through the barracks door, doesn't remember going to the second floor, doesn't remember finding his room. Just remembers lying there in the dark, ceiling less than a foot above his head, reminding himself over and over what a *bad* idea it would be to go down the street and knock on Liz's door right now.

Trevor, for the first time Jones can remember, got a girl to talk to him tonight. Patty, her name was. Not a day over seventeen, but they're not particular with the ID check at Bucks. She came with her cousin, just a year or two older. Patty said she was from West Virginia, living now in Newport News with her uncle and aunt and their daughter—this cousin, Tricia, who took a shine to Sid. Jones thought Patty had a cute face, a chubby little body, and could have been Trevor's sister. He tried chatting her up at the bar—*hey! aren't you too young to be in here? you're cute!*—and she politely turned away toward Trevor. Okay, fine. Go get 'em, Alphabet.

Staring at the dark ceiling of the barracks room, Jones convinces himself he's sober enough to call Liz when the door opens, two people come in, and then the door closes. He can see perfectly: there's a night-light rigged that bathes the floor in a green glow but keeps the bunks in total darkness. It's Trevor, and that has to be Patty. Wonders never cease. Jones wait for him to say something—*don't you have an appointment somewhere, Jones?*—but there's not a word. Trevor is either too drunk to realize his roommate must be in bed, or he's too drunk to care. Jones can't think of a polite way to announce his presence, so he keeps perfectly still, not making a sound. *I should make a sound,* he thinks—*it would be the right thing to do. I should get out of this bed and make some laughing apology and leave.*

He doesn't.

She sits on the couch, and Jones hears Trevor mumble something friendly to her about does she want a beer. She says no. Trevor pops one for himself and sets it down on the dresser.

Whatcha gonna do now, Alphabet?

Trevor excuses himself and leaves—going to the bathroom.

She gets up and looks in the mirror on the wall. It's dark, but she can see as much as she needs to. Jones is curious about this girl—this is no paycheck grabber. That's what Bob and Sid call the local girls around Newport News and Norfolk that hang out in the army and navy bars. Especially the navy bars. But that's not Patty, Jones could tell when he first saw her. So could Trevor—that's why he was interested. Trevor isn't a whore.

She plays with her hair nervously, drawing in close to the dark mirror to look at her face. Jones wonders if she'll take her clothes off. There's only one reason you go back to a room with a drunken soldier, and even she has to know that, but she's nervous. Jones wonders if she's a virgin. It's possible. He's glad she picked Trevor, and not Sid.

Or me.

The sound of Trevor walking down the hall comes through the closed door, and she quickly retreats back to the couch, in the same position she was when he left. The door swings open, Trevor smiles to see her still there, the door swings shut. And now Jones realizes something in the drunken muddle of his brain—that's why he really left, this Trevor Alphabet. It wasn't so much to piss, it was to give her a chance to change her mind, to give her a chance to leave.

Trevor takes a long swig from his beer, then sits next to her on the couch, putting his arm around her. Jones thinks: *I know Trevor, he doesn't really know what to do now.*

Kiss her, man, kiss her.

He leans into her face and kisses her.

Jones sticks his head over the top of the bunk—a risk, but he's engrossed.

Trevor kisses her and she responds forcefully. Jones can see her back arch from here, her hands come up around his face, pulling him down onto her.

Maybe not a virgin, Jones thinks.

Or maybe a virgin too long.

I'm glad she picked him.

They both stand, and Trevor sticks his fingers down her waistband, pulling loose the white T-shirt she's tucked into her jeans. It's a tight fit, but he does it. He pulls, and the T-shirt comes up, exposing her white belly and then up and over her head exposing a pink Kmart bra. She quickly reaches down to her waist and pops the top button—she's embarrassed that he'll think she's fat, she's taking the pressure off. Trevor doesn't know, though. She picked the right one. She helps him with his T-shirt, and there they stand, torsos pressed together. He gets her bra off, and there are her breasts, full and with large purple nipples, Trevor's hand reaching up to cup them, one after the other. He's leaning into her, kissing her hard, left hand cupping a breast, right hand trying to snake its way down the back of her pants. She's arched her back again, pressing solidly into him.

Trevor twists, then sits down hard on the couch, his eyes at her waist level now where she stands in front of him. He looks up at her face once, but Patty's eyes are closed. He pulls down her zipper, runs his hands down her sides, pulling down her jeans and panties in one swift downward motion. He lowers himself to his knees and buries his face in what's there, and now she arches her back so hard Jones think she's going to break it, for the first time a sound escaping her lips, a moan more like a grunt.

Jones realizes he's hard. Slowly he rolls his head back toward the ceiling and stares at it blankly. When he rolls back they've switched positions. She's sitting on the couch, both of them completely naked now, her legs spread wide, Trevor working with his fingers. Jones is astounded by the amount of hair she has down there, the thickness and fullness and spread of it, and has to bite his bottom lip to stop himself from moaning as he silently comes all over himself. On his back again, ceiling inches from his eyes, he thinks he's never felt so sorry for himself, or so completely disgusted with himself, so evil. Surely, Patty deserves better than this—surely she deserves to lose her virginity without a pervert watching from a dark corner, lying in his own fluids.

Trevor raises himself on his arms then, trying to get into her, but she's very tight—*what is she, seventeen?*—and Jones can tell Trevor just came, a loud sound coming from him, his shoulders sagging. But she's not done with him, she's on fire, and within minutes they're on his bed, the bunk under Jones, and he can't see them anymore but can hear them and feel the shaking and rocking of the old wooden frame. His eyes squeezed shut, lungs desperately wanting to sob with the sadness of it—of him.

When he wakes the sun is creeping through the little window. Jones sticks his head over the edge of the bunk—she's gone. But Trevor's awake, staring up, as if he'd been waiting for Jones to look down.

"Dude, I didn't know you were here." His face is flat as he says this, flat and blank.

Jones raises his eyebrows in a question.

"Last night," Trevor says.

Jones shakes his head, another question. He tells him he never heard him come in.

Trevor looks at him, rolls over and faces the wall.

That afternoon they leave for a week of maneuvers, a surprise FTX, down the James River into the Intracoastal Waterway. Four of the 1098th's fourteen Mike Boats will go, two of them already fired off and idling when Jones gets down to the can docks at Third Port, making his way across to the end of the row where Bob likes to keep the LCM-8594. The air and water so cold Jones finally has to spray ether into the blowers to get the big V-12s to grudgingly turn over, the engine-room lights glowing weakly then shining bright as the engines finally catch and roar. Jones sits on his stool warming his hands near the port engine and doesn't go back topside until he feels the vessel moving, clearing Skiff's Creek, heading for the Dead Fleet shipping channel.

The whole time they're gone, four cold Southern days, Alphabet is distracted, his breath in short visible puffs on the quarterdeck, watching the first thin ice form on the edges of the Great Dismal Swamp, fretting that he wasn't able to call her. "She's a nice girl, man," he says to Jones. "She's gonna think I'm an asshole."

When they get back he calls the number she gave him, and a man answers. Patty's uncle? Must be. Trevor asks for her and this guy tells him to fuck off and then hangs up the phone.

A week after that Trevor sees her cousin, Tricia, back in Bucks Grill. Seems Patty had moved in with them because she was sent here by her mom. Patty was pregnant.

"Kidding, right?" Trevor told Jones he asked her, and Jones can picture him this way, sitting on a bar stool, beer forgotten in front of him, his face drawn up like it does.

"Nope," Tricia answered. "Pregnant. She came down here to get out of town."

"Can I see her?"

"If you go to West Virginia," came the answer.

Patty, it seems, had miscarried just a day or two ago, while they were on maneuvers, and went home to her mother—problem solved.

"You didn't do it," Jones told him later that night, signaling the bartender. "Getting laid doesn't make you miscarry."

"How do you know?"

Jones just shakes his head.

"She was a nice girl, man. A *nice* girl."

I'm so glad she picked him, Jones thinks, then finishes his beer.

6

It's already hot at seven in the morning when you live on the equator. Jones's eyes open to the remains of the bonfire, empty bottles littered around, two-thirds of a detachment sound asleep on the rocky ground. The other third—Norm, Schaeffer, those guys—had quietly roused themselves at four in the morning and made their way down the hill to the port for their sail to Mogadishu. They were supposed to drop lines and spin props by six thirty.

Jones sits up, raising a hand to his aching head, sees Bob passed out at

Trevor's feet, right across the bonfire pit. *Fucking Bob,* Jones thinks. *He deserves better.*

He looks around and thinks they all deserve better.

I don't know. He wipes his mouth, his unshaved cheeks. *Maybe we don't.*

Twenty minutes after waking they're all at the port, firing off the engines of the two remaining Mike Boats, half dressed and half sleeping and completely hungover. Lieutenant Klover is standing on the quarterdeck like a nervous hen, watching as they lift lines and pull rain covers off the fifty-cals for the first time since they got here.

An MP staff sergeant from 10th Mountain hops gingerly off the quay wall and onto the boat, dismissing the lieutenant with a glance, leaning in through the wheelhouse window toward Sid, pointing out across the bay in the direction of Kismaayo. The MP is completely dressed out, helmet and flak jacket and ammo pouches, desert goggles over his eyes, a grenade launcher slung under the barrel of his M16. Jones watches him nervously, wondering idly where he put his own flak jacket, wondering if he's going to need it. He pulled the rain covers off the fifty-cals as a matter of course, a movement of habit, from field exercises in the States. Even after seeing what was left of the Belgian squad after they got ambushed, it still hasn't hit home, and now as he watches this MP and tries to remember where his own gear is, leaning against the fifty-cal machine gun bolted to the deck, he wonders: *am I actually going to have to use this shit?*

What the MP is pointing at is a boat, half a mile across the bay, coming in the channel from the ocean, headed not toward the city but the seaport compound. It's not much of a boat. Wooden, just this side of a Viking ship. It's thirty feet long, enclosed, colorful sail. The deck is crowded with people.

"Refugees?" Sid yells to the MP over the roar of the diesels.

"I don't think so," the sergeant yells back. "Trading vessel. Used to trading between Kenya and here, up and down the coast. Gypsies."

Sid slides his sunglasses on, taking a better look. The lieutenant steps toward them, listening. Trevor is across the quarterdeck, holding in his hands the last line to the dock, waiting for Sid's signal.

Sid looks at the MP.

"What are we supposed to do?"

"Stop them."

Sid smiles.

"Clarify that, Sergeant."

The MP shakes his head.

"Just that simple. I don't think they're trouble. But they can't come in here."

"All right."

Sid circles his hand up to Trevor, and Alphabet pulls the last line in, Sid engaging the engines as they start to drift. He waves at Dom, driving the second boat, to tell him he's taking the lead, then signals to Jones and Trevor and Bob.

Gathered around and listening, he repeats to the lieutenant what the MP told him, his hands on the wheel, guiding the Mike Boat away from the port and toward the channel.

"I guess when we get out there we'll just yell at them through the bullhorn," Sid finishes, the MP nodding in agreement. "I think they'll get the point. Everyone put a rifle in your hand, but *don't* fucking point it *anywhere*—especially at them."

Jones glances at Trevor, and sees that he is staring at him, rifle loose in his left hand. He breaks eye contact, and glances down at his own M16.

The MP leans in closer, the sun shining bright off his goggles, and says, "Sarge, I wouldn't get closer than twenty feet to them, if that. They'll be able to hear us fine through your bullhorn. But you get any closer and we're begging for someone to throw a grenade in your welldeck."

Sid shakes his head, a pissed-off grimace set on his face. "I thought you said they're harmless."

The MP laughs, hard, slapping the lieutenant on the back.

"Stranger-danger, just like they teach ya in school, right L.T.?"

Klover nods uncomfortably.

The MP turns back to Sid. "We'll be fine, Sarge. Safety first, that's all."

Sid nods.

"Jones, Alphabet, you guys up on the ramp with rifles. Keep your bodies behind the bulkhead. And put your fucking helmets on."

Jones turns, pulling the M16 off his shoulder. The MP puts a hand on Jones's arm.

"You gonna put some rounds in that thing, buddy?"

Jones looks down at the empty magazine of the rifle.

"Good idea?" he says.

The MP smiles. "Good idea."

Jones thinks: *Should I be nervous? Is this when I'm supposed to get scared?*

He doesn't know how he's supposed to feel, but he is nervous. Slapping clips up into their rifles, Trevor and Jones drop into the welldeck, go forward to the ramp, clamber up it, and crouch down with barrels pointing toward the sky. Over his shoulder Jones sees Dom's boat behind them, Dom's engineer Meier on the bow, crossing himself. He sees Jones, smiles, and flips a peace sign. Then he ducks behind the ramp so all Jones can see of him is a strip of desert camouflage on the top of his helmet.

7

They got significantly closer than twenty-five feet from the gypsy boat. Once the shouting was done, once the confusion ended, once the nerves were calmed, they all tied up together—the two Mike Boats and the wooden trading boat—floating in the middle of the channel. They were traders, and they traded. Jones got a carved juju mask and three big skunky buds of weed in exchange for his old and smelly Nike running shoes. Trevor made out the best: he came home that night with a carved stone chessboard and pieces, all that for just a pair of his combat boots. He had three pair with him, he didn't give a shit.

Within half an hour port control is on the radio, wondering what the hell is taking so long. Sid waves good-bye to their new friends, making it abundantly clear that they can't come back, and points them out the channel. The MP staff sergeant—a new carved-bead necklace hanging over his flak jacket—grins up into the sun and lights a cigarette.

Lieutenant Klover leans against a stanchion line as Sid pushes the throttles up and spins the wheel back toward port. Klover stayed removed during most of the exchange, but in the end even he got in on it, trading a five-dollar bill for some masks and carved animals.

"Nice enough folks, don't you think Jones?" he says as Jones unsnaps his helmet and pulls off the hot, heavy flak jacket.

"Nice enough, sir," he says.

Nervous? Not yet. Just stay awake, he tells himself. *Stay awake, and all will be well.*

JONES:
Thirty Days in San Francisco, *Part Three*

California—May 1993

Chinatown has become my favorite section of San Francisco, and I go out of my way to walk through a corner of it as I head to the BART that will take me back across the bay to Berkeley. The sun is low, rush hour thick and buzzing in the streets, a warm breeze pushing through, ginger and garlic carried on the air. I'd walked into the lobby of some big hotel and found a bathroom and scrubbed at my face and hands for what seemed like fifteen minutes, trying to wash away the smells of the basement I'd spent the afternoon in. As I came out of the bathroom door I realized I was probably in the hotel that my high-tipping customer had invited me to, and I went into a panic, looking around quickly, almost running out of the lobby and back to the street.

I stop for spring rolls at a kiosk, standing at the counter, dipping the things in a puddle of duck sauce and mustard I'd mixed up on a napkin. I pull out a notebook I'd been carrying around with me since well before Somalia, writer's notes and lines and phrases and chord progressions, and I flip through it. There's pages and pages of my handwriting, all dated, right up until March. After March, not a word. When my meal is done, I put the notebook on the napkin with my sauces, roll the whole thing up in a ball, and toss it in the trash on my way out the door.

Tower Records is on the way to the BART, and is big enough to have an acoustic and folk section. I'm flipping through the stacks of CDs, something I've done almost every day since I've been here, but I can't even pretend to concentrate, to relate, to understand.

What do you do when you're young and broke and don't care and need to make cash? Sing folk songs? No one gives a shit for that. No one's in a union, or cares. There's no war on, you know. Twenty-year-olds spread our legs to aging and groping Baby Boomers and get fucked backward while yawning, idly thumbing through a textbook or chewing our nails—actions as mindless and automatic as cleaning a rifle in a peacetime army. It's not big enough to protest; it's hardly worth a mention, let alone a song. It's fucking boring, is what it is. It's not a metaphor for anything bigger, it's not anything at all. It just is, and we just are.

In one afternoon I've earned enough traveling money to go where I please, courtesy of Big Black Gunther. Liz is being a soldier in Mogadishu, Trevor is wearing corporal stripes in Virginia, and my baby daughter is almost certainly better off without my presence. The road leads north, to Seattle, and within the week I've left San Francisco behind.

On the Mike Nine-Three

Jiliri, Somalia—Late March 1993

1

Seventy-some miles south of Kismaayo.

Deepest Africa, Jones thinks. *Deepest Africa, yes sir, there we were. And here we is.*

In the cramped wheelhouse of the Mike Boat the marine-band radio slung under the throttles crackled to life.

"Mike nine-three, mike nine-three, position report."

Trevor was closest to the radio. He stood up, pulled the mic toward him, and keyed it.

"Alpha-alpha-charlie two, this is mike nine-three." He glanced at the chart laid out over the engine-reading gauges, made a line with his finger, then gave their position. Jones, sitting with his knees pulled to his chin, his back against the inside of the starboard hatch, yawned and took another bite from a stale MRE cracker.

After a pause, "Roger that, nine-three." They heard another crackle of static, then it cleared.

"Nine-three, status?"

Trevor bent his knees, sitting on the deck next to Jones, pulling the mic and its cord down with him. "Stoned and psycho. You?" he said, winking at Jones. He hadn't keyed the mic. He put it to his lips, then said, "Charlie-two, we're five-by." He drawled it, and winked again. Trevor detested radio lingo, and exaggerated it whenever possible. "Sergeant Mason is on the ground with the U.N. civilian, Mister Simpson. We're at anchor. Over."

A third voice came over the radio, it was Sid. "Charlie two, charlie two, this is Mason. I'm here with your civilian and the nurse. We're secure for the night here in . . ." The radio gave a sound that was clearly Sid messing with a map; Jones could picture him squinting through his glasses, trying to make out the tiny village names. "Here in Jiliri. The nine-three is secure and at anchor. We'll continue unloading at dawn. Over."

The voice of command came back quickly: "Nine-three, we have you scheduled to sail out of there tonight. Verify, over."

"Not likely, jackass," Jones mumbled. He had never been to 7th Group's radio shack in Kismaayo, had no idea who worked there, but always pictured someone like the idiot corporal Dale Scruggs they had met on their first night in port. That seemed to be the intelligence level of charlie two.

The radio stayed quiet for a long pause. On the shore, within their sight if they had stood up and looked through the wheelhouse window—and had there been any daylight left—Jones knew Sid was talking quickly with the U.N. civilian who was running this little relief operation. Finally, the static cleared and Sid's voice came back.

"Alpha-alpha-charlie two, this is mike nine-three. That's a negative, charlie two, say again, a negative. I've got Mister Simpson here with me on the beach. He's quite familiar and experienced with this region. He highly recommended, I say again, highly, that we close it up for the night, lock down, and finish in the morning. They've been having trouble down here." A pause, then, "It's only the four of us down here, it's too risky to keep unloading, too risky to sail back out the river. We'll lock it up where we are, and finish unloading in the morning. How do you copy?"

"I copy with *this*," Trevor said, and flipped his middle finger up in the air. Jones smiled weakly, the best he could do on the amount of sleep they'd had—none. The unsaid in Sid's last transmission was quite clear to the two privates: *Charlie two, shouldn't you guys know this shit already?*

Kismaayo, seventy miles away as the crow flies but a solid twenty-four-hour sail, finally came back with approval. *Like they could disagree?* Jones thought. Followed with: *Cynical? I have not yet begun to get cynical.* He smiled to himself, and lit a cigarette. Trevor reached around and clipped the mic back on to the radio.

*   *   *

They had sailed out of Kismaayo the day before with sixty-some tons of grain in burlap sacks, a few packages of medicine, a pale Belgian nurse who didn't speak a lick of English, and an American civilian from the U.N.—Simpson. The route took them twelve hours down the coast from Kismaayo, then upriver to this little inlet. The American civilian and the Belgian nurse had spent the entire time on the open water vomiting, heads stretched over the sides of the boat, hands clinging tight to stanchions. When Bob finally guided the LCM out of the sea and into the river the nurse had started praying loudly.

They had run this type of mission for Simpson maybe six times before, but never to this village. Trevor called it a "Here ya go, stop shooting your neighbor" mission.

"Essentially," Simpson had explained to them in his white, all-American voice, "the technicals that roam around here raid the small villages, steal the food, shoot a few men, maybe have fun with the women at gunpoint, then slip back into the night."

Simpson had one of those tones of voice that let you know he had a mustache, even if you couldn't see him talking.

For a while Simpson's plan had been for a Special Forces ODA from Kismaayo to patrol the sector to stop the raids, but it wasn't enough. There was too much ground to cover, too many guns, and too great a need for the main body of American troops to stay near Mogadishu and famine-ridden Baidoa in the north. So the new plan called for bribes: the U.N. would go to a village, drop a load of food and medicine for the locals, then drop a similar-sized load next to it with the understanding that the technicals would take the extra food instead of killing the villagers for it. If they followed the rules, there'd be more freebies later.

"Let me get this straight," Bob had said to Simpson on their first run out, the two of them standing on the front ramp while the boat slowly plowed up the river, "our job is not to drive them to their knees, but to feed 'em, and *hope* they stop killing people." Simpson smiled, tightly. He didn't care for his plan to be reduced to basic description; it was obvious that Bob wasn't the first to do so.

At first, they preferred these missions with Simpson to the other things they'd been called on to do. Generally the villagers they met were friendly and thankful, and the river runs were quiet. And Simpson himself, once his arrogance abated, turned out to be not bad company; he shared his cigars and whiskey. He and Jones would sit on burlap grain bags in the welldeck, talking about Mark Twain and Woody Guthrie—and, strangely enough, the others started seeing Bob and Simpson talking quietly together on the bow ramp, about what none of them could imagine. They would, like here, anchor the boat fifty yards from the beach, drop the ramp, and wait for the villagers to come out in their tiny wooden vessels and collect up the bags of grain. Simpson would accompany them on their last trip in, ensure the grain was divided equally, half going to the village, half left on the beach for the technicals to get after the sun set. *Like vampires—with rusty machine guns,* Jones thought.

But the last two runs had been different, and the four soldiers were getting nervous. Up north, in Baidoa and Mogadishu, 10th Mountain and the Marines were coming under sporadic but increasingly stronger and more accurate fire every day. And here, the rumors out of Kismaayo were that Adid had moved his operation down to the south, and on missions like this it seemed to show. Twice they had been shot at; not accurately, but enough to scare them. On the last trip they had been boarded—sort of.

The sun had set right before they finished unloading, and—like this time—Sid hadn't wanted to run the river after dark, so they went to anchor and took shifts watching over the boat. About 2 A.M., while Bob was on watch, they had been wakened by a loud yell, and a thump. Bob was down in the empty welldeck, a tiny twenty-ish-looking Somali man held at arm's length in his grip. Bob was slamming him into the bulkhead, screaming at him something unintelligible. The man had swum over from the shore and crept on board, probably looking for food or, more likely, a loose pair of Nikes. Bob had been dozing in his beach chair at the front of the wheelhouse, and when he opened his eyes he saw the little man rooting around in a deck box. The surprise of the moment got the better of him.

Later, Bob, jumpy and still pumped, had said, "What if that fucker had had a gun? Oh, this is *all* going FUBAR. *Jesus Christ,* Sid, thank God he didn't have a gun in his hand!"

Sid, under his breath, so that only Jones heard him, replied, "No, thank God *you* didn't have a gun in your hand."

They had only opened fire twice in the three months they had been in-country, both occasions they were shot at first, both times while running this river. Sid had ordered first Jones, the next time Trevor, to rake the shoreline with one of the fifty-cal machine guns. They had no idea if they had hit anyone or anything, but both times they didn't get shot at again. After the second time, Trevor—pale and sweaty—said to Jones, "My Uncle Ralph was in Korea, y'know? When I was a kid I asked him if he ever killed anyone." Trevor wiped his lips. "He said, 'War doesn't work that way. I have no idea. I pulled the trigger. I might've killed fifty, I might have killed none.'"

"There was no one out there, Trev," Jones said. "Lighten up." But he had taken the first shot with the fifty-cal the week before, and had a good idea of the thoughts going through Trevor's brain. Jones remembered that feeling, standing at the tripod-mounted fifty-cal, putting pressure on the trigger, the incredibly loud cough of the gun, realizing he was shooting at something—*someone*—but having no idea what or who it was, or if he'd hit anything. As he'd approached the weapon from across the deck—slamming his helmet on his head, gripping the trigger guard, swinging the mighty machine gun on its tripod—he'd never felt more like a soldier. Seconds after he let the trigger go—the echo of the blast ringing in his head—he'd never felt less like one.

I am an American fighting man, and I have no idea what the hell I'm shooting at.

Or why.

They were more than nervous: they were scared.

It didn't show on the surface. They still took slugs out of the hooch canteen at night, still paged through their dog-eared *Playboy*s in the wheelhouse, still blasted "Welcome to the Jungle" out of their tape player when they approached a village on the river, imitating the cavalry from *Apocalypse Now.* But no one had dropped a fishing line in the water for quite a while and, although he couldn't be sure, Jones didn't think a one of them had written a letter home in weeks. He knew he hadn't. He really didn't have anyone to write anyway—just simple and happy words to his daughter—but it was inconceivable for the other soldiers; letters mailed and letters received were the lifeline, the thing that kept you going. But Jones had noticed that Sid's notebook sat unopened on the dash of the wheelhouse long enough to gather dust, and once when he was in the lazarette, rooting around for a carton of Marlboros, he found a whole stack of envelopes addressed to Trevor, with Michigan return addresses, unopened and forgotten. He almost asked him about it, but in the end didn't.

The headquarters building in Kismaayo port had a satellite connection, and in the poor-excuse for a dayroom the support staff had set up a TV that was kept on CNN all day. Of course, they watched it. And what they saw was not what they expected: What they saw *wasn't* them.

At first, there had been a lot of updates from Mogadishu, especially after the fiasco of the Marines and navy SEALs being met on the beach by the press corps that first night of the invasion—they had watched that from their hotel room in Kenya. But now, pretty much nothing. The occasional political report on Somalia from an on-camera journalist who more often than not wasn't actually filing the report *from* Somalia, and the occasional feel-good film clip showing a minor celebrity on a USO tour visiting the troops. No mention of Belgian casualties, no mention of *American* casualties, certainly no mention of Somali casualties. The biggest report they saw was when some dumb fuck of a Marine in Baidoa had killed himself—suicide. That had kept CNN's interest for a whole forty-eight hours.

"Do you suppose it's possible no one knows we're here?" Trevor asked one night, crossing the quay wall toward the boat. "What's my mom gonna say when they come to tell her I'm dead? 'Who? Killed where?'"

The smaller and smaller Somalia became on CNN, the weirder and weirder life got in-country. That's how it felt to Jones, anyway.

The week after the Belgian squad was slaughtered in their own truck, the night Jones and the LCM-8593 had arrived in Kismaayo, CNN had reported a "minor skirmish" in a "southern Somali city" involving "U.N." troops. They *did* report three Somalis were shot in the port by the Belgians, but not that they had been executed at point-blank range, without a trial. No one knew, because no one asked.

The Mike Boat would sail a mission, gone anywhere from two to three days. Every time they got back to Kismaayo it felt different somehow, changed. Bob, for reasons known only to him, called it "the Octopussy Garden"; the weird feeling that would slip over you as you stood on deck at night, or walked along the edge of the pier—that someone had his sights between your shoulder blades, and you wouldn't be able to duck fast enough to avoid the bullet. They'd be walking along, and all of a sudden Bob would just stop talking, his face tightening. "Octopussy Garden,

Bob?" one of them would ask. He would nod, and pick up the pace. The first time they had been shot at Bob was on the helm, and he started yelling out the window, toward the shore. Jones, who had been on the bow at the time, then running toward the fifty-cal, wasn't sure but could have sworn Bob was yelling "In the Garden! They're shooting from the *Garden!*"

2

Tonight, in the middle of nowhere—Jiliri—their divided situation had come about following this progression: Mr. Simpson had decided he wanted to stay in the village overnight, since they had to be here anyway, and take the time now available to him pumping for local information. This would require getting him drunk, and he paid Jones ten dollars for a bottle of Kenyan hooch. But the squad was under orders to protect this civilian at all costs, which meant Sid had to join him. That scared Sid, and if he was going to spend the night in a goddamn Somali village he wanted the M60 machine gun to make him feel better. Since Bob was the only one in the squad half reliable on the M60, he got the ticket to join. Which left Jones and Trevor to guard the boat.

"What, are you kidding me?" Trevor had said when told the news. "We gotta sit in this floating target all night, only two of us to split the night?"

Sid, exhausted and distracted and nervous all day, had at that point pulled rank for the first time ever.

"Did you fucking hear me, *Private?*" Tiny little Sid threw himself into Trevor's face, his index finger poking his chest. "Yes, that's exactly how it's going to go, and you won't be splitting the night, you'll *both* stay the fuck awake so we don't have any more fuckups like last time."

Trevor stood there without a word, Sid backing off, looking hot but like he couldn't quite believe he'd just raised his voice and actually called somebody "Private."

"Don't worry about it, Alphabet," he said, quieter. "We'll finish offloading this thing tomorrow, and then you and Jones can sleep. Me and Bob'll sail her home."

"Dude," Trevor said, surprised and red-faced. "I'm sorry. No biggie, right? I was just talking. Really."

They separated themselves and Sid went to gather his gear and wake up Bob from his nap.

Mr. Simpson, bag over his shoulder, blue U.N. ball cap on his head, stepped to the corner of the wheelhouse where Jones and Trevor stood. He pointed over the stanchion line to the little wooden Somali boat tied to their port quarter, two bare-chested men in dhotis looking up at them smiling and patient with oars in their hands, a boy of maybe ten reaching up to the deck of the Mike Boat, trying unsuccessfully to reach a stanchion pole to haul himself up. "These gentlemen are going to take us over to the village in their boat," Simpson said. "Don't sweat it, I'm quite sure that any technicals in the area have seen us—" and with this he rested his hand on the mounted fifty-cal "—and won't come a-knockin' at the village tonight. I'm going to tell the locals here to keep their boats clear of the water tonight, and we'll come back at first light."

Trevor raised both of his huge eyebrows in one great movement. "Yeah, okay then," he said, and Jones thought he looked just a little . . . funny. *Maybe the thing with Sid,* he thought. "But you tell 'em," and with this Trevor pushed his open palm into the air, "you tell 'em absolutely no fucking boats in the water tonight. They take all those little wooden dinghies they have and beach 'em until dawn. *Nothing moves in the water.*"

Simpson nodded, chuckling as he did. "We'll be all right," he said again.

"I'm sure you will," Trevor mumbled, then turned and climbed down into the lazarette.

"We'll be fine," Jones said, and lit a cigarette. Waiting for Sid and Bob, Jones looked down into the wooden boat, raising his hand at the two Somali men. They both grinned and waved back and Jones said "Jambo!" He didn't know how to say hello in Somali, figured the Kenyan greeting would be close, and the two men rewarded him with a "Jambo!" in return. The boy in the little boat's bow started yelling "Jambo! Jambo! Jambo!" and smacking his hand on the side of the Mike Boat. Jones reached down for his arm and hauled the boy up on deck, laying an easy arm around his skinny shoulders. The boy grinned maniacally, pulling on Jones's hand, looking up at him. "Jambo! Jambo!"

"Jambo, indeed, little man," Jones said, laughing, looking up at Simpson, then down at the boy. He pushed him back a pace so he could see what he thought he saw on the boy's chest: torn, filthy, but undeniably a Stray Cats concert T-shirt, circa 1983, hanging down almost to the boy's knees, a pair of dirty purple shorts sticking out.

"Brian Setzer!" Jones yelled, and high-fived the boy. "Bine Sessah!" the boy yelled gleefully in return, swinging his arm around for another high five, Jones catching his wrist, reaching down, then swinging the boy up off the deck and holding him there on his side. "Bine Sessah!" laughed the boy, thrilled with his two new American words. He was light, too light, too small, his bones too prominent under his skin, and Jones's laugh caught in his throat, and then the boy was grabbing at Jones's dog tags and babbling incoherently and laughing and pointing at everything on the boat. Jones swung the boy around, then carefully bent over the side of the Mike Boat and deposited the boy back with the two men, waving, then reaching deep into his pocket for a handful of root beer barrels and filling the boy's waiting hands with them.

The sun was gone before the little wooden boat made the beach, and the only way Jones knew for sure they had made it was because Sid had, as promised, flicked his red light twice in their direction. "I'll be monitoring the radio, too," Sid had said, standing in the middle of the sailboat as the two Somali men untied from the LCM, "and either Bob or me will be up all night. If something happens, call. If something bad happens, lay on the foghorn." The little craft started to drift away. "And don't forget to check the anchor line every hour!" he called back over his shoulder, losing his balance for a second, grabbing the shoulder of the boy, almost falling into the water. *Didn't anyone tell that sergeant you shouldn't stand up in a boat?* Jones asked himself, raising his hand a last time to wave good-bye to his new little friend. The boy cupped his hands and yelled, "Bine Sessah!" and Jones yelled a "Bine Sessah!" right back at him. Lowering his arm, he turned toward the wheelhouse and the beginning of a long night's wait. Bine Sessah indeed.

After dark, Trevor spent the first hour planted in front of the wheelhouse, scanning what little he could see. His feet were almost parade-regulation on the deck, back straight, eyes moving left and right.

"You look like you're reviewing the troops, Alphabet," Jones yelled up at him from the welldeck, where he was sweeping up loose grain. Trevor shot him the finger and didn't move. When the radio call from Kismaayo had come in they both moved into the wheelhouse, and after that Trevor's comfort level seemed to rise. They stayed in there, one of them always standing, scanning out the open windows. Trevor put Pearl Jam in, and it played low behind them as they talked.

They talked easily, about everything and nothing, the way two people can when they have the whole night ahead of them and a whole world together behind them. In that way, with that between them, they could skip seamlessly from fishing to unwanted pregnancies to shock executions in Kismaayo to fear to promotion to life after the army. All of this touched on at least once, certainly to be touched on again, added to, gathered together in their shared understanding of each other.

Trevor had never been out of Michigan before he joined the army. He would get Jones to talk about Greyhound buses, youth hostels, sleeping in open apple orchards under a Vermont sky; pieces of Jones's prefatherhood life that felt like failure to him, high-school teenage runaway wanderings, seemed romantic to Trevor. Even the forced domesticity that followed seemed different—interesting. Jones told Trevor about his father, and he'd never talked about him with anyone before—not even Liz.

And Jones, born in New Jersey, had never been hunting. He would listen carefully as Trevor detailed grease and powder, scent and tracking, knives and rope, dirt and hunger, fathers and sons and things they were supposed to do together. At one point, with the sound of water lapping the sides of the boat, soft green and red lights in the wheelhouse outlining their faces, Jones jokingly asked Trevor if he actually *enjoyed* hunting—he didn't know why he asked, but it occurred to him that in all of Trevor's talk he knew all the answers, yes, knew the black-and-white, but Jones had never heard Trevor actually say how much he *loved* hunting. Trevor looked at him for a moment, his brown Polish eyes connecting with Jones's mongrel blues, the two of them now both crouched on the floor of the wheelhouse, a forgotten game of chess spread between them, a forgotten window unwatched above. Trevor looked at him that way, held it, then broke the moment by looking down, reaching for his plastic bottle of water, taking a swig. "What is there to *enjoy*, Jones?" he asked. "It's hunting. You *do* it, or you *don't* do it. I do it. You don't."

Trevor stood, knees popping, and swept his gaze across the dark horizon through the window. Jones wanted to say something, but didn't know what it was. Trevor crouched down again and said, "Tell me more about Guthrie—wasn't he in the army for a while?"

"Yeah. Him and Jerry Garcia too."

"At the same time?"

Jones reached over and swatted his friend on the back of the head.

The night crept on.

Jones shook himself out of a doze sometime later, checking his watch, suddenly nervous they'd let their guard down. 0200. Trevor was snoring quietly, a thin line of drool running from lip to collar, his back to the portside hatch. Jones pushed himself to his feet, scanning the darkness through the window, and picked up the pistol Trevor had set on the dash. It was a pistol that once belonged to a pimp in Mombasa, stolen and cleaned up nicely by Alphabet, some fine touches Jones didn't understand performed by Bob on the firing mechanism. He turned it over in his hands, figured out how the safety worked, and shoved it in the right cargo pocket of his BDU pants.

He stepped out onto the quarterdeck, warm dark breeze, the sky clear and overflowing with stars. Jones was still quietly stunned by what this part of the earth did to the night. The northern and southern constellations met here, and mixed, in a nervous and overcrowded conglomeration of points of light. The Big Dipper and the Southern Cross in the same sky. Constellations overlapping, fingers from two immense hands intertwining. This place was the curse of the ancient sailor; you couldn't get your bearings, couldn't figure it out. No order, just a mess of stars, daring you to try and fathom it.

He tugged the anchor line, then stepped to the break in the stanchions, unbuttoned, and pissed into the water, enjoying the breeze. This was a hot fucking country, a brain-crushing dry heat, but the nights were sweet and tolerable. He had a sudden flash of a sea monster, or the ghost of a dead Somali warrior, reaching up out of the water to drag him in. But he always made himself imagine things like this, and he didn't get spooked. He finished, buttoned his BDU pants, and with a last look at the stars went back into the wheelhouse.

Amazingly, in the middle of all of this chaos of Somalia, even in the face of this horror, he found for the first time he could think clearly about himself, even if only for brief moments at a time. He missed his baby Emma, and took comfort in the thought; he didn't want to be someone who played lip service to how he felt about his child. The only other parts of his previous life he had any connection left to were his guitar and his writing, and both of those things seemed . . . ridiculous. Who cares, anyway? He took great pleasure in this *not caring*. His dreams consisted of an apartment, a little apartment, maybe in Hoboken or Weehawken—somewhere with beer and art in close contact—and weekends with baby Emma, and cooking her spaghetti. Going to the library. And being in his twenties and feeling that way. He'd felt fifty since the day he turned fourteen—most of his old friends wouldn't settle for that, he knew, and he was jealous. They seemed to get younger with age. He wanted to taste that.

And Liz. He didn't know how this would play out, but he felt the closest he could come to peace in the thought of unburdening himself to her, of falling into her, of surrendering. *Giving up*, he thought. If she would let him.

Jones sniffed the dry, diesel African air. He was exhausted. They all were. There was no sleep on these three-day missions.

Fuck it, he thought, making himself comfortable on the steel deck in the wheelhouse, placing his outstretched feet around Trevor's. *It'll be fine. I'm going to sleep. Bring 'em on.*

He hesitated once, then closed his eyes.

Outward peace was one thing—remaining sane and even improving sanity in the face of this country was one thing—but the inner, involuntary dreams were something else completely. Jones didn't know how Trevor was dreaming these days, one subject they hadn't touched on, but he knew how his were going, and it was always a variation on the same theme. It scared him, sometimes so much he shook himself awake, but you had to sleep, *had* to, no matter what Drill Sergeant Rose once said, so the dreams, like everything else, had to be endured.

Jones drifted, then fell asleep.

3

He who sleeps, dies.
  (Who's knocking at the door?)
  Say it again, Private: he who sleeps—

BOOM!

—*dies.*

BOOM!

Trevor's voice, yelling: "Oh you FUCK!"

Jones's eyes pop open, Trevor is on his knees, M16 in his hands, pointing up and out, the barrel a straight line for the open window, smoke drifting from the muzzle, hot brass in Jones's lap. Trevor raises the rifle to his eye and shoots again out the window he is three feet below, the explosion of the shot in the wheelhouse beyond anything Jones has ever heard and it deafens him instantly. From where he sits on the deck he can see the mast of one of the tiny wooden sailboats, bobbing. Calculating in a second he knows that puts the boat right up against theirs. And there must be something wrong, it must be clan militia, technicals, because Trevor is *shooting* in the fucking *wheelhouse*—

"Oh my GodOhmyGodOh" Jones stammers frantically, his muscles, all of them, letting go at once, warm urine streaming down his leg. He realizes very suddenly he does not want to die sitting here in the wheelhouse of this boat. He has tried hard, with success, to not think about his own death, a foreign concept, but here it is and Jones knows right now he will probably die right now and he doesn't want to die. His hand pushes into his pocket, gripping the pistol, ripping it out *(thank God, oh thank God I put the fucking safety on)* and bringing it around in front of him, both hands wrapping around it, dropping the safety with his thumb, screaming at Trevor, *"What the fuck am I shooting at?!!"*

Trevor raises himself from his crouch in one swift motion, his M16 still up to his shoulder, and as he reaches his full height a face, one round black face, appears from nowhere, perfectly framed in the forward window.

"THAT!" Trevor screams, and they both shoot at once, shoot *as* one, two hammers slamming down on two weapons, two bullets exploding from barrels, two screaming straight shots from the unbearable noise, two slugs that pass in a fraction of a second over the lip of the window, knocking back the face—back, and out of their view.

JONES: Two Privates

Jiliri, Somalia

More than two hundred miles south of Mogadishu—where children still have parents, where villages struggle to remain villages—I found a nice rock to sit on. The water lapped gently around the rock, the tiny beach behind me a scrabble of pebbles and coarse sand, wooden sailboats pulled up on it, resting above the tidemark. From the village fronting the beach came sounds of confusion, people rushing around in the night, a woman crying, screaming, a man arguing with another man, all of this barely heard by me—I was deaf from the blast of an M16 in a Mike Boat wheelhouse. The boat was on the beach now, too, jammed into the sand, ramp down—but I couldn't see it from this rock.

Since I couldn't do anything but wait out this deafness, wait for my hearing to come back, I figured I would wait it out right here. On this rock. It's a nice rock, and it's a nice night, anyway. Warm breeze pushing gently on my face, the water lapping up toward my boots, cigarette smoke thick and soothing to me. I could wait here, wait for my ears to clear, while someone higher ranking than me deals with the confusion in the village. The villagers seem to have lost something, and I think I might know where it is. But, like my hearing, the knowledge is elusive and slippery. It will come, though, I think to myself. It will come. And when it does I'll get off this rock and go tell them.

I flicked the butt of my smoke into the water, and as the red glow sizzled and then went black the knowledge came to me, suddenly and fully, like a rude smack from a wave. I think my face must have gone white, my muscles limp, almost sliding off the rock into the water, the power of knowledge driving me to my feet, and as my boots slammed into the sand I said, out loud, *oh God,* my voice leaving me in a gasp. I raised my head, yelling the name of my friend, Trevor—it's now very important that I find him—then turned and ran to the village, leaving the water and the stars behind.

I found Trevor about a quarter mile past the village, sitting hunched in a stand of dying grasses. He was stock still—in the dark of night I almost missed him. I came up behind him and put my hand on his shoulder. He didn't flinch.

Staring straight ahead, he said, "What are we going to do?"

He wasn't asking about tangibles—logistics, actuals. It was a deeper question. Not really *What are we going to do,* but *How do we live now?*

I had no answer for him.

PART TWO

Shadowtime

Mogadishu and Kismaayo, Somalia—Late March 1993

1

In a land that has no electricity, the night settles with a firmness and finality most of the world has forgotten.

The night here rises from the sea and pushes across Mogadishu, shadows digging in and taking hold. Some face it head-on, in shattered high-rise flats with gaping holes where walls and windows used to be. Some hide from it, in back alleys and burned-out basements where the jumping shadows of small brush fires built for warmth and light and company create a different kind of darkness that exists on its own level.

The dark, the night, molds to the city, and embraces it, feeding off the deep crimson brilliance of the sun's final bloody retreat into the Indian Ocean. Once, not long ago, Mogadishu welcomed the night and all it promised. The central avenues—laid out by Italian engineers—bustled with it, the clubs and casinos depended on it. But now, the night brings nothing but the night, steady and relentless. Pressing on.

In the outlying stretches of the city lie the homes and manors of the once well-to-do, and in these neighborhoods this shadowtime is most dangerous of all. Even the clan militia and technicals that hold power in this land don't go here; not at night, not anymore. Bands of children—boys mostly—have taken many of these houses for their own, these houses of the exiled, and the dead. At the approach of dusk they move out in squads of miniature soldiers, knives and clubs and pistols in hand, spreading out across this suburbia, looking for whatever might catch their eye or cool their appetite. The last few adult survivors in this neighborhood—and, outside the militia, there are few adults still alive—bolt their shutters and lock their doors, rifles and pistols loaded and ready, guarding their possessions and listening carefully for the high-pitched sound of a child's giggle. They will shoot these children if they try to enter. But in this country, in this city especially, there are more children than there are bullets. If the children decide to come in, they will, in the end, come in.

The dark devours Mogadishu and presses on from there into the desert. Here there is nothing for the dark to grab on to and it slides, slowly and gracefully, across the hard-packed ground. There were once trees here, fields here, but no more. There are no animals. There is no life. There is nothing but the ground and the night and one does not travel the ground without first consulting with the night.

In this land, however, the night sometimes lies.

In this land the northern and southern constellations meet, joining in an uneasy peace that leaves lonely night travelers confused and lost. In this land, in this night, it is not wise to find yourself lost.

Shadowtime slides on and finds a village. In their huts, the Berberi, descendants of the nomads, draw flimsy curtains across doorways to hold back the shadowtime. They see it like their fathers saw it, and their fathers before them. These people know the night, can use it—but they don't trust it.

In the shelled remains of what was once this village's school, four white reporters pull out sleeping bags. They share around a bottle of whiskey and play cards and smoke cigarettes and fight over who will sleep first and who will watch. The foreign soldiers were here, briefly, but are gone now. The reporters complained about restrictions and freedom of the press while the soldiers were here, but now they miss the protection. The soldiers might come back, and they discuss this. Or, maybe, they should move to where the soldiers are now; they have a jeep they share. Nothing can be done until morning, though. It is night, and the road is not safe. Especially for white men.

In this land, in this time, the night slides on.

A mile east of the village the dark catches a small dog, still alive, curled up in a ball next to a long-dry stone well under the only tree for miles: a baobab, huge and reaching out with its gnarled branches. The dog lifts its head and growls softly, hearing something. In the distance, in the shadow-time sky, a red light appears, pulsing slowly. It grows larger and a breeze kicks up, then a sudden explosion of sound and movement. A foreign thing, this Black Hawk helicopter, it slices the night and is gone almost before it was there. It flies west, back toward the coast.

In their huts, the villagers mumble and roll over, returning to uneasy sleep. The reporters pause in their argument, four necks looking upward to a sky they can't see through the roof.

In the seaport, where Mogadishu meets the ocean—where the dark and night came from—a female soldier standing at the gate looks up at the sky as the helicopter passes and then leaves the land behind, moving out over the water. In less than a minute its blinking red light is gone, the silence returned. The soldier looks back down and out through the gate toward the darkened city that is her home now, her thoughts an easy and unhurried mix of responsibilities on her shift tonight, letters she must write, and wondering about a friend who is far to her south, in Kismaayo. She sees the scurry of a rat through the shadows and pulls back, disgusted. She turns toward the water, and decides she doesn't have enough time to get a sandwich before her shift starts.

There are electric lights at the Mogadishu seaport—and the airport, two miles south—because the foreign armies have brought their own. They are not comfortable without them. The lights cast a pale, yellow glow over the buildings and warehouses and out onto the water; the noise from the generators keeping many awake at night until the body and brain become accustomed and you forget they exist at all.

Soldiers stand under these lights, waiting in line for their one-minute shower, waiting for their food, waiting for their mail. They talk while they wait, laughing and slapping each other on the back. These soldiers waiting tonight are Rangers, and they like that they're Rangers. It is who they are, and what they do, and they're restless to see this land they've been sent to. They're new here, and have yet to leave this compound. In this land, in this port compound, you are new if you've never been in to the city, or beyond to the desert. You are a veteran, and feel that way, if you've been in this land for more than a week. These soldiers, laughing as they wait, are new, and they enjoy the coolness the night brings.

From their lines, waiting, they can hear children. The port is surrounded by tractor-trailer and Conex vans, stacked three high and stretching around the perimeter of the compound. The children climb them from the outside, the city side, and crawl through to where they can sit, up in the air, looking down on the soldiers and their electric lights. They look, and the soldiers can hear them giggle. There seem to be more of them every night. The Rangers have been told by their officers and by the infantrymen and Marines who have been here for months to ignore the children, and to be wary of them. But this is absurd. How much of a threat can a child be?

The children will stare and giggle all night, moving swiftly from one trailer-van roof to the next. They will be gone at sunrise, along with a few cases of MRE rations and some fatigue jackets and one loaded M16A2 rifle that a lieutenant put under his cot before he went to sleep.

2

The twilight of shadowtime slides east to west, but the Black Hawk—like all man-made things—pushes its own course. West to east, out of the desert. Over the Mogadishu seaport. Then south, hugging the coastline, a two-hundred-mile flight to Kismaayo. The wink of an eye for a Black Hawk pilot. Flying asleep, they call it.

Kismaayo appears as a glowing ruby of light, warm reds and yellows twinkling off the ocean. Not Kismaayo proper—the city is as dark as Mogadishu, a black hole of empty as gone as the day. It's the seaport that glows, a weak glow, but enough for the Black Hawk pilot to see and correct course, suddenly there, oblivious in his cocoon to the maelstrom of wind and dust his helicopter raises as he sets down on the largest concrete pier.

Two soldiers sit just inside the door of a warehouse, hiding their faces behind brown scarves from the hurricane of blowing grit as the Black Hawk lands.

"I wish they wouldn't do that," the one soldier says. He is instantly filthy from the storm of the landing, and had just showered an hour before, in the plywood lean-to up on the hill. With water rationing, he wasn't likely to see another shower for a week. "Goddamn," he said. "Goddamn."

3

The two soldiers spent most of that late winter—what would have been winter at home, February, March—playing chess. There was some movement, two days up this river, three days at that village, but in between only time to kill in the Kismaayo port compound.

They started playing chess to pass the time back in January, usually setting the board where they were most comfortable—on the quarterdeck of their Mike Boat. But by February they were looking for any reason not to be on the boat. Moving the game up the rocky hill to the American camp lasted only a day: too many people around from the same unit, too many chores to be given to too many bored privates, and no real relief from the sun that beat down on them relentlessly.

They found a shady spot for their game right inside the door of one of the huge warehouses down in the port area. Up in Mogadishu, warehouses like these were now soldier hotels: rows and rows and rows of mosquito-netted cots, most with overturned boxes or scrap-wood tables between them, holding pictures of wives and tattered paperbacks and rounds of ammo and half-empty plastic water bottles. Over the door of one of these warehouses someone had erected a sign: MOGADISHU MARRIOTT. But down in Kismaayo, both of the two port warehouses were filled with bags of grain waiting to be picked up and trucked in-country. The grain was filthy with rats, so you didn't dare venture far into the warehouse; but right inside the house-size door—where you still had a view of the boats and the city, and the shade and the breeze took the temperature down ten degrees—there you could be comfortable, setting the chessboard on a milk crate, facing it from either side with two folding chairs that could be stashed under a grain bag after the game was done.

The more time that went by—days, then weeks, then two months—the more chess they played. The more games they played, the quieter they got. By late March it seemed all conversation had ceased. A game, won; then another, won by the other; then another. No words during play. Even a call of check or checkmate felt unnecessary—you could see it right there in front of you. And certainly no words between games. If one soldier had to piss, he just got up and stretched and walked to the piss hole behind the warehouse, then came back and started the next game. Or, if the games got boring—when the afternoon got too long—one soldier would check his watch, point toward the HQ building, then saunter off in that direction to watch CNN. They almost never went together, and when one would come back—usually finding the other right where he'd left him, sitting at the chessboard, staring at the comings and goings across the port—there didn't seem much reason to pass along the day's headlines to his friend: it was all the same.

The soldier from New Jersey smoked, and he tapped his ash carefully in an empty tin of Spanish anchovies; you had to be wary with flame in a warehouse like this, even near the door. The other soldier, who was from Michigan, didn't smoke but dipped. He'd make a small wad under his lip, and it usually lasted the whole game. He kept an empty water bottle next to him and would spit in it every thirty seconds or so, the juice building up over time until the bottle was near full of brown, foul liquid. When it got to that point he'd stroll over to the quay wall, dump the contents into the ocean, then walk back for the next game.

The two soldiers were evenly matched. Neither was particularly good, but they knew their own game well. Neither was much better than the other.

Like most soldiers everywhere, they played cards, too; with the other members of their squad and their platoon, especially the two buck sergeants who were their friends and boat mates. But as the weeks went by, all of the soldiers started drawing back, from comfortable groups of five or six to smaller cliques of three or four, until finally most everyone either just kept to themselves when off-duty or stuck with just one other guy. Cards got boring with only two, and neither of them were strong on cards anyway, so chess became their pastime. You could play it silently, and that was important.

They'd be gone for a while—firing off the Detroit Diesel engines on the Mike Boat before sunrise, out of sight of Kismaayo by nine, back by sunset two or three days later—and when they got back they'd find their chessboard and table where they'd left it, stashed behind a pile of grain bags, their two clanky metal chairs folded flat under another pile.

Once, they tied-up the boat after returning from a three-day mission to a village called Jiliri—a mission that had gone very wrong—and walked silently right to the warehouse without even a stop for chow; it was only seven and neither soldier was hungry or tired. They were both out-of-uniform for the port area: desert BDU pants stuffed into jungle boots caked with dried beach mud, brown T-shirts loosely tucked in with no BDU top—one soldier had no belt because he'd used it to tie a loose pipe in place in the boat's engine compartment—rifles locked and loaded slung over their shoulders, unshaven faces, bare heads. As they approached the warehouse they saw their table and chessboard had been found and pulled out; two older soldiers at their table, playing on their board, sitting in their chairs. One was an American captain, Quartermaster insignia on his collar, new and pressed desert BDUs, face and haircut squeaky clean. The other was a master sergeant, looking almost as fresh, a cheroot jutting from his lips, a Big Red One combat patch on his right shoulder. The two young soldiers walked up to them; "That's our game," one of them said without emotion. The sergeant and the captain looked up at these two privates, the sergeant's mouth opening, then quickly closing. The captain looked them both up and down, eyebrows raised, and seemed about to say something when his sergeant kicked him lightly under the table. The master sergeant pushed back his chair and stood. "Sorry, fellas. We just found it here. Didn't know it belonged to anyone." The officer and his NCO left. Without a word, the two returning soldiers sat down, resting their M16s on the ground beside them, cleared the board, and started a new game.

4

As a hot February had turned into an even hotter March the two soldiers began extending their time at the board into the evening hours. Before, they might have been found up in the camp after dark, drinking with the other boat crews, writing letters, reading, enjoying the dark and silent ocean breeze, watching the fireworks display of tracers that lit up the city of Kismaayo every few nights one mile across the bay. But as the months changed, so did the situation; slowly, slowly, so you might not even notice your comfortable routine was different: the hooch they had brought up from Kenya in December was about gone, letters received became harder to relate to so therefore harder to respond to, paperback novels got so torn apart you couldn't follow the story even if you were interested. And no one—none of them—wanted to watch the nighttime firefights in the city anymore.

Slowly, slowly the two soldiers stopped making the long climb back up the hill right after evening chow. They might watch a movie in the VCR tent, or stop to smoke cigarettes and drink bug juice with friends in the SF hut or the Dive Det camp at the end of the pier, or on the big floating army BD crane that had been brought in to clear wrecks from the channel; all soldiers—like them—removed from the mainstream by the nature of their duties, separate from the lumbering dinosaur that was 10th Mountain Division. Either way, by ten or so these two soldiers would both be back at the warehouse, one of them dusting off their chairs, one setting up the board, cigarette lit, dip can packed down, BDU tops off, first move knights out.

Where they sat in their warehouse doorway they faced the quay wall at the deepest part of the port: Kismaayo harbor was only big enough to handle one or maybe two large ships at a time, and here is where those ships would tie-up, sit for a few hours or days, then be replaced by another ship. The two soldiers would sit and smoke and chew and sip at their canteens—bitter from iodine tablets—and watch the progression of maritime work. Most of the work was done at night now, too hot in the afternoons.

Big clunky, rusty cargo ships were there mostly, all of them bearing more and more bags of grain to be stored in the warehouses. The two soldiers couldn't recall a time when any trucks had come to take the grain away, and they found this curious, but still the ships would come, delivering even more piles of the overstuffed burlap bags to be placed, forgotten, in the deeper regions of the warehouses. Hundreds of Somali men from Kismaayo and the environs would be trucked in to do the unloading at night, under bright lights on poles running off the generators, turning night into day on one small circle of the dock. Tiny, skinny black men with blue eyes and no shoes, some with large and clumsy turbans, most bare-chested, sweating and straining as they sang and chanted and heaved the grain bags from pallet to shoulder to shoulder to pallet. During breaks in their labor they would stand in groups of fives and sixes, chirping quietly to one another in their sing-song language, eyeing the Belgian and American MPs that stood loosely around them, rifles in their arms but pointed to the ground. The Somali men would chew their *chat,* long and stringy sticks of it, picking at their teeth, rubbing between their gums, breaking into laughter from time to time over something one of them had said.

One night the two soldiers had their game interrupted by a sharp howl, both of them immediately down and grabbing for rifles, forgetting the chessboard in front of them. But it was nothing: one of the Somali laborers, deep inside the warehouse, stacking bags onto piles, had his finger bitten viciously by a rat. When he instinctively drew his hand to his mouth to suck the wound there was no finger there: the rat had ripped it off in one mighty bite. He fell to his knees, screaming with the pain of it, and three American MPs ran over to him. But they would not pick him up to help him walk to the infirmary tent: blood was gushing from his hand, African blood, maybe AIDS blood. The three MPs looked at one another nervously, one finally taking a step toward the injured man. But his sergeant stopped him with a hand to the shoulder, drawing him back. "No, stay away." Finally, a group of the Somali man's co-workers came running in, picked him up, and carried him out of the warehouse; his surprised howl slowly turning into an extended whimper.

The two soldiers at the chessboard took all this in, looked at each other, then went back to their game.

One day, not long after the worker lost his finger to the rat, a new order came down from on high: no more Somali nationals in port. Period. Too dangerous, too impossible to root out troublemakers among them, too risky. There had been problems in Mogadishu—Purple Hearts handed out like party favors for shrapnel wounds incurred within the port walls from pipe bombs—and even some close calls here in Kismaayo port.

This meant there was no one to unload the grain. At first, the U.N. civilians came to the army for help. One bright young captain from 10th Mountain sent a squad of his troops down to the port uninvited to assist—they stood around for a few hours in the sun, kicking at pebbles on the dock, softly cursing this betrayal by their ass-kiss of a commander. But the colonel in the HQ building, backed up by the general in Mogadishu, countermanded this with one stroke: no soldier would unload grain. It was too dangerous, it was too dirty, and nobody flew five thousand miles over here to heave bags of shit around a seaport.

The two soldiers at their chessboard watched as the last grain ship sat in port for almost a week, fully loaded, its Portuguese crew standing around on deck all day, reading movie magazines, tossing their cigarette butts into the water, the grain in the ship's holds not going anywhere. One morning as they readied their Mike Boat for sailing one of the two soldiers looked over and saw the big ship had gone. It had never been unloaded and was never replaced.

But other ships came and went.

Twice, a Belgian ship in naval gray called for a day. Its arrival was greeted by cheers among the Belgian infantry: this was their food, and more important, their beer. The Belgians laughed at the Americans, so *gung ho,* so *crazy-man-crazy,* and yet so conservative and unsophisticated that not only didn't they supply their troops with beer, there were actually regulations that said Americans weren't allowed to drink at all. *Mon Dieu,* G.I. Joe; fuck you, Charlie. The huge pallets of canned beer would be swung from the side of the ship by crane, hanging precariously in the air over the dock, American MPs in guard towers eyeing the Belgian shipment dryly and wordlessly behind their reflective sunglasses, tightening the grip on their rifles, then looking elsewhere.

Once an Indian gunboat called for twenty-four hours; the two soldiers interrupted their game long enough to join with their two sergeants to go on board for samosas and papad, the spicy smells wafting through every passage and compartment of the little ship, the Indian sailors gracious and excited hosts who sat their four guests in the wardroom, even after polite protests from the small squad on their enlisted status.

An American M.S.C. ship came in one night; unloaded its belly in less than four hours, and was gone again before sunrise. It left four stacks of metal Conex containers on the dock, two of them labeled US ARMY COLD WEATHER GEAR. Sitting at the chessboard, the soldier from New Jersey—without looking up, concentrating on his move—said, "That is either the biggest fuckup we will likely ever see, or the first part of bad news we don't want to hear." He moved his last bishop and realized he would lose the game in the next move.

The two soldiers knew each other's chess game, knew how the other was likely to play, but never got bored with it. They played on anyway, almost the same game each time, not really noticing or caring. The soldier from Michigan made ticks on the wooden door frame with his K-Bar for each win from one of the two; the columns were almost equal.

5

The night they had found the Quartermaster captain and his old master sergeant sitting at their board, playing their game, the two soldiers had just returned from Jiliri, seventy miles to the south. It had been their first mission to that village, and although it wasn't supposed to be the last, neither of them ever went back. Neither of them sailed on the LCM-8593 again. Things changed quickly after that mission.

The second chess game that evening they returned from Jiliri was interrupted by their harried-looking lieutenant, himself out of uniform in running shorts and sneakers, looking like he had just woken up. He probably had; Lieutenant Klover spent increasingly more and more time alone in his tent. Some days the platoon never saw him at all. And although he didn't have it now, he'd recently taken to carrying a pocket Bible with him everywhere he went.

He pointed at the soldier from Michigan.

"Alphabet, come with me?"

Then he looked at the soldier from New Jersey, taking him in.

"And Jones, go clean up and shave, then come back."

The lieutenant led the one soldier away toward the HQ building, while the other sat there in his folding chair at the chessboard, staring across the port, not making any move to go clean himself up. Later, the lieutenant would come back for him, too.

It turned out not to be the end of the world, as the lieutenant feared it was: just a few questions, and of course some paperwork. Then some more paperwork. Amazing, really, how much paper the army had managed to ship over here. The two soldiers sat side by side at a long metal table, their two sergeants sitting across from them, all four scrawling out long and meaningless lines of ink across never-ending paperwork. Their concentration was interrupted occasionally by loud, punctuated bursts of belches from the mouth of the least-ranking of the two buck sergeants—Bob, his name was; he was swilling his fourth warm Pepsi of the evening while he wrote, and it wasn't going down well. The lieutenant stood over them, nervous and almost twitching; he gave off the distinct impression that something terrible—an explosion maybe, or some other sort of sudden death—might occur at the conclusion of their writing.

But it didn't. They finished, all about the same time, and handed their work to a clerk sitting at the radio desk.

"Thanks, fellas," the warrant officer in charge of the port ops center said as they filed out. "That should do it. Get some sleep, y'all." He smiled warmly and patted them each on the back as they passed him.

The lieutenant rushed forward toward the warrant officer as the soldiers filed out, questions upon questions in his mind, wondering about what came next and what was he responsible for and who should be talked to.

"That's it, L.T.," said the warrant, turning back to his desk, taking the soldiers' statements from the clerk then shoving them into a drawer. "Done deal. We're through here. Fire's out, go home."

The lieutenant pressed. He needed answers, he said. He'd have to answer questions when he got debriefed in Mogadishu. The details from Jiliri were hazy, and the four enlisted men had been evasive.

The warrant, a tall and soft-spoken West Virginian with tight-combed gray hair, looked down into the lieutenant's eyes.

"Son, whose side are you on?" he asked quietly, the hint of an unfriendly smile playing at the corners of his mouth.

"Side?" the lieutenant said, annoyed by this distraction. "There *are* no sides."

"There's always sides, L.T., you should know that. Besides, you as an officer got only one side—your boys." He pointed out the window of the office where they could see the two sergeants and two privates walking across the port. "Them are your boys walking out there, and you're supposed to be on *their* side. Always."

He turned back then, and sat at his desk.

"It's late, I got a movie to go watch, and these reports is filed. We're done here." He paused, then added, "Sir."

The lieutenant opened his mouth, then shut it, then opened it again. "Thanks."

"No problem, L.T."

6

The four soldiers separated as they approached the large chow tent; one of the two sergeants spoke quietly to the other three soldiers for a moment, and then—in turn—grabbed each on the shoulder, one after the other, with his right palm, and squeezed. He looked at each of them, and then when he felt it was right, that *they* were right, he and the lesser-ranking sergeant turned and walked into the mess tent.

The two privates watched them go, then finished the walk back toward the warehouse and their chess game. It remained where they had left it, unmolested. They sat down and faced the board.

"Start again?"

"Yep."

"All right."

The soldier from Michigan cleared the board and reset it while the soldier from New Jersey lit up a smoke, cupping his hand over the match to guard against the night breeze from the harbor. When he looked up the lieutenant was standing over them.

"Need a smoke, L.T.?"

"I don't smoke. You know that."

"Just being polite."

"Yeah," the lieutenant sighed, then looked away, stuffing his hands into the waistband of his running shorts. Down the dock a hundred feet or so a squad of Belgians were setting up a volleyball net under a string of bare lightbulbs. The lieutenant watched them for a while. A look of not-understanding was etched on his face. He turned back, looking at the two PFCs.

"You fellas . . ." he started, then cleared his throat. "You fellas got anything that maybe we should talk about?"

The soldier from Michigan stood straight up, his folding chair falling over backward, never looking at the lieutenant, his face bright red and tight and angry, and said, "Excuse me, sir, I gotta go use the latrine." He turned and disappeared into the dark warehouse without waiting for an answer. He was angry because he thought it was cheap that an officer, even a second lieutenant, would come to privates looking for answers.

The soldier from New Jersey took a drag on his cigarette and watched as the other disappeared from view. He agreed with his friend's sentiments, but in his case it didn't make him mad. He was willing to wait out the lieutenant. They'd been friendly once, but not so much now. Now, it seemed all dealings with the lieutenant were adversarial. He felt bad about that. This was important to him, now: finding trivial things to feel bad about. He'd come to understand over the last forty-eight hours that the only way you could get through this, the only way to keep yourself breathing, was to find the trivial and concentrate all your energy on it. Ignore the forest, and the trees, and stare at the blades of grass.

The lieutenant picked up the fallen chair and sat down in it, heavily. He tried to raise his shoulders up, to level them with his chest, to attain the air of authority certain sergeants had, but he had been trying and failing at that since the day he was commissioned. It bothered him only a little bit; he wasn't fooling himself, let alone anyone else. That wasn't who he was, or what he wanted. He just wanted to go home. Things were out of control. They'd always seemed a bit out of *his* control, he expected that. But they weren't just out of his control now, they were simply out of control. He didn't want control back—he'd never had it, he understood that. But his worry was now greater than ever, and the worry, he thought, was for his soul.

He opened his mouth, but was cut off by the private before he could get his thought out.

"John?" the soldier from New Jersey asked him quietly, looking at the lieutenant carefully as he ditched his smoke in the anchovy tin.

The November night they'd left Ft. Eustis, waiting forever—hours upon later and later hours—through the night for the bus to Langley Air Force Base, the lieutenant had amused himself at the piano in the USO lounge where they sat locked-in for deployment processing. This soldier here, the smaller of the two chess players, had walked up and sat down next to him on the bench, joining him in a duet of "Heart and Soul," the two quietly laughing as they tried to impress each other with their amateur keyboard skills. An hour of playing duets, two hours. Three in the morning, four in the morning, drawing close to 0500 and the bus to the plane to Africa. Talking quietly between tunes, about nothing. And then, "Scared?" the lieutenant had asked the private finally, as the clock clicked past 0400. "No," came the answer. "No, not scared. Nervous, though. You?" "Yes." A laugh, from both of them. "Yes, both things." The private didn't say anything. A twinkle, a flourish on the bass end where the lieutenant sat, to the left, his hands twinkling the black keys. He kept his eyes straight ahead of him, fingertips pressing down carefully on ebony, and said, "When the time comes, if I'm—" He paused, his fingers pausing too, then pressing down again, a sour note from the ancient USO piano. "If maybe there is a time when you, not as a private, but as a man, um . . ." The lieutenant looked down at the keyboard, then closed his eyes and finished. "If you think you need to talk to me, if you think I need to know something, if maybe I'm not seeing something . . ." The private started playing "Chopsticks" on the high end of the keyboard, cutting him off. "L.T., if I gotta get through, I'll just walk right up and say 'Hey! John Klover! Wake up!'" He laughed. The lieutenant opened his eyes, and looked at him. They were exactly the same age. "Yes, something like that." He started playing "Imagine," and half an hour later they were on the bus.

The soldier from New Jersey said it again now, here in Africa, over the chessboard. "John?" It was a question, not a statement. A one-word question, almost lost in the sound of a big Volvo truck cruising slowly down the pier.

"Yes."

"Do you think you're a good man?"

"What?" the lieutenant answered, but his eyes were on the chessboard, then on the truck, then on the water that separated them from Kismaayo.

"Do you think you're a good man? A good person?"

"Yes."

The private put his elbows on the crate, leaning in. "Well, there you go, then. There it is."

"I'm not following you."

"You didn't do anything wrong."

The lieutenant sighed. "I know that. I wasn't there. I didn't do anything at all."

"John?"

"Yes."

"Neither did we."

The private said that, but he didn't mean it. It didn't matter: he'd made his point—that's all he wanted to do.

The lieutenant looked up at him now, his eyes red, his skin drawn like a mask across his face.

"This is so fucked up."

The private didn't say anything to that, just pulled another cigarette from the pack, and lit it. Then: "John?"

"Yes."

Taking a chance, but suddenly the private needed to talk it out. "I'm scared now."

"Now? You're leaving soon. The last mission is done. We're through. Going home."

The private blew smoke out of his mouth in a ring, then looked down.

"I'm not scared of that. That's done."

He picked at a scab on his wrist, then stopped. He looked the lieutenant dead in the eye, hoping the officer would get this, understand this. He was putting himself out on a limb, taking a chance this man would see, would understand, and that the understanding would be good for both of them. But the harder he tried here, the more he felt it slipping, slipping, and now he didn't think this lieutenant understood. He tried once more.

"I'm scared for Trevor. I'm even more scared for me. I'm scared for . . ."

But he didn't finish, just turned his head toward the bay.

The lieutenant took that in, then sat back.

But he didn't get it.

"Could I . . ." He looked at the private, waited until he was looking back at him, then started again. "Could I have done anything if I had been there?"

And then, right then, the PFC hated this lieutenant so much, hated him with all of his heart for asking that. *Fuck you, man,* he thought. *Just fuck you and your conscience. You want to believe that, don't you? That you could have it in you . . .*

And then it passed. Everyone wanted to believe that. It didn't make any difference.

Finally, he said, "No."

Believe what you will, and sleep well, sir, sleep well.

The lieutenant looked down and let a moment pass. When he looked back up again the private was shredding the butt of his cigarette with his fingernails.

"You want to play, Jones?" he asked, pointing toward the chessboard.

"No sir. Thank you, but I think I'm done tonight."

The private from New Jersey stood up, grabbing his and the other private's rifles from the ground, slinging them both over his shoulder, then turned and walked out of the warehouse and toward the camp up on the hill, leaving his lieutenant and the chessboard behind.

The Art of Dishwashing, *Part One*

Huley, Washington—October 1993

1

There is a certain Zen to professional dishwashing, if you allow it to come.

There is a surrender.

What's the Buddhist saying?

First, dishes. Then, ecstasy.

Perhaps not ecstasy; not doing someone else's dishes. But you can draw into yourself, find a comfortable seat there, sit in it, and—as you sit and think whatever thoughts you might have for the thinking—watch with detached interest as your hands perform the task you set them to.

Jones had discovered you couldn't *always* do this—some nights the brain wouldn't let go; and there you were, stuck with your hands in boiling water, scraping shit off plates, loading the industrial dishwashing machine, keeping up with the pots stacking in the far sink.

But, on good nights, it worked out. Either way, it passed the time.

Louie stepped from behind the line, arms loaded with sauté pans and one big steel pot. He tossed them all in the sink to the right of Jones.

"Catch up, Crash," he mumbled, turning back toward the line, scratching his ass through checkered chef pants. The sink was so full the tower of pots threatened to fall over onto the greasy kitchen floor. Jones had been concentrating on plates for almost an hour, lost in thought, and had let the pots go.

"Crash" was Lou's name for Jones, appearing from Lou's mouth a few months ago after Jones told him the story of how he came to be looking for work in this restaurant. Jones hadn't actually been the one to crash, but never mind—he appreciated the humor, or at least where it came from.

Lou was Louie Rado, a Hungarian-born, Brooklyn-accented, mustache-sporting, thick-glasses-wearing, usually even-tempered man in his early forties who had a small genius for cooking northern Italian cuisine. Louie owned this joint fifty-fifty with a skinny, older guy in a bad suit that Jones had seen once, but never met. The man owned the Chevy dealership in town. Lou did the cooking, bad-suit paid the salaries; both profited—and relatively well for this backwater of Washington, almost a day's drive from Seattle.

Jones was living with Lou in a spare bedroom in the cook's small house three miles south of town. He got docked thirty dollars a week in pay for the bed—cheap, even for Washington. Lou had space to spare, and didn't mind the company. Jones had spent the three nights previous to this employment, back in May—almost five months ago—sleeping illegally in the cold, dark, and locked Huley bus depot—after that, he thought the deal with Lou very reasonable indeed.

Louie led an ordered, structured life that Jones found fascinating. For months now he'd waited for a break in the schedule, but none ever came. Jones doubted much one ever would.

Lou woke—with a yawn like a low-timbered moan—at nine every morning. By nine thirty he was showered and sipping coffee on the back step. By nine thirty-five he had a Bud pony opened next to him, alternating between sips of his second cup of coffee and the tiny beer bottle. By nine forty Lou sparked his first joint of the day; in the unlikely event that Jones or any other house guests were up yet, Lou always shared this. By nine fifty he was back in the kitchen, at the tiny gas stove, frying three scrambled eggs. At ten, he sat on the dog-smelling old brown couch in the dark living room, plate of eggs propped on a knee, third cup of coffee resting precariously on the arm of the sofa, second Bud pony opened and sitting on the small coffee table, first Marlboro fired up and resting in an ashtray. Oprah came on at ten, and Lou never missed Oprah. "I love this broad," he'd mumble in his low growl, if you asked. By the time Oprah ended at eleven, there would be another empty pony bottle on the coffee table, a few more dead cigarettes in the ashtray, and Lou invariably would be snoring, sitting upright, head back on the couch, sometimes drooling. But, as if he had a silent alarm clock in his head, his eyes would pop wide open within a few minutes of Oprah's departure, and Lou would look around, confused, blink, then get up. Within five minutes of that, he'd be off on the ten-minute drive to Huley and an afternoon's prep at the restaurant.

After work they were usually out of the kitchen by midnight. A stop at Miller's Tavern with whoever of the kitchen staff wanted to go along, maybe a game of pool there. Then home to the couch, six-pack of ponies in easy reach, joint lit and again shared with any hanging out, a few hours of *Love Connection* (*"That fucking Chuck Woolery, I love this guy . . ."*) and *Star Search* (*"Ed McMahon! Who can beat this fucking guy?!"*), then a long, slow crawl to bed by two or two thirty. After that, Jones—almost always still awake—would switch to CNN; after months of nonreporting, there was new and heated interest in Somalia. Things were not going well there. Jones always turned the channel back to 2 before he finally went to sleep, so Lou wouldn't have to switch to get to Oprah in the morning.

During the day, between 11 A.M. and closing, Lou would methodically work through two six-packs of Bud ponies and one, maybe two joints. Wednesday through Sunday. On Monday and Tuesday, when they were closed, Lou sometimes fished, sometimes worked on his Harley in the garage, but usually sat on the couch (*"Colonel Hogan . . . you know this guy got whacked and killed by a camera tripod? I love this fucking guy . . ."*).

Jones put down the spray hose, and moved from the dishwasher to the row of three deep sinks. The sauté pans he could do right away; the big steel pot would have to soak for a while. He looked up at the clock: 10 P.M. He was hungry. Finish up these pans, then maybe take a break on the back step for dinner and a beer. Lou would cook whatever anyone wanted for dinner, as long as he wasn't busy.

Jones had first walked in here looking to cook, but Louie wasn't hiring—no one but Lou ever went behind the line. Jones wondered what happened when Lou got sick; after a month there, he decided Lou never got sick.

"You can wash, though, if you want. I need a dishwasher. Mexican just quit. No one but Mexicans know how to wash right, but I'll take you awhile if you need it."

Jones had given up trying to find work on a fishing boat—he took Lou's offer.

Louie was paying six bucks an hour. On their Monday and Tuesday nights off, Jones could play cover songs at Miller's for tips. He usually played three or four hours, Creedence and Gordon Lightfoot and a lot of Jim Croce, and went home to Louie's with thirty or so bucks in his pocket. He had a ways to go yet, but was getting closer to what he needed to save to go home. It was slow going. He sent most of everything he made to Katy, for Emma's child support. He couldn't complain. At this point, he considered himself lucky to be alive.

"Crash!" Lou yelled from behind him. "Watch out, deliveries."

Lou deposited another five pans into the sink, and this time the pile did collapse, three of them hitting the floor with a loud bang.

"Catch up, Crash, catch up."

Jones got to catching up.

Scrub, scrub, wipe, scrub, plop, reach, scrub, scrub.

He tried to get the Zen back, even a light Zen, but it was harder at the pots sink than it was at the dishwasher and hose. Too much distraction with Louie right behind him, waitresses passing by, cooking smells getting in his nose. And this work was different, too: with the plates and glasses, you could get a fluidity to your movements—reach, scrape, swoosh, drop in rack, repeat. With the pots, there was too much confusion, too much change: some needed scraped, others not; some needed scrubbed, others needed intensive scrubbing; some had to soak—and reaching into that sink, which had its own heating element to keep the water bubbling, was painful enough to wake you from even the deepest of Zen dreams.

The hostess, a mid-fifties woman—sweet, friendly—named Linda, came back and yelled in Jones's ear over the kitchen noises: "Sweetie! There's someone out back said he has to see you!"

Jones mouthed, "Who?"

"Dunno. Young guy, your age. Black raincoat. Said he had to see you."

Jones went back to scrubbing. "Tell him I'll be out in five?" he asked over the pot.

"Good enough." She walked back out.

George. Had to be George. He didn't know anyone else in town—except the employees here—and he'd been waiting all summer for George to show up again.

Well, George could wait outside a few more minutes.

Scrub, scrub, rinse, plop, scrub.

Jones gathered a pile of clean, dry sauté pans from the rack into his arms and sneaked behind Lou to return them to their shelf over the broiler. This was the only time anyone was allowed behind the line, to return cleaned pans, and Jones did it quickly.

2

Jones had been in Huley, Washington, all summer, the time creeping numb and painless into fall and winter, one day at a time.

Retreat from San Francisco in May had come swiftly. Sitting on the attic bed—the reds and maroons washing over him as the sun set through the curtained windows—he had counted his money, down to the pennies. He added to this a one-hundred-dollar bill he'd found laid flat in a copy of *Firestarter* downstairs on the communal bookshelf—someone's long-forgotten (Jones hoped) struttin' money, put aside for a rainy day. Well, it was pouring on Jones, so he'd helped himself. He packed his things, sat unmoving on the bed until midnight, then quietly went down the stairs and slipped out. He wasn't sure why he was being secretive—there hadn't been any official mention made of rent—but he figured he wouldn't take the chance. Better to just go. Thanks, Cliff. See ya. Jones cocked his thumb and headed north.

He had some phone numbers and names with him, scribbled from the papers in California, some of them taken from a book he'd immediately realized was a rip-off when he got it—a photocopied sheaf of papers adver-tised in the classifieds for forty dollars—promising guaranteed leads for *"High Paying Fishing Jobs In Washington!!"* Bullshit. But, rip-off or not, it was a start. The recurring theme in most of the company names was a town called Huley. He'd never heard of it, but that's where he went.

Huley, Jones learned over his first few days in town, led a dual exis-tence. The area was based—and still relied heavily—on fishing. But an artists' colony had popped up as well, over the last ten years or so. No one would ever mistake Huley for the East Village or Soho, but Fairley Street—which cut a half-mile swath diagonally across the town—was a string of quickly changing art galleries, New Age stores, a few record shops, a head shop, a summer-stock theater. Jones learned that the cottages and houses you could see on the mountainside to the east were mostly summer homes of the Seattle and Vancouver rich, and these folks were the main customers on Fairley Street in July and August. This time of year, not much doing in the hip section; but Jones, in his wanderings, saw a few hippied and gothed kids, younger girls mostly, hanging and strolling on Fairley, maybe left behind or stayed behind when their parents went home. Maybe they came on their own. Who knows.

But the main trade of Huley's year-round residents always had been and still was fishing and boating. There was a small fishing fleet at the docks, and pilots and tugs for some of the big tankers sailed from here as well.

Jones had blown ten dollars on breakfast the morning he got here in May—so sure in his knowledge of soon-to-be windfall. At a small shack at the top of the curiously unbusy docks he'd had steak and eggs, it was a real steak, and it was really fucking good, crisscrossed with black grill marks, juicy pink in the middle. Three coffees with it, push back, light a Marlboro, man of the world. Payphone outside, able to keep an eye on his backpack and guitar through the window, it was noon back home; after a few very cold, very brief words Katy put Emma on the line, and it made him wince. But it was going to be good here, and he felt good, so he was able to be happy on the phone and have it sound real. Then a quick call to Virginia, checking in with the CQ at HHC 24th: "No, Jones, Liz is still in Mogadishu. Call back in September."

He got a room over a bar a few blocks away from the docks, dropped his stuff. He'd have to make money quick to pay for this, within days really, but he wasn't expecting any trouble with that. He was *here*. He'd done it.

Failure, when it comes, is almost always so stupid, so silly. So easy to avoid in the first place—it seems, in hindsight—if you'd have been paying attention; so incredibly hard to get out of once it grabs your ankle and digs in.

There was one small but important point Jones had failed to consider:

Why would any skipper hand out a high-paying fishing job to some kid from New Jersey who claimed an army Mike Boat as "experience"? Especially when there was no shortage of men in town to fill the bills.

Jones spent six hours on the docks, going boat to boat. Most of them were closed up, empty, dark. Those with life on board gave him, at best, a blank stare; at worst, a laugh.

Washington.

Jesus wept.

Jones sighed now—five months past his failure on the docks—wiping his hands on the dishrag he pulled out of his apron pocket; straightened it, folded it, then stuffed it back in. George was waiting outside, he couldn't put it off any longer.

"Takin' a break, Lou," Jones called over his shoulder, walking toward the door.

"Ya want eats, Crash?" Lou asked over his Coke-bottle glasses, leaning over the line, the dinner rush long done.

"Maybe I'll bring something home."

"Lafuckingsagna tonight."

"Sure, Lou. Thanks."

"All right."

3

By eight o'clock on Jones's first night in Huley—back in May, just days after leaving San Francisco—the reality and absurdity of the general situation—and his personal situation—had become abundantly clear. Standing at the end of the Huley pier, out of cigarettes—he'd gone through two packs already today—he thought very lucidly about the pros and cons of stepping off and dropping into the water. It was night, it was Washington, he'd heard it would take less than a minute or two to lose consciousness in the water, even in May, less than five to quietly die. And sink.

He looked down.

He was a coward.

Jones turned and walked back up the pier.

That night, he met George for the first time in the same shack where he'd had his steak and eggs for breakfast.

Sitting in a back booth, long-neck Bud in front of him; better to drink quietly and burn the last of his money here than in a crowded bar where

he wouldn't know anybody, and where everyone had jobs and a couch to
go home to because they were smart, and sane, and with it, and it would
never even occur to them to drop everything and haul ass across a conti-
nent chasing *escape* dressed up in a dream's cheap clothing, chasing something all the time thinking nervously that maybe something is chasing
you—

—a face, in a window, a flash of skin—too quick, too fucking quick . . .

On the pier that day, one guy—a boat's mate he'd said—told him:
That looks like an army haircut.

Yes—hard to break the habit, right? Jones laughed. *I keep thinking I'm
gonna cut it, then I wake up in a barber's chair.*

Oh, yeah? The guy looked at him funny—too much information. *I
wouldn't know.*

Sorry—the way you asked, I thought maybe you'd been in.

Nope.

The guy wiped his nose on his sleeve.

So you was? In?

Yes. Somalia. Just back from Somalia.

SomaWhat? Where?

A sudden, hot rage spiked in Jones, raw steel in his mouth.

Then— it was gone; resigned to defeat.

'Nuff said.

Jones saw George through the window of the restaurant, barely noticing him, only paying even the slightest bit of attention to this man at the
payphone because he'd seen him today a few times on the dock and recognized him now, and because it suddenly dawned on him that this guy was
staring back through the window at him.

Jones dropped his eyes and raised the beer to his lips.

"Ya want something to eat, honey?" The waitress talking to him. Sure,
what the fuck, burn the money. Breakfast served twenty-four seven? All
right then, bring me a steak and eggs. And a coffee. And another beer.

He lit a cigarette, coughing loudly, the waitress swooshing away toward
the counter.

Jones's feeling and mood of despair had left him. Now he just felt . . .
dark.

He looked up and this man, this painfully ugly man, was sitting down across from him in the booth, Mariners ball cap tight and backward on his head, long hair falling over his shoulders. Thirty, maybe? Hard to tell.

George.

"Dude, I been watching you all day."

"Yeah?"

"Yeah."

George grabbed Jones's new pack of smokes and shook one out, only then looking up, asking, "Y'mind?"

Asshole.

"No, man. Help yourself."

George fired it up with the matches on the table. Jones could see this guy had a pack of Winstons in his breast pocket.

Asshole.

"You're not from around here, are you?" George asked through a cloud of smoke.

Jones shook his head, smiling, not kindly.

What am I, in a movie? "No, I'm not from *around here*."

But he couldn't keep it up. Even knowing he already didn't like this George, he couldn't keep it up. "Sorry. Bad day. Bad week. Bad year."

"Yep, me too."

Great. Good for you, pal.

George looked over at the counter, waved at the waitress, and yelled "Coffee!" across the mostly empty room.

He tapped his ash.

"So, look, you need a job?"

"Need? I dunno," Jones answered, sighing inwardly. Of course he needed a job. "I've been looking."

"Not much work on the boats, not if ya ain't connected," George said.

"I'm learning that."

The waitress set George's coffee down in front of him, and he emptied four packs of sugar in it, then stirred it with his index finger, whipping his finger out quick, then sucking on it in his mouth.

"You got an AB?"

Jones had learned today, the hard way, that an AB was the very thing he didn't have to get a job on the boats. It was an able-bodied seaman card from the coast guard. He'd never heard of it before today, but had certainly heard a lot about it this afternoon.

"No."

"Any experience?"

Jones looked up, opened his mouth, then closed it again. Shook his head. "No, not really. Mike Boats. In the army."

"Army? I thought so. The hair. What's a Mike Boat?"

"Not a fishing boat."

"Yep, gonna be hard to find a job for you."

A regular Sherlock, this guy.

George slurped half his coffee in one gulp, his Adam's apple bulging as his head went back.

"You'd be surprised," he said, putting his cup down. "Lotta guys—chicks, too—show up here, all times of year, looking for work. Most of them ain't got no experience. I don't know what the fuck they're doing here . . ." He trailed off, looked at Jones, then laughed. "I mean, Washington wouldn't be my first choice of destination, if ya know what I mean, if I was from down below and needed work. Or was maybe running away—"

"Don't I look a little too old to be a runaway?"

George nodded, quickly, but with a smile on his face.

The waitress brought Jones's second beer, and let him know his meal would be out shortly.

"I could see Seattle, I guess. Everyone's going there. Center of the universe. Pearl-fucking-Jam. But Huley? The peninsula?" George shrugged. "People hear you can make money on the boats. It's all bullshit, though."

"Yeah?"

"Yep. Look at you, am I right?"

"Yeah."

George nodded.

"Well, look . . . what's your name?"

Jones told him.

"Jones, huh? Just Jones? I like that."

George smiled. It was gruesome.

"If you're hard up, I can help you with some work. Ain't what you're looking for, of course, but we've already seen you ain't experienced for that.

But we can use some help up at the place, not too hard. We could definitely use a guy who knows how to hold a gun."

"I don't know much about guns," Jones said.

"I thought you was in the army?"

"Yeah, well—what's the pay?"

"Good." George said simply. "The pay is good. We can put you up, too. Some harvesting, some delivering—easy!"

"Dude, I don't even know you."

"You know me better than you know anyone else here, right?"

"Yeah."

Jones took a long swig from his beer, then said, "Okay, so thanks." The waitress set down his plate. "Um, look . . ." Jones forked a piece of potato. "I got a place to stay tonight, so I'm thinking I'll poke around more tomorrow. If it don't work out, maybe then we can meet up."

"Yeah," George said, getting up from his seat. "Good deal, good deal. You poke around. You're just wearing out shoe leather, but I understand. You poke around, then I'll meet you here about four tomorrow, right?"

Jones nodded, mouth full of food.

"Yeah, see ya later, Jones."

George walked out, then disappeared out of sight of the window.

At least he was gone, Jones thought. And, if everything fell through on the fishing boats tomorrow—as he was now sure it would—maybe this guy had something useful for him. If only for a few days, make some cash, move on.

Where?

Too early to ask that yet. George had said "the place." A farm, Jones thought. Or a ranch. Hauling moose shit to fertilize George's dope garden for a few days or something. That'd be fine, just fine.

4

Louie had taken to calling Jones "Crash" because that's exactly what had happened to the boat Jones and George took out that night to deliver a bale of dope.

Four o'clock in the afternoon, the day after he'd met George, Jones's second full day in town. And of course Jones was waiting for George to show up at four, because of course he'd gotten nowhere during the day—no work, no fishing, you got no AB, son have you checked your brain lately?

George had come running up in a hurry, from around the back of a warehouse—looked up and down the docks, found Jones waiting by the payphone, and rushed up to him.

"Change of plans, buddy, change of plans," he'd puffed out, winded and excited.

"No work?"

George had laughed.

"Oh, we got plenty of work, don't you worry. And we'll get up to the farm later. But I got a last-minute thing, just came through. You want boat experience? I can give it to you. And a wad of cash, too."

Jones stubbed his smoke into the side of the payphone.

"You didn't tell me you had a boat. I thought there was no fishing now."

George laughed again.

"No, no fishing. And I sure as shit don't do it even if there was—nasty job, fuck that. No, I got a delivery to make. Could you use four hundred dollars?"

Jones looked at him, hard.

"You serious?"

"Serious as a heart attack."

"What exactly are we delivering?"

"What do you think, Jones? Look, I ain't got time to dick around here. Either you're in, or you're not. Doesn't make a shit bit of difference to me either way, but I gotta sail soon to make it out there, and I could use a second on board, gonna be foggy as a bastard tonight, and icy."

Jones thought quickly. It was bullshit; stupid and reckless. But he figured this guy was too stupid, too scrawny, and too pathetic to be a threat. And he didn't figure George was going to shoot him—why bother? Jones had survived a month in San Francisco without getting shot, he didn't figure this bonehead had the balls to do something like that. So he must really just need some help and muscle. Four hundred dollars? Fuck. Yes, he could use it. And he was desperate—there was no hiding it, so why bother?

"I won't handle a gun."

"Naw, that probably won't be necessary—"

Jones's eyes met George's and narrowed. "No. Not at all. I won't handle a gun."

"Fine, man, fine."

Jones sighed. "Okay, yeah—I'll go with you."

George's face broke into a grin.

"Excellent!"

He rubbed his hands together, then punched Jones lightly on the arm.

"Good move, Jones!"

They walked a fast clip, half a mile to a smaller set of docks. Dark already now, streetlights on. Cold as a bastard.

"Jones, you got to get yourself a better coat," George quipped, stepping down onto a pier.

Thanks, pal.

"I thought everything was iced up," Jones said, keeping pace behind George, who was almost running, wheezing and out of breath.

"Out of the harbor, yeah—mostly it still is. We ain't going out there. Right out there in the channel is as far as we're going. A little dangerous, but that's why I need you—you gotta be my eyes at the front of the boat, so we can avoid becoming the *Titanic*."

"I can do that."

"I know you can, buddy, I know you can."

Most of the pier was empty, this dock used for personal boats mostly, pleasure cruisers and small fishing boats, most of them out of the water and safely tucked away. There were a few tied-up, though, and George stopped at one toward the end of the pier—a small cabin cruiser, badly in need of a paint job. George reached into his pocket and pulled out a set of keys.

"This yours?" Jones asked.

"Nope," George said, and didn't elaborate.

"Where's our . . . delivery?"

"Already on board, Jones, already on board. You ask too many questions."

Jones shook his head, and climbed on board behind George, who was already making for the helm—key in, engine fired off. George hugged himself—it was getting colder.

"We gotta let this shit warm up," he said. "Wanna see something?"

Jones shrugged. George unlocked a storage case right next to the helm, and motioned for Jones. He looked in—it was a big bale, wrapped up in newspaper and twine.

"Is that as much as it looks?"

George laughed, slapping Jones on the back.

"Bet ya ain't seen no shit like this, huh? Yep, this is the real deal, and a fuck-lot of it. Why do you think I'm paying so good?"

Jones hadn't really expected to see a full four hundred dollars tonight, but didn't say this. But maybe he would, he thought now, maybe he would. It was a big bale.

They made the trade at an anchor buoy a mile down the shipping channel—it went fine, but they waited a long time for the other boat to show, an hour past when George expected them. They'd tied up to the buoy, and George passed the time by getting extraordinarily high. Jones sat shivering in a deck chair, turning down even a hit, watching nervously as George smoked two fatties.

"Dude, you going to be able to drive this thing straight when we're done?" he asked.

George laughed. "Forward, never straight, Jones my man."

When Jones spotted a shiver of light in the distance, a boat approaching from farther out in the channel, he had a flash of something—bad TV cop shows, *Miami Vice* or something. He waited for a Colombian to appear on the deck of the other boat and open fire at them with an Uzi, or some great argument to ensue where George ends up getting thrown overboard by a goon in a bad suit.

But it didn't go like that.

Five minutes, less, they were done. A fat white guy in an orange all-weather suit, his compadre thinner but dressed the same—George heaves the bundle over to their deck, fat guy tosses a padded envelope to George. The other boat pulls off, disappears into the night, George has Jones untie from the buoy and turns the helm back toward Huley.

Fifteen minutes later their cabin cruiser is sinking, slipping under the waves while Jones is helping George climb up to the surface of the pier he's clinging to for dear life.

"Jesus Christ, it's cold!" George, shivering uncontrollably, his skin blue. He was only in the water a few minutes, but it was enough. "Help me to the truck, man, gotta get the engine started. I'm fucking freezing." This came out *"f-f-f-f-f-fuck-k-king f-f-f-freezing."*

They never saw what they hit—a rotted piling maybe, but Jones never saw it. He heard it, though; a slick crunch from the bow, the nose dipping immediately, never to come back. They had enough time for George to get the boat back to the end of the pier—Jones jumping from the deck with a foot of water swirling around his feet and ankles, hearing George yell from the direction of the helm but not taking the time to turn around and see him, or wait for him. When Jones got himself up on the pier and did turn around only the top of the cab was still visible, and George was in the water, hanging off the pier supports, yelling for a hand.

Jones got George the three blocks back to his truck, turned the key for him to get the engine going, then slammed the door and took off running down the street. He heard George yelling at him from the truck, but he never slowed down to listen. It was about half an hour later that he realized he hadn't been paid. *Fuck it,* he thought, gripping white-knuckled to a cup of coffee at the bus depot, *stoned bastard probably wasn't going to pay me anyway.*

5

That had been four months ago. Since then, Jones managed to keep his profile low, with no signs of George. Until now.

Jones opened the back door off the restaurant's kitchen, the wind beautiful on his sweaty, greasy body for about two seconds—then just damn cold. He'd never felt cold like this before he came here, never.

George was sitting on the bottom stair, pegging pebbles at a rusted-out old Ford on cinder blocks. He turned and rose as Jones lost the door to the wind, slamming closed behind him with a bang.

"'Bout fucking time," George said.

He was tall, skinny, with a long, black leather raincoat on. He was shivering in it. He wore the same backward ball cap, and had grown a light beard that peppered his chin and cheeks.

"What's up?" Jones asked. He didn't expect trouble from George—and he guessed he could handle himself if trouble came. Still, Jones hated confrontations, would go way out of his way to avoid them these days, and found himself tight with adrenaline just standing here with the guy.

"I got your money, Jones. I got it for you."

Of all the things Jones thought George might say tonight, this was the last one he expected. He knew George had collected that night in May, he'd seen the envelope. But it was comical to think this guy would track him down and give him the money—why? Why bother? Jones hadn't wanted it bad enough to look for George.

Jones, nervous to begin with, felt it build. Slow but sure, unease spread up his spine.

"Is that right?" he asked. He really didn't know what to say.

"Yeah, man, that's right."

George bent over and tried to light a cigarette in the wind. It took him four matches to get it.

"Look, I thought you'd be more happy than this. I didn't have to come, you know."

"No," Jones said, "no, you didn't. Thanks." He hated this.

Liz, he thought suddenly. *What the fuck am I doing here?*

No answer.

Jones stuffed his hands down in his apron pockets, his bare arms freezing in the wind.

"So . . . so, okay, cool. The whole four?"

"Yeah, yeah, the whole four," George said. "And a chance to make more."

Jones couldn't help it; he laughed out loud, quick and nervous.

"I had enough trouble making the first four, George. How 'bout we leave it even?"

George dragged on his smoke.

"Well, this would be different. But yeah, whatever. So I just wanted to tell you I got the money, and let you know where to go to get it."

"Go?" he asked. "You don't really have it, do you?" He turned back toward the door. "Look, man, it's all right. I got a job. We'll just call it even. Thanks for coming by."

His fingers touched the knob, and George's hand fell on his shoulder.

"Wait."

Jones tensed, waited, but didn't take his fingers off the doorknob.
Fuck.

"No, look, I just don't have it with me, that's all. A lot of people are looking for me, I didn't want to come into town with cash. That's all." He coughed a cloud of smoke. George wasn't healthy. "I got it stashed up at the farm, friend of mine I told you about. I'm doing some work with him. Camera work. But it's real safe, no drugs. Good money. Not too far from where you're staying."

Jones turned, pushing his face up into George's.

"How do you know where I'm staying?"

"I saw ya, that's all. I saw you was working here, just happened to be going the same direction when ya went home." George shrugged. "You're staying out at Louie's place, right?"

"You know Louie?"

"No, man, not really. But everyone knows who he is. Chill, dude. You don't want the money, fine. Fucking great. More for me. But even if it got all fucked up, I said I'd pay ya, and I will. You pulled my ass to land, I figure I owe ya. Besides, I'm throwing a little party, some kids I know from down on Fairley, they got nowhere to live, and it's getting too cold to have nowhere to live. Seeing as you probably don't know no one in town, I thought you'd wanna come and hang."

Jones stuffed his hands back in his pockets again, backing off. He was *really* freezing now. He tried to think quickly. He could use the money. Six bucks an hour, even over the course of a whole summer, doesn't get you far. He wanted to leave, go back East. Liz was home now, back in Virginia, and he desperately wanted to see her, desperately wanted to stop spinning his wheels—four hundred dollars would help pay his way and get him started back East.

"All right, where do I go? What's the deal with this party?"

George relaxed, his shoulders falling back into place, and smiled.

"I'll pick you up Saturday night, man. What time you done?"

It was Thursday. "Eleven. I'll be done by eleven."

"Fine, cool. I'll be here eleven, Saturday. Across the street, in my truck."

"All right."

"Cool, all right!" George smacked him on the back. Jones hated to be smacked on the back.

"Yeah," George said, walking down the stairs now, "we'll have a little party out at the farm. Good times, good times. We'll have a laugh."

He raised his hand, then was gone around the corner of the building.

"Fuck," Jones cursed silently to himself. *"Fuck."*

But he needed the cash. He needed to start living again, and if this guy was gonna share it around, then what the hell. George was a sorry bastard—maybe he just wanted someone to drink with.

Yeah, maybe.

Whatever. Jones needed the money. He was a big boy. It'd be all right. If the place really was near Lou's, he could just hoof it home when things got stupid. And Jones was sure that—one way or another—they would get stupid; hopefully, after he'd gotten his money safely into his pocket.

And, he thought, maybe the guy will smoke himself numb again, and I'll grab the whole stash and hop the 6 A.M. bus to Seattle.

"Fuck," he said again, shivering.

And a whole new line of work! George had said.

Camera work. Jones had a good idea what that meant. He'd talked to a couple of kids down on Fairley Street.

What the hell—he was tired, tired of his journey to nowhere. He wanted to go home. If George could provide the means, then what the hell.

Jones rubbed his arms and walked back up the stairs into the kitchen.

Endgame

Mogadishu, Somalia—Late March 1993

1

They rode Mr. Rintel's LCU transport to Mogadishu together: Jones, Bob, and the lieutenant. It was a thirty-six-hour run up the coast, on the same boat that had towed the Mike nine-three from Mombasa to Kismaayo three months ago. The lieutenant spent the entire time in the head, bent over a toilet bowl. Jones didn't hold it against him: the ride was horrible, against a ripping south-flowing current and twelve-foot swells; they were all sick. But the enlisted men spent more time on the water than this officer did, and they were able to ignore it—or mostly almost ignore it, once their stomachs were emptied.

While they made this sail north on the LCU, the Mike Boats were being taken back south to Kenya by a skeleton crew, for transport home. Most of the rest of the platoon had flown directly out of Kismaayo for Frankfurt. The lieutenant was under orders to report to Mogadishu for his platoon's final outprocessing paperwork and debriefing. When word came down that battalion was also looking for two enlisted volunteers to fill some emptied slots in Mogadishu for a few days before the main body went Stateside, Bob and Jones had raised their hands. *Unfinished business,* Jones said simply to the lieutenant. *I'll take the slot.*

Trevor had raised his eyebrows at this, but didn't question it. "I'll see you home, then, Jonesy. Home, discharge, fishing."

Jones stood on the fo'c'sle of the LCU as it steamed into Mogadishu harbor. Even in port the water was rough; the engineers had designed the port with its mouth north instead of south, so the sea current flowed right in. *Must've been military engineers,* Jones thought idly.

The LCU dropped its huge ramp and finally made head-in contact with the concrete pier on the fourth try. Crew members in orange life jackets raced to tie the thing off before the swells could push it back out.

Jones saw Bob skip right off, jumping the last foot before the ramp made contact, then moving out toward one of the warehouses, his duffel, ruck, and rifle slung on his back. The lieutenant—with a group of warrant officers from the former HQ in Kismaayo—followed a few minutes after they'd tied off, headed down the pier then out of sight.

Lieutenant Klover and Jones had passed no more than a handful of words together since their conversation in the warehouse a few nights previous; the lieutenant carried the look of a man who thought he'd said more than he wanted to and is just now realizing it, turning nervous but friendly discomfort into a cold and businesslike demeanor. Jones could relate to that. He was starting to appreciate Trevor's ability at distance, his ability to get up and walk away, like he'd done that night in Jiliri. Sometimes it was just better to say nothing. Jiliri was a week gone now. Neither of them had spoken of it since.

Maybe it didn't happen?

Jones pondered that for a moment.

I will it not to have happened.

Done.

Jones ditched his smoke in the water, leaning against the stanchion line toward the bow of the LCU, and looked around. It was a different place, Mogadishu. There was order here, military order. Everything dress-right-dress: the Humvees parked on the pier, the mess tents lined up next to the warehouses, the latrines, everything. The U.S. Army Transportation Corps in all its glory. The American and U.N. flags flew briskly in the wind atop the 7th Group port ops building in front of him.

A lone soldier, American desert BDUs but blue U.N. beret, was walking toward the LCU. It was a woman. Something else in short supply in Kismaayo.

As Jones looked, the female soldier suddenly waved at him, then cupped her hands and yelled.

"Jones!"

He pushed up his sunglasses and squinted.

It was Liz, trotting now toward the LCU's ramp.

"Jones!" she called again, and Jones felt something catch in his chest.

He hoisted himself over the stanchion, dropping the seven feet, and hit the cement hard, wincing as his right ankle twisted under him. He recovered, and walked the last two steps toward her. Both stopped awkwardly, six inches between them. Scared, for different reasons. Jones looked at her, feeling the weight of her absence. "Liz," he said simply, then reached out and put his arms around her, drawing her close, feeling her tight against his chest. She squeezed, pulling him in. Then pushed him off.

"Back off, Romeo," she laughed, quickly glancing around. "You been in the field too long, wild man."

She stepped back, and looked him up and down. He had showered on the LCU—his first in two weeks—but his uniform was tattered and dirty; fresh water was a commodity in Somalia, even on the boats, and the LCU crew had made it clear that these Mike Boat Seadogs were not welcome to use their washing machine.

"You're a bit rough, buddy."

"Mmmm," he said. "Some of us are in the real army, y'know."

She slapped at his chest, laughing.

"Fuck you, Jones."

He smiled, then pointed at her blue beret.

"Nice chapeau, troop."

"Fuck you again, Jones."

Liz looked down at her watch, then said, "C'mon. I got about twenty minutes before I go on duty. I'll show you around. There's an empty cot next to mine, you can crash there."

"Gimme a minute," he said. "I gotta go back on board and get my shit."

When he came back from his cabin, crossing the LCU's welldeck with both his duffel and ruck on his back, his rifle in his hand, he saw her waiting on the pier where he'd left her. She was standing sideways, facing the closest warehouse, shading her eyes, looking at something.

Liz was an inch taller than Jones—*that's why we could never date,* he'd told her once with a small smile—dirty-blond hair pulled up in a bun off her neck, a few wisps sticking out free from the beret she wore. She didn't have a BDU top on, just the standard brown T-shirt tucked into the desert-pattern BDU pants, which in turn were tucked into a highly polished pair of jump boots. From the side, the swell of her breasts pushed out from her T-shirt, impossible not to notice—no matter how hard you'd trained yourself not to look. Her complexion, normally Ohio-pale, was darker than when Jones had last seen her in Kenya. She was beautiful. Hard, tough, and beautiful. As he approached, she turned to him and smiled.

Get a grip, he thought. *Just get a grip.*

"I've missed you," Jones said quietly, stopping in front of her.

"No you haven't either," she replied, not unkindly. "You're just glad to see me. But you haven't spared me a thought in months, Benjamin. I'm a tree in a forest, falling alone."

He smiled and said nothing to that—he hated to be called Benjamin, she used it when she wanted to get under his skin. He hitched his duffel to a more comfortable position on his shoulder, then asked, "Warehouse bound, ma'am?"

"Hell, no!" She turned and walked toward a small building next to the port ops shack, Jones following one step behind. "The warehouses are unhealthy, not to mention low-rent." They crossed the empty pier under the bright morning sun and Liz opened a wooden door into a tight, cramped room with four cots. Duffels were open, uniforms and other clothes scattered here and there, hanging from clotheslines strung from window to window. "We got laundry here, but no dryer," she said.

Liz was the daytime voice of Mogadishu Harbormaster, the northern equivalent of Kismaayo's charlie two. She was one of only two lower enlisted in a small team with three warrant officers and a captain. Also, the Harbormaster's office was now officially tasked to the U.N., not 710th, 7th Group, or 10th Mountain. The company you keep had its privileges: while most of the troops in Mogadishu seaport lived uncomfortably in one of the warehouses, Liz and the PFC who had the night shift on the radio—a 10th soldier girl named Booker, from Philadelphia—had convinced the Harbormaster to let them stay here. "We'll be closer to the ops center if you need us in an emergency," Liz had argued. It wasn't hard. The building belonged to Harbormaster, but he didn't need the space; he and his officers had rooms on the second floor of the ops building. "Don't make a mess, and don't draw attention," was all he'd said.

Jones brushed a pile of purple and black bras out of the way and sat down heavily on the cot closest to the far window. Liz gathered the pile up in her hands, checked for dryness, then stuffed them down into one of her duffels. "Girlie things," she said. "Sorry." She sat down opposite him on a footlocker, peeling the wrapping off a granola bar.

"Wanna bite?" she offered.

Jones patted his belly, shaking his head. "Sea stomach," he said. "It'll be a while before I can eat." He popped the clasp on his pistol belt, releasing the belt and pulling the LBE suspenders off his shoulders. He picked the belt up and started pulling M16 clips from the ammo packs, stacking them next to him on the cot. It was habit: count and clean the cartridges once a day.

"Are those loaded?" she asked.

He just looked at her. There were six clips, all full.

She shook her head. "You can't have those here, Jones . . ."

Jones kept looking at her, not understanding.

"You're in port. Mogadishu. This isn't the field. You can draw an ass-chewing at best for walking around with all that ammo. Three bullets, in one magazine, is the S.O.P. Not six fucking mags all fully loaded!"

Jones shook his head, then put the clips back in his ammo packs. "Different world," he muttered.

Liz eyed his LBE as he pushed it under the cot he was sitting on. "You got to turn that stuff in." Jones nodded.

He pulled out his Zippo and shook a smoke free from his pack, lighting it.

"You know a Sergeant Cowens?" he asked, squinting his eyes as smoke brushed by them.

Liz nodded, swallowing.

"Why?"

"I'm supposed to report to him tomorrow afternoon at the gate. I've got three days working for him before I fly home. Let no man not have a job to do, I guess."

Liz nodded again. "You won't like him," she said.

Jones raised his eyebrows.

"Cowens just got here. The colonel's driver got ringworm so they sent him home. Cowens flew in from the States to replace him."

Sent him home for ringworm? Jones thought. He didn't know anyone in his platoon, including the lieutenant, who *didn't* have ringworm. It was in splotches all up and down his inner thighs. It had pretty much stopped spreading, though. After countless creams and pills from the Belgian doctors, a medic from a commo detachment of the 82nd that was in Kismaayo had offered the boat crews Monistat. Jones remembered Sid turning the tube over in his hands and asking the medic, "Isn't this—"

"Pussy cream?" the medic had finished. "Yes. Don't laugh, and don't ask why. Just trust me." They had, and indeed Monistat was the first stuff that stopped the spread of the ringworm.

Jones guessed they didn't have Monistat in Mogadishu. Whatever.

He asked Liz, "Why won't I like Cowens?"

"He's a clerk, at home. But he's on the colonel's staff, so now he's the driver."

"I know some very nice clerks, Liz." Jones smiled.

"This one thinks he's Rambo," she explained.

"Is that right?"

"Um-hmm."

Jones didn't break his smile, just placed his palms on his knees, then reached up to take his smoke from his lips and tap the ash in an empty soda can.

"I'm a new man, Liz," he said, slowly. "People don't bother me any more. I'm all about people. I'm a people lover. Power to the people."

"Yeah, okay," she said, laughing nervously.

"I've got three days, and then I go home, Liz. Three days and a wake-up. Week after that—I'm out. I got no problems with no one."

He stretched his neck, then smiled again.

"You on that plane?" he asked. Hopeful, trying not to let it show.

She shook her head. "Soon, though," she lied.

Liz reached over to her right and grabbed a BDU top from a pile and started putting it on, buttoning it from bottom up.

Before Jones could press more on her particulars, she asked, "Where's Alphabet?"

"I dunno. Kenya, home, somewhere. Not here. Most of 'em are gone."

"Why not you?"

Jones increased his smile to take up his whole face. "I wanted to see you!"

"Fuck you, Jones," she said flatly. "How was Kismaayo?"

"I dunno. What did you hear?"

"All sorts of shit, but I don't believe half of what I hear anymore. I heard from one person that the Mike Boats spent the last three months tied to the pier in Kismaayo while you guys sat around and drank without a job to do. I heard from another guy that you were sailing all the time and got attacked somewhere down the coast and were all dead."

"I'm not dead."

"I see that." Liz smoothed down the front of her BDU top and looked at him.

"I'd go with story number one," he said, sighing. "That one sounds good to me. Drunk and jobless, that's what I'm going to tell my grandchildren I did in the war."

Liz nodded but didn't say anything.

"How's Schaeffer?" he asked. Schaeffer had been on the one Mike Boat up here in Mogadishu. He'd wrecked his left arm in a freak accident tying off the boat to an offshore ship a few weeks ago—that was what Jones had heard, anyway. He liked Schaeffer.

"Bad," she said. "I saw him the afternoon it happened, as they were carrying him off the boat. It wasn't pretty."

Jones nodded. "And how's you?" he asked.

"I'm good, Jones," she said, honestly. "I'm good. It's a good group of troops, no one fucks with us. I write my letters and drink my vodka and walk around. Liz-things, like you say." He smiled. "It's good. There's talk of keeping the Harbormaster Det here longer than the rest of 710th, but I don't mind. Being attached to the U.N. is a whole different world. And nothing better to do, right?" She smiled at him, then—without having planned to—asked, "What are you doing tonight?"

He drew a thin notebook out of his front pocket—his tide tables from Kismaayo—and studied it carefully. "Oh, I dunno, let me check my schedule . . ."

She reached over and smacked his chest.

"I don't have to report to that Cowens until later tomorrow. Whatcha got in mind?"

"I'm done in the commo shack by 2100 or so. Wanna take a ride out to one of the ships?"

"Out there?" Jones pointed in the general direction of where the ocean would be through the wall.

"Yep. I got some friends on an MSC ship out there. A few times a week I take the Zodiac out after work, spend the night out there."

Jones laughed. "They let you do this?"

"C'mon, Jones. I learned from the best, right?" She pointed her index finger at him. "As long as you look busy and carry a clipboard you can do pretty much whatever you want in the army, right?"

Jones dropped the butt of his cigarette into the soda can. "So you cruise out to the ships at night, clipboard in hand?"

She laughed. "Something like that."

He shook his head. "All right, all right. Yeah, let's do that."

Liz stood, looking down at him. "You look tired, Jones. Unhealthy."

Jones stood up, and they were face-to-face now, just an inch separating them. He was close enough to smell the sweet scent of her sweat, and a hint of her deodorant. A line of freckles crossed her nose.

"I am tired," he whispered.

She put her palms on his cheeks, gently, then drew them back and put her hands in her pockets.

"You okay?" she asked.

He looked into her brown eyes, wanting to close the gap between them, to kiss her, to feel her soft lips under his. He forced himself to stillness. Tried to smile, but couldn't. "I am . . . yeah, I'm okay. I'm alive, right? We're all still alive." He tried again to smile, but it still wouldn't come.

Hands in pocket, she leaned forward and kissed him on the cheek, then put her lips to his ear. "Three days and a wake-up, Jones," she whispered. "Three days." He looked at her, and she stepped back.

"Yeah," he said. "Three days." He raised his arms to shoulder level, like a plane flying away. "Three days, then I sit in Virginia and wait for you to come home, too—right?" He sat down on the cot again.

Liz didn't answer. She picked up a pile of black plastic binders and turned to the door. "I'll be back to collect you at 2200. Sleep, pal."

"Right," he said, leaning back, bringing his feet up on the cot, then lying down fully on his back, putting his hands under his head. "I'll be here."

She opened the door and left, leaving him alone.

Jones took off his uniform and was asleep within five minutes. He slept undisturbed most of the day.

2

Bob was sitting at a corner desk in the commo office when Liz walked in, phone pressed to his ear. She dropped her binders on a chair, walked over to him, leaned down, and kissed him quickly on the cheek. He smiled up at her, putting his hand over the mouthpiece of the phone, and whispered, "All circuits are busy, please stand the fuck by."

She laughed and went to check the port status board to see what had changed overnight. Eight ships at pier, another eleven at anchor. The last army boat, Mogadishu's lone Mike Boat from 710th's LCM platoon, had sailed out at midnight for the long haul down the coast to Mombasa, Kenya. She had said good-bye to Norm, Burr, and Jimmy Two-Balls the previous afternoon.

Liz sat down at the radio console and got her paperwork in order.

A few minutes later Bob slammed the phone down in disgust. Tired and slow, he pushed his bulk out of the chair and walked over to her.

"Queen of Africa!" he said.

Liz swiveled in her chair and smiled up at him.

"What's up, Cowboy Bob?"

"Trying to call home. Jones scammed an access code from a major down south, guy was going home and took pity on us."

If you were one of the few privileged with a phone access code you could use it to dial in direct to the switchboard at Ft. Bragg, whose operator in turn would forward your call no charge to anywhere in the States. It was for official business only, but the codes were traded back and forth between soldiers like they were drugs or other contraband. Jones had struck up a friendship with a doctor, a major, in Kismaayo, who had given Jones his code when he flew home.

"Anyway, trying to get through to my wife, but can't get past Bell Atlantic. Lines are down somewhere or something."

"How's that going?" Liz asked.

"What?"

"Your wife."

Bob didn't say anything for a moment, just scrunched up his face. Then, "Well, y'know . . . I dunno. Who knows? Who knows. I'm trying."

They talked awhile, about nothing. Liz asked once about Kismaayo and saw the same hesitancy she'd seen in Jones, so she let it drop. After five minutes or so, Bob went on his way.

Liz got herself a coffee from the pot in the corner, then got busy with her paperwork.

She liked her job here, and she was good at it. The only drawback these days was that no one was allowed outside the gate of the port anymore unless they were going somewhere on official business. The whole city had changed, it seemed; the tone of it, the feel of it, the mood—both the Somalis and the Americans here to do whatever it was they were doing. It was tense; tense and uneasy. The arrival last week of the Ranger battalions had done nothing to help the mood. Although the Ranger presence and mission was supposed to be secret, everyone—from the other troops, to the few reporters left, to the Somalis themselves—knew why they were here: to catch Adid, and anyone associated with him. The Pentagon, everyone figured, was tired of looking stupid, and the Rangers were their cure. It wasn't exactly like throwing a firecracker into a crowded room, but it was close. The newly arrived Rangers were quickly learning what the 10th Mountain infantrymen and the Marines had slowly come to discover over the last few months: they might be the Pentagon's "cure," but in Somalia there was no cure-all. There was no support here; you—whether "you" was a single soldier, a platoon, or a battalion—were on your own. This wasn't war games in New Mexico, or even "real" war in Iraq. This was a situation where "you" were told to accomplish something, and there would be no big stick to wave when the going got hairy. The Rangers—trained to work alone—were learning that there was a whole new, and even lonelier, definition to that word.

Tense? You could call it tense.

Liz missed the Mogadishu that had been, the city she had arrived in. Her first month here, January, she would hop on board a Humvee any chance she could, checking out the city, driving around with whatever patrol she hooked up with, snapping pictures on her little camera the whole time. She had brought fifteen roles of film with her to Somalia, and had already burned through half of them. This, this place, was like nothing she had ever seen before; or would ever see again, she imagined. She didn't want to forget, she didn't want it to become a hazy memory. She was changing, had changed, and knew it and liked it. She was confident here, she had purpose.

Since the gate had closed, though, she had found other diversions. She'd made friends with a lot of the civilian ship crews, and now instead of cruising the city when off duty, she went out to the ships. Most of the men out there were nice, polite. They treated her well. She knew most of them wanted to sleep with her, but they weren't pushy, and when they saw she wasn't giving it away, they relaxed and enjoyed her company. For most, she was the first woman any of them had seen in months. These MSC ships that had brought all the American equipment into Mogadishu were under orders to just sit at anchor, a mile or so off the coast. Weeks, months, however long it took. They were paid well to sit there and do nothing, but it got boring. Poker, booze, a little dope, a little music, these things all passed the time. Liz liked their company—far more certainly than the American officers she worked with, who were either fumbling and ridiculous in their affection for her, or worse (and more likely) bullying and testosterone-driven and arrogantly unable to imagine why she wasn't throwing herself at their feet. No, the boys on the MSC boats were much more pleasant company; blue-collar and rough, but once spurned they didn't react with arrogance. Instead, they took her in as a sister.

And then there was Thomas.

Thomas was the captain of the largest of the MSC ships. Fifteen years her senior, he was a big man, bearded, rough hands. Not at all her type— but then neither was Jones, was he? But Thomas was gentle, smart, and very funny. They'd met four weeks before, and within a week his was the only ship she would go to anymore. She was on a first-name basis with his whole crew, and they treated her like a queen. She was pretty sure Thomas ordered them to treat her like a queen, but that was all right. It was good to be the queen.

And now here was Jones, sleeping on her cot next door. She'd known he was coming—she'd seen his name on the movements roster. She felt mixed when she saw his name on the board. Their good-bye in Mombasa hadn't been exactly warm; in fact, she had decided shortly after it was probably in her best interest to just cut ties with Jones. She was tired of this. But, then she saw him on the LCU, leaning out over the stanchion the way he always seemed to be doing—he loved to sail. She hated to admit it, but her heart jumped when she saw him today. And she knew she wasn't fooling herself: he'd looked like he wanted to melt into her, like seeing her was his main reason for breathing. But there was something wrong—well, there were two things wrong. The first thing was her, but she'd figure that out later. The second was Jones—he was not right. She didn't know why but he was not right.

A few minutes after one, Lieutenant Klover came in, a pile of paper in his hands. He was freshly scrubbed, shaved, and his uniform looked brand-new. He nodded at her. "Hey there, Specialist Ross," he said, sitting at an empty desk. Most of the staff had gone to lunch, and they were alone in the commo shack.

"Sir," she answered, nodding back.

The lieutenant nibbled at the tip of his pen, then looked back up at her. "Ross, you seen Jones? You know where he is? I couldn't find him after we docked this morning."

Liz thought quickly. "No," she lied. "I saw him this morning, but I'm not sure where he's at now." Jones needed sleep.

"Problem?" she asked.

"No," he said. "He's supposed to report to this . . ." he paused, looked down at one of his papers, then continued, "this Sergeant Cowens tomorrow."

"He knows," Liz said, swiveling her chair so that she was facing him. "He'll be there."

Klover nodded.

"Sir?"

He nodded again.

"What happened to you guys in Kismaayo?"

The lieutenant's face paled, he looked like he'd been punched. "What do you mean? What did you hear?"

"Nothing, really, sir," she said. "Rumors, whatever. Nothing solid. But Bob and Jones came in here looking like ghosts, y'know, and I just wondered." The lieutenant didn't say anything, so she continued. "I just wondered if they were okay, what had happened, or whatever."

Lieutenant Klover looked at her for a minute, then busied his hands straightening his papers and said, "Nothing happened, Private Ross. Nothing happened at all. They're tired, I'm sure, and it was a rough sail up here. Rumors are rumors. Keep them to a minimum."

"Yes sir."

Liz swiveled her chair back to the radio, turning away from him. *Asshole*, she thought.

3

The Zodiac cruised over the dark of the ocean, leaving Mogadishu harbor and heading for the lights of the ships anchored in the distance. The outboard motor buzzed at a high pitch. Liz turned the nose of the plastic raft into the waves, causing it to ride up then splash down with a thud every few seconds.

"Waterborne!" Jones yelled, laughing, the spray hitting him in the face, the smell of the ocean overpowering everything he felt, saw, or heard. "You're a god at sea, Liz!" he said into her ear.

The dark city retreated behind them, and they were alone in the black, warm night. *It's all right*, he thought, *it's all right*.

They cruised silently for a while, just enjoying the ride and the night and the company.

"You come out here every night?" he asked, finally breaking the silence. They had to yell over the noise of the outboard.

"Every few nights."

"Long ride, huh?"

"I don't mind," she answered. "Worth it."

"I'll bet," he said.

Liz looked over at him, startled, trying to see what he meant behind his comment. But Jones was staring straight ahead, his face in a grin, nose to the wind.

Water boy, she thought. *All these fucking guys, water boys.*

"It's a great day to be sailing, Liz!" he said stupidly, catching her looking at him.

"It's night, idiot."

"Yeah, that too!" He laughed again, and turned back forward, Liz shaking her head.

She'd finished her shift—Booker from 10th relieving her half an hour early, the two of them chatting and gossiping for fifteen minutes or so. Liz had left the commo shack, making for her little room, then changed her mind and went to the chow tent. She boxed up a sandwich and a few pieces of fruit for Jones, then crossed back over the pier.

When she walked in it took a few seconds for her eyes to adjust to the dark. "Jones?" she'd called out quietly. "Ben?" No answer. As her vision got better she saw him: he'd removed all his clothes except his boxers and was sound asleep where she'd left him on the far cot. He was lying on his back, snoring gently.

Quietly, she'd put down the food, then sat on her footlocker and unlaced her boots, taking off her socks, trying to make noise to wake him up. But he didn't stir.

Bastard probably hasn't slept in weeks, she thought.

She didn't know what had happened in Kismaayo, and had decided she didn't care; she wasn't going to push it. Like Jones had said, they were alive, all her friends were alive, everyone was okay.

She leaned back and looked at him, eyes now fully adjusted to the dark. He had a long scar on his lower leg, purple and ragged, and blotches on his shoulders from the sun poisoning he'd gotten in Kenya back in December. She remembered that: Jones sitting on the roof of the Mike Boat wheelhouse, eating a candy bar, shoulders all bandaged up like he'd been in a fire. He had suffered second- and slightly third-degree burns, and they'd almost sent him home with a reprimand. He'd fought it, though—insisted he was okay, insisted he wanted to stay—and recovered.

He fought to stay here, she thought. *What exactly does that say about him?* She didn't have an answer—she knew she would have done the same. After all, who had just volunteered to stay on in Mogadishu? *We are alike.*

He was skinny, even skinnier than he'd been, ribs sticking prominently out, veins bulging on his forearms not so much from muscle but lack of a place to hide under his tight skin.

Liz looked at him, seeing that he wasn't going to wake up, then sighed, then laughed to herself. *I'll wake his ass up,* she thought. She stood and took off her BDU top, then her brown T-shirt, leaving just a black bra on.

She looked down at her chest and adjusted her breasts in her bra. She reached down to unbutton her pants, then thought better of it and left them on.

She quietly lay down on the cot next to him, pushing her chest into his side, letting her fingers wander over his stomach. He murmured, barely a whisper, and his breathing shifted. She put her lips to his ear.

"Jonesy," she whispered, then moved her lips to his cheek and kissed him softly.

Like a shot, Jones's eyes flew open and he let out a howl—in a second he was on his knees grabbing the M16 that Liz hadn't seen lying next to him. He moved so quick she was shoved off the cot, landing hard on the concrete floor with a gasp.

"Ben!" she yelled.

He howled again, raising the rifle in a snap to his eye, the barrel pointed down in her face, then—suddenly, instantly—he recognized her. His whole body tensed, and he let the M16 drop from his fingers to the cot.

"Jesusfuckingchrist!" she yelled, jumping to her feet.

"Oh my God," he stammered, "Oh my God, I'm so sorry. Liz, Liz, I'm so sorry, are you okay?"

He drew himself up and stood, putting his arms around her.

"What the fuck, Jones?"

He didn't say anything, just held on to her, his whole body shaking like a live wire. She pulled back, keeping her hands on his shoulders, steadying him, and looked him in the eyes.

"What the fuck, Jones?" she asked again, evenly. Quietly.

He shook his head.

"I'm sorry, I was sleeping . . . I . . . you woke me. Thought I was somewhere else, got confused."

He wiped his forehead with his hand.

"Dreaming. Got scared."

"Yeah, I guess so."

He looked at her, waking up.

"Liz?"

"Yes?"

"You don't have a shirt on," he said.

She looked down, and quickly drew her arms up over her chest.

"No shit, Jones."

She turned and grabbed a T-shirt and quickly drew it down over her head.

Jones sat down on the cot. She turned back to him. She was mad, but didn't want to show it.

"I brought you some food. Are you hungry?"

"What?" he said. Then, "Yes. Yes, thanks." He took the box from her and unwrapped the sandwich. His face was still pale, she saw, his forehead beaded with sweat.

Liz sat down on her footlocker again, and watched him eat. Finally, she said, "Jones, are you psycho?"

He looked up over his sandwich.

"No, Lizzie. Not psycho."

"It's not—normal—to shoot half-naked women who crawl into bed with you."

He smiled, thin but as real as he could make it, and didn't say anything, finishing his sandwich.

Liz sighed, then said, "You still want to go? We can just stay here. Maybe you want to sleep more?" She had been thinking this through all afternoon, and now what had happened here finished it for her—she didn't want to go to the boats with Jones tonight. Things were not at all as she had thought they were.

"No," he said, wiping crumbs from his mouth with the back of his hand and standing up, reaching for his clothes. "No, let's get out of here."

She almost argued, but couldn't. "Okay," she said, "let's go then."

Jones's mood had improved steadily from there, especially once they jumped down into the Zodiac, fired it off, and made for open water. And now, here, more than a mile out, he was someone new, someone different—someone laughing.

Well, not really new, Liz thought. *New for here, but it's just the old Jones.*

Liz pondered that this should be a good thing—so why was she uncomfortable?

Well, that was obvious; Thomas. But she couldn't do anything about it now.

Maybe this is best, she thought. *Maybe he needs to see how it is.*

The ships were taking shape in their sight now. They hadn't said anything in a while, when Liz cleared her throat and looked at him. "Jones?" she half yelled over the engine.

"What?"

She looked at him—looked at him smiling, enjoying the ride.

"Nothing," she said. "Forget it."

"Okay." He turned his eyes back forward, watching the ships and the night.

That was the problem with Jones, Liz thought. He could let you let it go too easily. Sometimes you *shouldn't* let it go, sometimes you should insist. Made things easier later, in the long run. But Liz couldn't deal with that now. Problem was, the closer they got to the MSC ship, and the easier Jones's mood got, the more and more she realized what a mistake this was. Her mistake had been in believing him, or believing what he projected: that it was cool, that it was all cool—they were friends, nothing could be more cool. It obviously wasn't cool, any idiot could see that now, but there was nothing she could do.

Fuck it, she thought. *No regrets. No regrets.*

Liz, steering with one hand now, grabbed the handheld radio out of her cargo pocket.

"MSC five, Motor Vessel Frances, this is Harbormaster three," she said into the radio.

There was a pause, then, "Go ahead, Harbormaster three."

"Frances, permission to approach on your starboard side, permission to come aboard."

This time the reply was immediate.

"Permission granted, Harbormaster three."

The ship was immense. Designed to carry an entire armored regiment—although not used for that here—it rose up and over them like a floating city, brightly lit and endless in its gray length.

Liz swung the Zodiac in a wide arc, Jones grabbing on to his seat to keep his balance, then she pulled even with the pilot's stairs that came from the main deck down to the waterline. Jones grabbed the line and tied them off to the stairs.

They crawled off the Zodiac, Liz grabbing Jones's hand to pull herself up. Jones started up the stairs, but Liz put her hand on his shoulder, stopping him.

"Jones, I—"

He turned and looked down at her, raising his eyebrows.

"Nothing," she said, pushing him forward now. "Nothing. But let's have a good time, hey?"

"That's why I'm here," he said, mounting the steps.

It was like climbing the Washington Monument—something they had done together the previous summer—and they were winded at the top. The pilot's stairs opened onto the main deck, empty except for a man waiting for them. A big man, bearded, handsome, in rubber boots, Levi's, and a blue MSC T-shirt that bulged from his muscular bulk underneath. He walked right for Liz, put his arm around her, and kissed her on the mouth.

"Liz," he said, breaking the kiss.

Jones, two steps to her left, took this in without a word, his head tilting to the side.

Liz brushed at her mouth with her hand, uncomfortably, then made a move to step away, just a bit.

"Thomas, this is my friend Jones I told you about."

Thomas crossed the distance with one step, sticking out his hand. "It's a pleasure! A pleasure. Welcome to my castle," he said, chuckling.

Jones shook his hand. "Thanks for having me," he said.

"Any friend of Ms. Ross is a friend of ours," Thomas said, stepping back to Liz, putting his arm around her. "A friend of *mine,* I should say."

Liz crawled out from under his arm again, trying and failing to be discreet. Thomas seemed not to notice. He turned and led them toward a hatch on the side of the superstructure. Jones and Liz were a few steps behind. Jones grabbed her hand, whispering in her ear, "What's the deal?"

She shushed him, dropping his hand, and picked up her pace.

Jones raised his eyebrows again and followed them into the ship's house.

4

They played poker most of the night, Jones and Liz and Thomas joined in the wardroom by the ship's steward, a burly Texan named Lance, and the second mate, a skinny, friendly engineer in blue coveralls named Joe who talked with a light stutter. Thomas and Liz were next to each other on a plastic couch pulled up to the table, his arm around her most of the evening, planting a kiss on her cheek from time to time, with no resistance. The bottle of tequila in the center of the table, full when they started, was almost finished three hours later, along with some bottles of Amstel Lite.

Jones sat hunched over the table in a plastic chair, growing quieter and quieter as the evening went on, stealing looks at Liz, eyebrows raised, not getting an answer.

Thomas, on the other hand, grew louder and more boisterous as the evening rolled, telling stories and jokes and bragging good-naturedly about ports he'd terrorized in younger days. He ran out of the room at one point and came back with an acoustic guitar, a Martin, and shoved it into Jones's lap: "Play!" he'd laughed, sitting back down next to Liz. "Play for us, Jones! Liz talks forever about how good you play." Jones plucked at it for a few seconds, then put his hands up, laughing politely, "It's been too long, I'm afraid."

"Jones!" Thomas yelled later, reaching across the table, pushing the tequila bottle closer to the young soldier. "What's on your mind? You haven't said a word in an hour."

"I'm good," came the quiet reply. "I'm good. Tired."

"Drink up, buddy!"

Jones took the bottle and tipped it up. He looked at Liz over the mouth of the bottle, saw her glance at him then look away quickly.

Lance called it a night around three, followed by Joe a half hour later.

"Just us chickens," laughed Thomas, stretching his arms out, yawning. "Jones," he said, piling up his chips, "I do believe I administered an ass-whupping on you tonight."

Jones smiled. "You're not the first," he said. "You won't be the last." Jones was trying very hard to not like Thomas, but it wasn't easy. He was a nice guy.

Thomas stood up, rustling Liz's hair as he got to his feet. "I'm gonna go try and track down a bed for our friend here. Be right back." He stumbled drunkenly toward the door, catching himself on the counter, laughing, then was gone.

Liz awkwardly gathered up the cards from the table, stacking them into a neat pile, not looking at Jones.

Jones lit a cigarette, and leaned across the table toward her. She was about to speak, about to say what she'd wanted to say for an hour now: *I'm sorry, Ben, this was a bad idea, I don't know what I was thinking,* but he spoke first.

"Are you sleeping with him?" he asked.

Liz looked at him; she was angry now, her face growing red.

"Fuck you, Jones," she whispered. "Could you be a little less polite?"

"I'm just asking a question—this guy is old enough to be your father. Are you sleeping with him?"

Liz dropped the cards and grabbed at her own cigarettes, her hands trembling.

"You know," she said, lighting a match, "you're a fucking asshole, pal. You know that?"

Jones sat back in his chair, not saying anything.

"You got a lot of fucking nerve, Ben."

"I don't know what you mean," he said.

"You don't know?" she almost yelled. "You don't fucking know?"

Jones shook his head.

"What *business* is it of yours who I choose to fuck?" she hissed.

"Jesus, Liz," Jones said quietly, "I just—"

"You just *what*, Jones?"

He didn't say anything.

"Where the hell have you been, Jones?" she asked. "Just where exactly have you been the last two years?"

Jones shook his head once, his mouth closed.

"Well, I'll tell you," she continued. "*I've* been right here. I've been right here for you—with you. And where is Jones? I don't have a fucking clue! You know what? You had your chance at me, pal, and you blew it. You *blew it off,* is what you did. Your buddies—your guitar—mostly you being a fucking class-A better-than-anyone-else soldier—all of these seem a bit more important to you. Or maybe just *being Jones* is what matters to you most, living like you're the only one on earth. Either way, you fucking blew me off, and now you've got the nerve, the fucking *nerve,* to comment on me and the choices I make?"

Liz ground her cigarette down into the ashtray, knocking it on the floor with the force of her hand. She stood, pointing at him.

"You know what, pal?" she asked. "Yes, I am sleeping with Thomas—

if that's what you want to know. He makes me moan and tremble and I love it. Is that what you wanted to know? Well, there it is. And you know what else? He makes me feel good about myself, he treats me with fucking dignity, and that's more than I can say about you."

She was crying now, tears running down her face, her cheeks flush and hot. Jones opened his mouth, understanding—too late—wanting to tell her, tell her how it was with him, tell her what he felt for her, about her, tell her what she meant to him.

But she was gone, gone out the door, leaving the ashtray smoldering on the deck next to his feet.

Jones jumped up to follow her, but there was Thomas, looming drunkenly in the doorway, turning his head to watch Liz storm down the passage.

"What's with her?" he asked, turning back to Jones.

"I think—" Jones stammered, his voice catching in his throat, "I think she had to go to the bathroom."

Thomas shrugged his shoulders, then smiled. "I found you a bunk! Follow me, trooper."

He turned and left the wardroom. Jones stood there, watching Thomas's back recede, his heart in his mouth, his hands shaking.

Then he bent to the table, grabbed his pack of cigarettes, and followed Thomas to a cabin at the aft of the ship's house.

5

The ship was so big that you couldn't feel it rocking when it was at anchor. It was just like a big hotel, a big economy hotel.

The master's quarters were nice: a suite of two connecting rooms, an office and a bedroom, with the only double-sized bed on the boat.

Thomas rolled to his side, taking his weight off Liz, whispering a song into her ear, pleasantly buzzed, pleasantly sleepy. He brushed at her face, her hair. It was too dark for him to see her face clearly, and that was good, Liz thought—she didn't want to hurt him. She didn't love him, but she'd never want to hurt this man—this good man. The truth was Thomas didn't make her tremble—she remembered throwing those words spitefully into Jones's face—but he was kind and gentle and giving in his love-making. And, more important was what he did for her beyond the physical. She felt whole with him, she felt warm, she felt wanted.

Thomas's tape player sat on his desk in the next room, turned down soft . . .

> *Gimme the beat boys, and free my soul,*
> *I want to get lost in your rock and roll*
> *and drift away . . .*

She slipped out from under the sheet, padding naked across the deck, feeling for her beer and her cigarettes by touch on his dresser top. She lit a smoke, the brief flare of light from the match outlining her form for him, small breasts, rounded hips, freckled and Irish skin. She set her lighter back down, next to the framed picture of Thomas's wife that she didn't even notice anymore.

"Baby, you good?" he crooned.

"Of course," she whispered, sitting on the side of the bed. "How could I not be?" She rubbed his calf with one hand while she smoked, staring into space.

"Your friend there, Jones," Thomas said, rolling over onto his stomach, laying his head on his crossed arms. "He's a quiet one."

"He was in Kismaayo," she said simply, as if that explained it. "For a long time."

Thomas grunted, getting himself comfortable. He stayed silent for a while, enjoying her presence in the room, listening to her inhale and exhale, feeling her fingertips on his skin.

She thought he had fallen asleep, when he said, "You're mad at him. How come?"

"You think so?" she asked.

"Yes."

Liz shrugged her shoulders.

"Yes, I am mad at him."

The sealed marine clock bolted to the wall clicked away, the moon showing itself through the port window.

> *Oh, gimme the beat boys, and free my soul . . .*

"Liz?"

"Yes," she said.

"Do you love him?"

No answer. Inhale. Exhale.

Finally, "He's my friend. My good, good friend."

Thomas grunted again, but she could tell from the tone it wasn't a mad or irritated sound; it was what it was—taking in information.

Her cigarette out, she crawled up next to him, slipping under the sheet, feeling him envelop her body with his, warm in his comfort and size and shape.

"Sleep good, baby," he said, kissing the back of her head.

"Yes," she said, drawing closer to him. "Yes."

6

Jones lay on his back on the bottom bunk in an empty cabin. Blank-faced, he stared at the underside of the bunk on top. Someone had scrawled with black marker: TOO LONG IN THE COUNTRY, LORD.

Too long, indeed.

He couldn't sleep. Surprise.

He felt like a man might feel when he's been handed the plate to his salvation, looked it over, carefully turned it around in his hands, then set it on the ground, unzipped his fly, and casually pissed all over it.

Too long in the country, Lord—too long indeed.

He thought of Thomas's Martin guitar, and wondered if he'd left it in the wardroom. He tried to remember how the wardroom had looked when he left, if there was a memory of a guitar there. All he could remember, though—the only thing he could see in the wardroom in his mind's eye—was red-hot emotion flooding like a torrent across the land.

Jones sat up and grabbed for his boots, pulling them on, leaving them unlaced. He stepped out of the cabin and tried to figure out how to get back to the wardroom and maybe the guitar.

He found the door, opened it, and saw that the steward, Lance, was back and sitting alone on the couch, watching a video on the TV. Propped in his lap was a big plastic travel mug, bagel-company logo on the side, filled with ice and a liquid Jones could smell from five feet away—rum.

"Drink, my friend?" Lance asked, moving only his eyes in Jones's direction.

"Thanks."

Lance pointed to the table, a few cans of Pepsi, a large bottle of Captain Morgan. Jones crossed the room, pulled a plastic cup from a stack, and poured himself a drink.

"Ice is in the freezer."

"Thanks."

"Turn that off?" Lance pointed at the TV. Jones pushed the button, cutting off the picture.

The room was quiet, Lance yawned, Jones sipped his cup, sitting down in a chair.

"Jones, right?"

"Right."

"You a chess player, Jones?"

"A bad one."

"An honest man. Me too. Wanna play?"

Jones sipped his drink some more, thinking. He couldn't think of a reason why not.

" 'Me too' an honest man, or 'Me too' a bad chess player?" Jones asked.

Lance laughed. "Me too, a bad chess player."

"Then bring it on, Lance. By all means, bring it on."

Too long in the country, Lord.

Too long, indeed.

He lowered his head to cough into his hand, and he wiped the water from his eyes while he was down there. He coughed again, squeezed his eyes quickly, then looked up, smiling tightly.

"Let's play, Lance."

7

It was her day off—one out of every ten for Harbormaster troops—and when Thomas crawled out of the rack at 0600 to go to the bridge, Liz rolled over and went back to sleep. Before the blowup last night she and Jones had agreed he would take the Zodiac alone to the pier in the morning to meet Sergeant Cowens. Thomas could get Liz back to port later in the day in his ship's launch.

She was still sleeping when Thomas banged open the door to the cabin at noon.

"Liz," he said, sitting next to her on the bed.

She looked up.

"You have to get dressed."

She looked at him, then at the clock on the wall, then back at him. His face was a mystery. He handed her a cup of coffee as she raised her eyebrows in a question. Her head pounded from the drinking the night before.

"Your friend, Jones—"

"What?" She sat up.

"He's at the hospital, the TMC at the airport."

"What?" The covers flew off her, coffee sloshing out of the mug all over her and the blankets.

"Something happened, something in town, I don't know what—Harbormaster just called it in on the radio."

The cup fell from her hand, coffee everywhere, not feeling it, her fingers raised to her lips. "Is he—?"

"He's alive," is all Thomas said, then left so she could get dressed.

The Art of Dishwashing, *Part Two*

Huley, Washington—October 1993

1

Jones sat alone in the ratty easy chair, bathed in the glow from the TV he'd turned down low when Lou dragged himself off to bed an hour before.

"You all right, man?" Lou had asked in his growl before leaving the room.

Jones had just looked up at him, his face blank, and nodded once, then twice. Lou nodded back, looked at him a second longer, nodded again, then went to bed.

And here was the TV—CNN, all you need to know, twenty-four hours a day.

The reports had come all day, but Jones had been waiting for the inevitable video feed, and now—right before 2 A.M.—here it came: Jones leaned forward and recognized a few places. Well, shit, it all really looked alike, didn't it? It was Mogadishu. But, yes, he knew that building, felt he knew it for sure. It was on the road to the U.S. embassy, but closer to the airport.

And then came the pictures of the naked body being dragged through the street, a barely contained crowd clawing at the dead American soldier.

Jones put his hand up to his mouth, a tiny sound escaping—*oh Jesus Christ what have we done?*

A scrubbed and lily-white reporter, standing in front of what had been the control tower at the Mogadishu airport: "First reports put American dead at thirteen soldiers—mostly Rangers—with scores of casualties." He looked down at his notes. "One source puts American wounded at more than one hundred. No solid reports yet on Somali casualties, but the unconfirmed figures we've gotten today are quite frankly astronomical . . ."

Too quick . . .

Jones sat and watched.

"Another unconfirmed report at this hour has it that the Somalis have taken an American prisoner . . ."

. . . too fucking quick . . .

". . . the longest and fiercest sustained firefight U.S. troops have been involved in since Vietnam, and the outcome at this point is . . ."

". . . Adid seems to have disappeared. He is *not* among the casualties, nor the prisoners."

A flash of a face in a window—

—Too quick!

An hour went by—more of the same, getting worse—and then the phone rang. Jones reached down to the coffee table and picked it up, his eyes never leaving the screen.

"Liz?"

Quietly, from Virginia, half a world away, "Yes."

He knew—he'd hoped—it would be her. They'd talked a few times since she got home in late September, long and quiet and careful talks. No apologies, just emotion. And longing. If she hadn't called him tonight he would have called her in the morning.

"How are you?" he asked.

"It's—it's hard to watch," she said.

"Yes."

She sighed. "The post is all fucked up. People walking around like zombies."

"I wish I was there."

"I wish you were here."

Neither of them said anything for a while, both watching their respective televisions.

"I feel stupid," Jones said. "I feel—castrated, useless—"

"I know," she said. "I know."

"I miss you," he said then.

"I know, Jones. It's hard—and I miss you so much."

"Liz, I—"

"I know," she said again. "It's all right, Ben. It's all right."

Jones looked up at the clock, 3 A.M. He got up from the chair and turned the TV off.

"Is Trevor there?" he asked. He walked to the corner where his guitar stood propped against the wall. He touched the neck, but didn't pick it up.

"Not now," Liz said. She had moved into an apartment with Trevor and Sid a few weeks before—four blocks down Warwick Avenue from the Ft. Eustis gates. "He and Bob and Norm and Meier went out right after we heard the news. I think they went to the Crystal Inn. I'm sure they're five shades of drunk by now."

"He's going to drag me out hunting over Thanksgiving—if I can get myself to Michigan."

She laughed quietly. "So I hear."

"How's he doing?"

"Oh, you know Alphabet. He's fine, fine."

She laughed again, small, then said, "He's mad at you for leaving."

"Leaving? Fuck him. He left me in Somalia."

"I'm kidding, Jones. Mostly. He just says he is—you know how he gets. I think he feels guilty."

"Guilty? For what?"

"You know."

Jones was silent a moment, then said, "Well—he's got no reason. There's a lot of guilt floating through the air tonight. None of it belongs to him."

Jones went into the dark kitchen and looked out the window, the frost setting on the field in the moonlight. Just a few more hours and it would be time for work.

"Ben?"

"Yes?"

"How are *you*?"

"Surviving," he said simply, then laughed. "Broke."

"You tried, Ben. I'm sorry it didn't work out."

"Yeah," he said. "Me, too. I should have known better. It's all right. I told Lou I'm leaving next month."

"He sounds nice."

"He is."

"Good. Ben?"

"Yes?"

"Take care of yourself—and get out of there."

Jones closed his eyes, trying to picture her, to smell her, to feel her.

"I love you," he said.

"I know."

2

What does it take? What does it take to slip through the tiny, hidden crack of normalcy, of reality?

A blink of an eye. The wave of a hand.

You saw them, sure, you saw them all the time. On the news, in the papers. Lost. Lost kids and lost adults. At rest stops, at truckstops, on a Greyhound, on the corner at Forty-second and Eighth Avenue. You saw them, flashing by, and maybe didn't know what you had seen.

A mother, a baby, a young man.

So solid, the ground under our feet. So solid.

Sometimes. Watch your step.

Jones's friends from childhood, from a life he barely remembered, most of them were finishing college or in grad school, or already starting careers. Most would never touch *disturbing*; and if it touched them, briefly, they wouldn't know it. Maybe a shiver, a bad feeling in the spine, that's all.

And that was good. Because most of them were *nice* people. Very nice, kind in their own way.

TVs, computers, dishwashers, dryers, cars, houses, dogs, cats. Things to paint, and things to feed.

Years ago, in a different generation, you waited for the phone call—it was inevitable that someone on the block was going to get that call, what were the odds it would be you? Fifty-fifty, maybe.

Ma'am? It's about your son. I'm his lieutenant, I was there when it happened—I just thought you should know he asked for you before he . . .

Well, you know.

But not anymore. Those calls didn't really happen anymore. It was a kinder, gentler world.

Noon on a Monday, you come back from lunch, and there's a crowd of strangers in cheap suits around your desk, your secretary looking flustered and nervous, they say they're from the SEC.

All gone.

A quiet Saturday afternoon, husband watching the football game, a phone rings in the kitchen, ma'am what kind of car does your daughter drive?

All gone.

Mom, I'm in trouble.

Dad, I'm pregnant.

All gone.

But probably not.

Probably never anything more disturbing than lost luggage, a flat tire, a speeding ticket, a nonmalignant skin growth—thank God, it was on his back, not his face.

Thank God.

3

Saturday night. Jones wore his Walkman radio the whole night at the pot sink and the dishwasher, tuned to the AM news station out of Seattle, waiting for more details from Mogadishu. Everything was still confused there, though, and details were sketchy—*and they're acting as if that was something new,* he thought. The only sure thing anyone seemed to know was that American casualties were huge and Somali casualties were staggering.

Right before midnight, Jones turned off the dishwasher, checked around to make sure everything was as it should be, told Lou he'd meet up with him later, then slipped out the back door.

George was waiting in his truck, as promised. Jones opened the passenger door and climbed up, warm inside, bordering on hot, cigarette smoke dense and thick, bad country on the radio.

"My man!" George greeted him. "I knew you'd come. Good times tonight, Jones, good times."

Jones didn't say anything, just nodded and strapped the seat belt across his shoulder and lap. The months since May had done nothing to improve George.

"You see that shit on the news last night, man?" George asked. "Isn't that the same fucked-up place in Africa you said you was at last year?"

Jones almost turned and punched him—his muscles tense and tight, blood rushing to his head.

He let out a breath.

"Yeah. I don't want to talk about it."

"Whatever, dude."

George put the truck in gear and pulled out, two blocks down, then a right onto Fairley, following it out of town then up the mountain.

There were no streetlights once they left the city limits, and the road ahead of them was dead dark. Jones recognized the turnoff for Louie's place, but they kept going, another mile or so up the road.

"So what's at the farm, George?"

"Good times, Jones, good times, and easy money."

"Speaking of which—"

"I got it for you back at the farm."

"George?"

"Yeah?"

"How come you're so gung ho to pay me? I just gotta ask. I left—you could have blown me off."

"Ah, we can always use help at the farm, we need ya up there—you got a marketable body, army boy. And I couldn't ask you if you and me wasn't straight in all ways. Right? This four hundred ain't no shit to me—you gotta know it's only a slice of what I took that night for the dope. And there's been a lot more since then."

Stupid, but reasonable.

4

Back at the restaurant, right before he'd slipped out the door to meet George. Phone rings—it's for you, Jones.

Not totally surprised, he'd sent a card and put this number on it.

But it's not his ex. It's his mother.

"What are you doing?"

"Working."

"Why?"

He laughs, not in a good way.

"I need money."

"No, why are you there?"

"Good question. Was trying to line up work, on a boat."

"You don't have to do this, you know."

"I know."

"When are you coming back?"

"I don't know. Soon, I think."

"I saw the baby yesterday."

"Good of you."

Sharp, she's mad—"That's not fair."

He's got no reply to that.

5

The farmhouse is old and looks from the outside like it's falling down. The porch has already fallen down; they have to enter through the kitchen door.

"Upkeep's a bitch," says George. "It's nice inside."

Warm, anyway. Peeling Formica, dishes piled in the sink, hunting rifle propped in the corner, open cereal boxes on the table—but it is warm.

George opens the fridge, grabs two Coors, hands one to Jones.

"Basement, that's where the party is."

George opens a door and they go down the stairs, fake wood paneling on the walls. Loud music, Metallica, and a small group of people. That one has to be George's partner: the only older man in the room, gray work pants, flannel shirt, sitting in an ancient La-Z-Boy, smoking a joint—raises a hand in greeting but doesn't say anything. Everyone else is a kid, or almost a kid. Three boys, four girls, seventeen maybe? Maybe. Sitting around, watching the TV, beer cans and overflowing ashtrays scattered about. Kids from Fairley Street.

"This here is Jones! Jones was in the army!" George greets the group, slapping Jones on the back, pointing him to a couch. A few heads turn and look at him, all of them completely stoned.

Zombies? Jones thinks. *A bunch of zombies. I'm in a movie.*

Then, *Welcome to the jungle, we got fun and games.*

Jones doesn't sit, leans to George and whispers in his ear, "How 'bout that money?"

George smiles and pulls four crisp bills from his pocket, hands it to Jones. *Fucker had it with him the whole time.*

George grabs a seat, Jones stays where he is, sipping his beer, watching. One of the boys is rubbing the neck of a girl sitting in front of him. She's in jeans and an unbuttoned flannel shirt, her pale breasts tight in a pink bra. None of the rest move, just staring at *Hawaii Five-O* with the volume turned down and the stereo blasting. They're mostly dressed alike, in jeans or black pants and combat boots, one girl with a Nirvana T-shirt cut off high showing a silver belly ring.

Not zombies, Jones corrects himself. *Vampires.*

Jones has met a few little groups of Vampires over the last year—some truckstops crossing the country in the Greyhound, but mostly in San Francisco and Berkeley. He figured they're runaways, but who the hell knows. You can't tell a runaway from his looks—*look at me,* Jones thinks. *I'm twenty-three, and you'd never know the difference.*

The ones he saw in San Francisco would group together at Fisherman's Wharf at sunset, ten or twelve of them, usually with little mutt dogs on string leashes, begging loose change from tourists.

What in the fuck are they doing in Washington? he thinks.

Octopussy Garden . . . I have returned.

George motions for Jones to join him on the couch, but Jones stays where he is. George gets up then, takes Jones by the arm, and leads him to a door in the corner of the room. One of the girls *(sixteen—maybe?)* follows them with empty eyes, pulls on a joint, and turns back to the TV.

The room George takes him into is dominated by a big four-poster bed, covered with a sheet that was white once. There's nothing else in the room but two professional video cameras, standing on tripods in the far corner.

"This is where the fun takes place, Jones," George says, waving his arm across the room.

"Oh yeah?"

"Yep. Big money, buddy. Not as big as dope, but a whole lot safer! And pretty much legal. Almost. You in?"

Jones looks at George.

"What—um—what exactly is my job?"

George almost explodes with laughter, spraying a mouthful of beer across the room.

"Dude, are you fucking kidding me? Did you see the pussy in that room? Think of sliding into that, Jones. Just imagine!"

Jones nods, forcing a tight smile.

"You're a good-looking kid, Jones. Army boy, muscles, tattoos. There's a market. They'll like ya just fine."

"They're all willing?"

"Sure, man. What, do you think—we got fucking slaves here? They get paid, just like everyone. Get a roof, good dope, burgers on the grill. It's a good fucking time, Jones. But I need more help—on tape and off. Someone with some brains. Distributors pay the big bucks for these amateur tapes." George turned and coughed violently into his hand. "You in?"

Welcome to the jungle, we got fun and games . . .

Jones blinks hard once then answers: "Yeah, George. Sure. Why not?"

They go back into the other room, nobody looks at them. The older-looking of the boys asks George's partner on the couch if they got any potato chips.

"Sure, man, sure, up in the kitchen."

"I'll go," Jones says, pointing at his empty beer can. "I need another. Got to take a leak, too." The kid asking for the chips looks at Jones blankly, then turns his attention back to the TV.

"Yeah, cool, Jones," says George, sitting himself back down on the couch, firing up a joint. "Crapper's off the kitchen."

Jones crumples the empty can in his hand, turns, and gets up the stairs into the kitchen. Finds the bathroom.

He's pumped, adrenaline pushing dangerously into his head. He pulls the string for the lights, stares at his face up-close in the mirror, then shuts his eyes and tries to get the picture right in his mind.

Envision it first, Drill Sergeant Rose used to say, that too-fucking-serious look on his face. *Envision your action before you take it. Like a movie,*

Privates. Watch yourself doing it, then correct what you did wrong, then watch again. When you get it right, that's when you move.

Jones pictures it, seeing himself in his mind's eye: *He leaves the bathroom, crosses the kitchen to the far corner, picks up the rifle he saw. Checks for rounds, checks the safety, sights it quickly against the refrigerator door. He opens the door to the basement, takes the stairs down two at a time, hits the floor, sights on—? George? No, Jones knows George is stupid—doesn't know about the other one. Take care of the unknown first.*

Back up.

Hits the floor, sights on George's big friend in his La-Z-Boy. And then—
What?

Shoot the man? Shoot George, too? Save the kiddies? Get them home to their loving mamas?

Save all the kiddies here, and then all the kiddies in the world? Is that the obligation now?

(. . . a flash, a face in the window—TOO QUICK!)

He blinks furiously, clearing his head. He runs it again—okay, something was wrong, backtrack to the beginning.

Bathroom, kitchen, rifle, stairs, George's friend, then—
What?

Jones opens his eyes, looks at himself in the mirror.

Then—

nothing.

There's nothing to save.

George wasn't lying—there's no slaves here. There's a lot of taking advantage here, a lot of fucking with someone's head. But that's all. Really, in the end, that's all.

Jones, looking in the mirror, sees a tear—then another, then another—slipping down his face. He's crying. He doesn't feel it, but there it is, right in front of him, he can see it. He's weeping like an old woman at a funeral. He wipes at his face with his hand, then pulls the string, turning off the light.

You don't have to redeem yourself—there's nothing to redeem.

Then a thought, crystal clear: *I want to go home.*

In the kitchen Jones quietly opens all the cabinets, searching around, not finding anything. There's an almost-full carton of Winstons on the kitchen table, and he slips this into his coat pocket. His hand touches the bills George had given him before, and he pulls them out, counting. Two hundred, three hundred, four hundred. Jones shakes his head. Son of a bitch played him straight.

He hears footsteps on the stairs, and slips out the back door into the night.

6

Twenty minutes later, shivering against the wind, making his way south down the road, he hears a truck engine behind him. He ducks into the bushes and waits. George's pickup finally appears, headlights on, driving no more than five or ten miles an hour. Jones can't see who's behind the wheel. He waits while it passes, waits a minute more, then climbs out of the bushes and starts walking again. Fifteen minutes later he hears the truck again, coming back. This time he knows where he is, though—the field to his right borders Louie's land. He leaves the road, ducking down, and crosses the field.

He finds Louie passed out on the couch. Jones shuts off the TV.

"What the fuck," Louie mumbles, rubbing his eyes, reaching for his glasses.

"Time for bed, Lou."

"Yeah, that's for sure."

He slips his glasses on and squints at Jones.

"Lasagna in the fridge for ya, Crash."

"Thanks, Lou. Thanks a lot."

Mogadishu

April Fool's Day 1993

1

A question from the past. Liz asked it—*When's the last time you saw your father?*

Jones sat and thought about it, not answering her then. But he knew the answer, he knew it like you know your name—how can you not remember when you last saw your own father?

I was seventeen, early autumn, a warm day but not sticky, with a sky overhead that said it would probably be cold that night, and then stay cold until next spring. We sat together on the porch of the halfway house in north Philadelphia—he couldn't leave the property with me, so we sat outside, enjoying the day and the light and the breeze, him with his old Gibson in his lap, making it work, me with my Yamaha, trying to make it work. My mother dropped me off, I remember; nervous and distracted, walking right up to him as I was still getting out of the old Impala she drove, she shot him a look and said, "I'll be back at four," then she was gone, that old car with the Jesus fish on the bumper weaving into traffic on Roosevelt Boulevard.

Bill hadn't wanted to come, I remember that, and Mom didn't argue with him. Since we'd come back to live with Mom, Bill had drawn away, from both of us—he was distant, a good student, concentrating all the time on his schoolwork, working as hard at it as I did not. When they let Dad out of jail and he called and said he'd be in a halfway house in Philly, Bill had slammed the door to his bedroom and turned up his stereo and stayed there all week.

And here's the old man, a guinea-tee tucked into black work pants, but shaved and clean and with-it and quiet and humble. He looks out of place in these clothes—my memories of him from early childhood put him in sharply pressed trousers, a tie and tie clip over a white shirt. I'm a clever teenager, and I think he's trying to cultivate something, cultivate the part, look how he ought to look—a con; but that's ridiculous. He's not cultivating anything, not anymore. This is who he is now.

He reaches over to the neck of my guitar and grabs my fingers and slides them down, one finger at a time, putting them into place. "You spend too much time with the technicals," he says. "That's good—yes—good to know, you know 'em maybe better than me. But don't forget style, don't forget style."

I strum the chord he's placed me on and I understand—I was on the seventh, because that's what you do there, that's what anyone would do, but he's got me on the sixth instead and now it's not just right, it's right and it's got style.

The old man listens to shit nobody listens to, leaving all those vinyl albums behind after he's arrested. After Mom gets through cleaning the house, they're the only thing left, the only thing that says he was ever here, the only thing that testifies to his existence—his ties, his shirts, everything in his closet cleared out and packed away, but the albums stay on the shelf. Utah Phillips, Jack Hardy, Stan Rogers, Roy Book Binder. There's straight old folk stuff, too—Woody and Pete; and Odetta; that stuff. And blues, scratchy old 78s he picked up at a yard sale that I find hard to listen to. But my favorites, and his too, I think, were these wandering gypsies, these nobodies with their records on labels no one ever heard of—Jamie Brockett, Liv Taylor, Dave Van Ronk, Greg Brown, Jack Williams, Anne Hills.

I remember he's squinting into the late-afternoon sun and sipping from a can of Sprite when I tell him that my girlfriend Katy is pregnant. He doesn't say anything for a long while, just puts down his soda and fiddles with his guitar. Finally he says, "Your mother know?"

I nod.

He nods back. He doesn't sigh exactly, but purses his lips and blows a short breath through them.

"What are you going to do?"

I shrug.

"Not much I can do to change it."

"How far along is she?"

"Six months or so."

He runs his fingers down the fret board.

"Well," he says, "that's about it, then."

"Yep."

I'm scared, and want him to say something, but he doesn't know what to say, and neither do I.

I play him a song I wrote, and I can see he's pleased—but he's distracted, and he's looking around, and I want to reach over and throttle him because he's got no right to be distracted, got no right to give me less than a hundred percent of his attention; after leaving me for five years he owes me undivided attention, and my knuckles curl white on the neck of my guitar and I don't say anything and then the moment passes.

And then my mother's back to pick me up, and he walks with her on the grass alone for a few moments, the two of them talking quietly, their heads together, walking in a circle on the lawn. I sit in the front seat of the Impala and raise my hand in a wave as we pull out, and he waves back, and as I turn and watch him he's sitting down again on the porch of that halfway house, sitting down with his guitar resting against the wall, just sitting and rocking and smoking and watching the cars go by.

Liz, I don't know where Trevor learned how to do it, but this is where I learned, this is where I learned how to shut down, right here, the old man giving me a lesson when he doesn't even think I can see him anymore—just sit down and smoke and watch the cars go by and pretty soon you'll just forget whatever it is that's troubling you. I can feel, Liz—I CAN feel. But sometimes . . .

2

Jones sat on an empty cot right inside the big door of the warehouse closest to the gate blocking them off from the anarchy that was Mogadishu. He was humming, under his breath.

Too long with no baby
too long, too long
Too long in the country
too long, too long

He could picture the changes in his head, how his left hand would shift: E to F#m to B7. Resolve at the end of the song not with the E root, or E7, but with E6, because it had more style. You didn't need a guitar to play guitar, you just needed a vivid imagination. Jones had no problem with that.

> *Yes, indeed*
> *Too long in the country*
> *Yes, indeed*
> *Too long, too long*

Sometimes, Jones thought, the words of the prophets aren't written on the subway walls—they're found scrawled on the bottoms of bunks on merchant-marine ships anchored off the coast of Africa.

He had a headache, but that was understandable—hangover. His skull itched, and he rubbed his hand up over his forehead. He'd not only shaved this morning, he'd also showered—a real shower—and then when he got back to port he'd found Bob and gotten him to shave his hair into a proper high-and-tight, so high it was almost a fuzzy mohawk. He'd dug this uniform from the very bottom of his duffel: an unworn set of desert BDUs, seeing the light of day for the first time since he'd packed them in November. His jungle boots weren't exactly shined, but they were clean.

Jones stared out into the hot morning, squinting and humming, not seeing anything. A shadow fell over him, and he looked up. It was Sergeant Cowens.

"You Private Jones?" the man asked.

"Sergeant, yes," he replied evenly. "Private First Class."

Cowens looked down at him, glaring.

"You gonna stand up, Private?"

Jones kept his face straight, and got to his feet. He locked to attention.

Three days, he thought to himself, keeping his temper. *Too long in the country, but short now and gone in three days—Lord oh Lord, I'm going fishin', yes I'm goin' fishin', and my buddy's goin' fishin' too.*

Jones was clean, but Cowens was spit-shined. Liz was right: this guy couldn't have been here that long—no one could stay that shiny for this long in Somalia, even desk jockeys. His helmet was perfectly centered on his head, chin strap tight and in place, LBE suspenders straight, BDUs starched. The M16 rifle over his shoulder looked like it had just come out of the factory box. He was a small guy—not as small as Sid, but almost. Judging from his apparent age, like Sid this Cowens couldn't have been wearing his sergeant stripes longer than four or five months. He had a look about him that Jones had seen before—the look of a man who has never seen danger but would like you to think he has, and that he will certainly know what to do if it comes again.

"I don't know who you are and what you used to do, Private, but for the next three days you belong to me. Is that clear to you?"

"Sergeant, yes," Jones said, clipped.

Three days.

"Private, I'm the driver for Lieutenant Colonel Aaron—your battalion commander."

Cowens looked at him, like he wanted an answer. Jones didn't say anything—*you looking for my gasp of awe?* he thought. Finally, he just nodded.

"We're all getting out of here, as you might know, and the colonel has to go meet with a Somali national—a Mister Pishu—about what's going to happen when 7th Group leaves and the U.N. takes over the port. This Pishu used to be harbormaster here. Anyway, normally we don't roll unless we got a three-vehicle convoy. Can't scare anyone up today, though, and the colonel says fuck it, we're gonna go anyway. I'm driving, colonel in the back, you next to me pulling shotgun, keeping your eyes peeled. Think you can do that?"

"Sergeant, yes."

Cowens looked at him hard, and waited a beat.

"You got an attitude problem, Private?"

This sounded like he'd wanted to say it to someone all day.

"Sergeant, no," Jones responded. "I hear you loud and clear. I'm your man."

"Fine, then."

Asshole.

Cowens turned to walk away, and Jones saw he had the 7th Group patch on his right shoulder. *Jesus Christ,* he thought. In the army you wear your unit patch on your left shoulder, leaving the right arm bare. If you ever go to war, then you put the patch of the unit you served with on your right shoulder, and keep it there no matter which unit you go to later. It's called a combat patch. Cowens was in-country less than two weeks and had already taken the time to sew his patch on.

Jones's own right shoulder was still bare. *Who has time to sew?*
I'm-a goin' fishin', yes I'm goin' fishin', and my buddy's goin' fishin' too.

They climbed in the Humvee, waiting for the colonel. Cowens reached behind his seat, grabbed an M16 clip and handed it to Jones.

"There's three rounds in there, and—"

Jones cut him off, pulling one of his own clips out of his ammo pack. "Got some, Sergeant, thanks."

Cowens looked at him, then at Jones's obviously full ammo pouches.

"What exactly are you packing there, Private?"

Jones swore to himself silently, remembering now Liz's words of warning.

"I'm just back from Kismaayo, Sergeant. It's all locked and loaded down there."

"Does this look like *Kissmyfuckingass* to you, Private?"

Jones shook his head—No.

"I'll turn this stuff in soon as we get back, Sergeant."

"You're fucking-A right you will."

Cowens shook his head, then shut up, seeing the colonel leaving the commo building, walking toward the Humvee. He got out to greet him. Jones smacked his clip against the side of his helmet, packing the rounds, then shoved it up into the M16. *Fuck you, man,* he thought.

The old man, Aaron, nodded at Jones as he got in and settled himself in the backseat. "Don't think I know you, son," he said, strapping on his seat belt.

"I'm with 710th, sir," Jones replied. "Was, anyway. Down south. Mike Boats, sir."

"Lieutenant Klover's platoon?"

"Yes sir."

"Hairy down there, Private?"

"No picnic, sir," he said. Then added, "Not exactly Normandy, either. Mostly boring. We did fine."

Aaron nodded.

Cowens started the engine, turning back toward the colonel.

"Private Jones here gonna fill in for a few days, sir. Unless you have someone you prefer."

"No, that's fine, Sergeant. Always good to have experience on board."

Cowens didn't like that, and Jones had to hide his smile behind his hand. They started for the gate.

Cowens leaned over, whispering. "Since you got a full clip, you keep that rifle on auto, you hear me?"

"Sergeant, I—"

Cowens looked at him sharply. "You what, Private? Keep that fucking rifle on auto and keep your eyes open, is that clear?"

"Sergeant, yes," Jones replied, making a show of moving his thumb, but not actually switching the safety down. He didn't give a shit what this guy said—M16s had a tendency to go off on bumpy Humvee rides. Not to mention you had more chance to think when your weapon was safed. Jones had decided in the last few weeks that maybe they all needed more time to think, to think things through just a bit more clearly.

The Humvee passed through three separate lines of Marines at three obstacle gates, then they were outside the compound and in the city. Jones returned the wave of the last Marine they passed—fully dressed in combat gear, M16 with grenade launcher slung underneath, thick goggles on, small ruck on his back. *Fucker's gotta be hot in that shit,* Jones thought.

"We're gonna make this quick, boys," Aaron spoke from the backseat, leaning forward as far as his seat belt would allow. "We've got no escort, but Pishu's office is only seven blocks away. I'll be in and out in ten minutes. Just leave the engine running, and keep your heads up. Should be no problems—this isn't Indian country exactly."

Cowens gave him a Yes, Sir, Jones nodding. *What the hell,* he thought. *What's a vacation in Somalia without a tour of scenic Mogadishu?*

The office was only seven blocks away, but they couldn't go straight there—twice they had to detour, once for a sickly herd of cattle led by a small boy with a big stick and once because of a huge crater in the middle of the road with the burned-out remains of a lorry sitting in it. Jones heard Aaron curse quietly from the backseat as they U-turned again, but the old man didn't say anything else.

They pulled up to what had once been a major intersection. There was an island in the middle of the intersection, two Marines there now, watching the traffic carefully, waving at them as they rolled slowly by. In front of them was what looked like a big hotel, eight stories at least, but all of the windows were gone, and it looked like some of the floors inside had collapsed down. Where the sign for the hotel used to be—a wide white marquee that ran the length of the entrance, almost the whole block—someone had painted in red SEMPER FIDELIS UNITED STATES MARINE CORPS GOD AND COUNTRY. Four Marines stood under the sign at an M60 nest, behind a concrete barrier and three rows of concertina wire. One of the Marines waved at them to stop, and Cowens brought the Humvee to the side of the road.

The Marine yelled something to them, but they couldn't hear, so he came out from behind the bunker. He had a pistol in his hand, and he leaned in over Cowens's shoulder. He was a captain.

"Sergeant, what the fuck are you doing?"

Aaron leaned forward, and the captain glanced at him, then gave a half salute. "Sorry, sir, didn't see you."

"Problem, Captain?" Aaron asked.

"Sir, vehicles in the city are only supposed to travel in convoy, three vehicles at least."

"I know, Captain. We got business, can't wait. We'll be all right."

"Yes sir," the captain said. "Where you headed?"

"Namjik Road, before the bazaar."

"That's a crowded section, sir. Lots of skinnies on the street today. Want me to send a squad of my guys with you?"

Aaron thought about it for a second, then said, "Thanks, but no. We'll be fine. In and out."

The captain nodded. "Drive safe," he said. He patted the roof of the Humvee, then turned to go back to his machine gun nest.

Namjik Road was indeed crowded. There was a bazaar at one end, and the road was filled with people and a few cattle and lorries. Jones turned and saw Aaron nervously looking out the window as they rolled through the crowd, but the colonel didn't say anything.

"Where's the kids?" Jones asked, quietly.

"What?" Cowens said.

"Kids. Not many kids. Everywhere else I've been in this country has been filled with kids. No kids here."

"Fuck if I know," Cowens said. "Maybe they're all in school."

Jones looked over at him, but Cowens was staring straight ahead—he didn't know he'd just made a joke.

Cowens stopped at number seven, a three-story stucco building with no windows, just a big wooden door facing the street. The building was crowded in on both sides by two others of the same type—number nine, on the left, had three women crouched down on the front step with a large jar of what looked like beads between them. The only other vehicle parked on the block was a tiny boxlike white car almost directly across the street. There was a man in a dirty loincloth leaning against it as they pulled up, but he straightened himself and slowly sauntered away.

Jones looked down and saw his knuckles were white around the M16. *Calm down,* he thought to himself. *Done, done—it's all done.* He took a deep breath and flexed his fingers.

The three soldiers got out of the Humvee, Cowens coming around the front to meet them on the sidewalk, leaving the engine running. Aaron had a sheaf of papers in his hand.

"I won't be long, no more than five minutes or so. It might be that he'll come out with me and go back to port with us—can't be sure."

Aaron eyed the street again. The main crowd was a block or so down, but already a few were making their way down to watch the Americans.

"Sergeant, you gonna be okay out here?"

Cowens nodded. "Yes sir. No problem. If I hit the horn, come running."

Aaron half-laughed. "Good."

He opened the big wooden door and went inside.

Cowens made a show of checking the magazine in his rifle. Jones slung his M16 over his shoulder and lit a cigarette. Cowens turned back, looking at him. "Hey, PFC Jones—did I tell you to put your weapon up?"

Jones took his rifle down again, holding it at a relaxed port-arms, his cigarette burning in his lips.

Cowens was nervous, it showed in his face. Jones actually felt better now that he was out of the Humvee. There was a small crowd, watching them and laughing and pointing, but most of them were half a block away. The soldiers were only a hop away from the Marine nest, a hop and a skip from the port, and Jones thought these people knew it—not that any of them were even slightly threatening. Only the three women going through their beads were close, and they kept their heads down and their hands busy. *Probably more nervous than us,* Jones thought.

But Cowens was agitated. He turned to watch the crowd for a second, then turned back.

"You see anything—*anything*—you shoot first, ask later."

Jones nodded.

Cowens turned back to the crowd, but he couldn't keep still. He looked at Jones again.

"So what the fuck was so gung-ho in Kismaayo?" he asked, sneering.

"Not a thing, Sergeant Cowens. Not a thing."

Cowens bit at his lip. "Yeah, I didn't think so."

He turned away from Jones again, and set his gaze on the three women sitting at their jar of beads. They were all skinny and poor, but not filthy, in full dress and turban, with earrings dangling.

Cowens whistled, startling Jones.

"Hey, baby!" he called, smiling wide, waving at the women. The women looked up, one of them giggled, then looked back down.

"Hey!" Cowens called again. "Any of you speak English? Speaken da fookin Englayse?" He waited a second. The women were all looking at him, but didn't reply. "Jambo! Fucking English?"

Jones shook his head.

Cowens turned and looked at him, laughing now. "Ain't these some bitches, Private Jones?"

Jones nodded his head once, to the right. Cowens turned back to the women, slinging his rifle up on his shoulder, gesturing now to the woman closest to him.

"Come here, sweetie."

He waved vigorously.

The women looked confused, unsure.

"C'mon!" Cowens yelled, smiling wide the whole time—friendly American soldier. He kept waving at the closest woman, and then started pointing toward his chest pocket, as if he had something for her. She stood, unsure, and her one friend stood with her.

"Hey, Sarge, I—"

Cowens whipped his head back to Jones. "You what, Private?"

Jones shrugged. This was ridiculous.

"Nothing, Sergeant. Nothing at all."

"I didn't think so."

Cowens turned to wave again, and the woman took two tentative steps in his direction. Her friend stayed where she stood, the third woman still crouching on the ground. She was older, and looked angry.

"Fuck," Cowens said, "I gotta come over here and feed their sorry asses, least I can do is have some fun with the chicks, right? Hey baby! Come over here!"

The woman stopped three steps away from Cowens.

"Whaddaya think, Jones? Nice piece of ass, this one—huh? Turn around honey, shake your skinny ass for me."

The woman took another step, smiling at him innocently, and Cowens reached out his hand, to touch her or grab her.

Then Cowens's hand wasn't there, and the woman wasn't there, and the tiny white car across the street exploded into a fireball, a dull *whump* slamming into Jones's side, pushing him against the wall of number seven, his left side and chest peppered with fiery small bee stings, his eyes seeing nothing but a white blinding glare.

Then a scream, then another, and then he could see.

(*. . . a flash of a face in a window, looking at his—TOO QUICK!*)

The woman was on the ground, a mass of blood covering her chest and arms, her eyes rolled up in her head, the other two women on the ground moving slowly, crawling into the street.

Cowens amazingly stood upright where he had been, his left arm outstretched, looking to see where his hand had been but was no more. His eyes opened wider than Jones thought possible and he screamed— "*Ohsweetjesuschristohchristohmyhand!*"

Jones dropped to a knee and thumbed the safety to full auto, raising the M16 to his cheek, but there was nothing to shoot, no one there. He twisted left and there was the burning car in his sight and he squeezed the trigger and his hand shook as he emptied the entire forty-round clip into the burning car. A wail built in the back of his throat, coming louder as the rifle rocked in his hand, flame shooting from the flash suppressor, hot brass falling to the sidewalk.

The rifle clicked, and he let his fingers go loose and the M16 dropped to the ground.

Cowens was down now, his face looking at Jones, pitiful and agonizing, crawling toward Jones on one elbow. "Jones Jesus Christ Jones get me in the fucking door *get me in the fucking door!*"

Jones reached behind him and pulled the door open, then flung himself forward, landing on the ground next to Cowens, looking him straight in the eye. The sergeant's eyes were red, bulging, and he was still screaming, but Jones couldn't hear him anymore, he had stopped listening, stopped listening to everything. Then Jones was gathering the Somali woman up in his arms, lifting her torso up like a rag doll, crawling backward, pulling her into the open door of the building, slipping in her blood.

"*What in the fuck are you doing?*"

Cowens, looking up at him, not understanding, not understanding at all why this was happening, why he was still on the ground. Jones nodded to him, heaved, and pulled the woman toward the door.

"*Private my hand what the—!*"

But Jones wasn't listening to him anymore, this man did not exist, and with one last surge of strength he got her in the door and he collapsed backward into the dark hallway.

He reached down with his fingers and wiped blood from the woman's face, pushing blood from her open eyes back into her hair, but she was dead, he knew it, he'd known it outside, she was stone dead, her midsection a mess of gore and tissue.

He sobbed once, like a scream, and rubbed at her cheeks—"*Oh please lady fucking please come on—*"

And then here was Aaron, coming down the long stairs, almost falling, his pistol drawn, bending at Jones's side, his hand on his shoulder.

"Where's Cowens?"

"She's dead sir she's dead I pulled her in here but she's dead."

"*Where is Sergeant Cowens?*"

Jones looked up at him, and they heard Cowens scream from outside. "Fuck," Aaron whispered, and stuck his head out the door, pistol first.

Jones didn't move, craddling the woman's head in his lap, rocking gently, but he whispered, "It's clear, it's all fucking clear, there's no one there, it was a bomb, a fucking car bomb."

Aaron took one step out the door, covering points up and down the street with his pistol, but there was no one there. The street was empty—

that quick. Just the other two women, huddled in the gutter now, hard to tell if they'd been hurt, and then Cowens, dead or passed out on the sidewalk.

Something flashed in the corner of Aaron's eye and he whipped to his left, finger pulling the trigger of his pistol before his brain knew what it was doing. He shot high, and that was good because the movement was a reinforced Humvee from the Marine nest back at the hotel, screaming up the street, a Marine's head sticking through the hole in the roof shooting straight down the street at nothing. And then Jones was behind the colonel, reclaiming his rifle from the ground.

Cowens wasn't dead, he was passed out, but he came-to as they lifted him to throw him into the back of the Humvee, screaming for mercy, and then there was a Marine there helping them lift and Jones fell off and sat down hard on the sidewalk, his legs giving out, his teeth clamping down on his tongue.

"Get up, man." It was a medic, a corpsman, and Jones did get up then, grabbing the corpsman by the shoulders, shaking him.

"She's already dead, she's in there, but she's dead, *you're too late*—"

"Who?"

"The woman! The Somali woman . . ."

"Fuck that," the corpsman said. "Do you see this guy's hand?"

Jones looked at him.

"It's gone."

"No shit—do you see it? On the ground?"

"There." Jones pointed. But it wasn't whole, it was no good, just two fingers, really, and most of Cowens's arm was gone from the top of the wrist down.

And then there were three Humvees in the street, and then six, and then a deuce-and-a-half with them. A squad of ten Marines had a perimeter around them, facing out, standing with M16s to their cheeks, locked into place.

Their Humvee pulled out then, a Marine at the wheel, Aaron in the shotgun seat, Cowens and a different corpsman in the back, another two Humvees following close.

The first corpsman was back.

"You're bleeding," he said to Jones.

"What?"

The corpsman pointed to Jones's chest, his uniform torn up where the shrapnel had hit, trickles of blood staining the fabric and running down his leg.

"Did you look at her?" Jones asked.

The corpsman looked at him blankly.

"Yeah, man, sure. Yeah, I looked at her."

"She's dead."

"I know, army. C'mon."

The corpsman directed Jones to one of the Marines' Humvees, and they waited for the captain to clear them to leave for port. Jones sat in the driver's seat, his BDU top open, the corpsman crouched down and swabbing at Jones's wounds. Jones looked through the windshield, at the Marines firming their perimeter, fanning out down the empty street, at the other Humvees—these from 10th Mountain—arriving, at a soldier and a translator talking to the other two women, now sitting on the curb, holding each other and wailing.

Jones looked down at the corpsman.

"Where's Alphabet?" he asked, calmly.

The corpsman didn't look up.

"Who?"

"Alphabet. Trevor—where is he? He can fix things. He's a strong motherfucker."

The corpsman looked at him now, his light black face staring up into Jones's eyes, tension gone, replaced with exhaustion.

"Dude, I don't know what you're talking about—"

"Trevor, man, Trevor. Is he around? He can deal with this—he just shuts down."

"I think you're in shock, man," was all the corpsman said, getting to his feet, putting a hand on Jones's arm.

Jones looked up at him, squinting against the sun. Then he looked down.

"Maybe," he whispered. "Yeah, maybe."

The corpsman looked down at him, not saying anything.

Jones fiddled with his dog tags, whispering, "He's a strong mother-fucker—he could fix this."

PART THREE

Two Soldiers

Michigan—Thanksgiving Weekend 1993

1

Crouched in a ditch, hard ground pressing into his stomach, the stock of this ridiculously heavy musket almost frozen to his cheek, Jones caught a glimpse of movement as Trevor passed from behind on his left, crawled from the ditch ten yards away, and melted into the twilight treeline. Had he seen something? Maybe. Jones doubted it, though. They'd been out here in the cold since before sunrise, the coldest Thanksgiving weekend on record in central Michigan, and had yet to see a clump of hair stuck to a tree, let alone a living, breathing deer. He shifted the stock of the rifle a twitch to make sure it wasn't *really* frozen to his face, then looked back to the left, trying to place Trevor. But he was gone.

2

Trevor had a 1991 Pontiac Sunbird; a comfortable enough car for two, livable with three, unbearable with four, especially when one of those four was five eleven and 220 pounds, especially when the trip in question involved fourteen hours of overnight driving. Bob, with the muscular weight, and Sid Mason—the skinny alter ego—had the back. Trevor—at the wheel—and Jones had the front, scrunched up with kneecaps busting on the dash. Whatever tiny bit of floor space was left in the car was taken up by empty bags of Fritos, microwave burritos, and the remains of a twelve-pack of Rolling Rock they had picked up at the West Virginia border. The car smelled, as Sid so aptly put it, like socks and ass.

Bob, Sid, and Trevor were on a week's leave. Jones had met up with them a few weeks before, getting off the Greyhound at the Ft. Eustis gates a little after midnight, Liz waiting there for him, collapsing into her arms, and she held him without letting go for three days.

I'm going to Michigan with Trevor, I'll be back in a week, he'd said later, *and then I'm not leaving again.* She bit his ear, then kissed him, pulling the blankets up to their chins, rolling lazily on top of him.

Bob got out in Ohio at 2 A.M., somewhere off the turnpike. A big Ford pickup with high beams on was idling at the side of the road just past the tollbooth, waiting for him. Trevor spun the wheel to pull away as Bob opened the passenger door to the pickup, dropping his duffel in the open well of the truck, and in the light of the cab Jones saw a man who looked to be future-Bob, a quick glimpse of a huge bear of a fellow, fiftyish, hunched over the wheel, who lifted his hand briefly in an almost-wave at the departing Sunbird as his son heaved himself into the truck.

Sid—at thirty, the oldest—they carried to his mom's house in suburban Detroit. Sleepy and mumbled introductions, hasty apologies for passing up breakfast, then the last two hours north to Michigan farm country, the sun rising pitifully against the freezing cold on this Thanksgiving morning.

They got to Trevor's parents' house a little after 8 A.M., pulling in on a near-empty tank of gas to the most ridiculous sight Jones had ever seen: a man—he assumed correctly Trevor's dad Peter—bundled up in what looked to be fifty layers of parka and coveralls, riding a lawn tractor over the frozen grass, breath pouring from him in white spurts, grass seed flying from the dumper in the back.

"Tell me he's not laying grass seed on Thanksgiving morning," Jones said with some wonder. It couldn't have been a degree over ten below.

"Yep." Trevor pulled hard on the parking brake. "Gets him out of the house, I think."

It started to snow lightly as Peter waved to the boys from the tractor, then disappeared behind the house.

"Polacks." Jones smiled, and ground his smoke out in the Sunbird's ashtray.

3

The sun, weak and worthless as it had been, was giving out its last gasp of light before slipping completely behind the treeline. Less than fifteen minutes of good light left in the day. *The only thing we're liable to shoot now,* Jones thought, *is each other.* He brought the stock down and laid the musket *(a musket! who hunts with a musket?!)* to rest beside his prone body, barrel sticking up a bare inch off the ground to keep the dirt out. Some training you never lose.

He sighed, shivered, then rolled to the left to relieve his aching rib cage. He wanted a cigarette badly, could have cared less about shooting a deer or anything else. He heard a crunch in the woods ahead and strained his eyes to make out Trevor's form, upright now, moving from tree to tree.

Fuck this, he thought, and tried to pull the collar of his borrowed camo coveralls closer up over his chin. *I ain't Robert De Niro, and I sure ain't a fucking deer hunter.*

He shivered, and waited for Trevor to come out and say it was time to go home.

4

Three Thanksgivings prior, hunting something slightly less tangible than deer. The rain poured down on the pup tent—endlessly, ceaselessly, relentlessly—in the cold Kentucky night. The tent had to be twenty years old, the weatherproofing long gone, but even that didn't matter: the tent was only two sides in a triangle, with no floor, so everything inside was already soaked. The only thing stopping it from freezing was that the water moved like a river in miniature, from the front to the back of the tent, never stopping long enough to freeze.

Two soldiers in the night, and this was basic training, so they weren't even allowed to be called "Soldier" yet—just Private. Private this, and Private that, and Privates in plural, and Private I cannot believe how completely and totally *FUCKED UP* you are. Two privates; two wet and cold privates. In Kentucky. Thanksgiving night.

The private lying under the pup tent in the mini-river next to him was called Trevor Alphabet. That wasn't his real name. His real name was something long and Polish and unpronounceable and Jones—in that long army tradition, which he didn't yet know was a long army tradition, of dealing with impossible names—called him Alphabet. He couldn't see Alphabet, even though they lay almost on top of each other, their soaked sleeping bags open to allow them to press their bodies against each other to get any kind of heat possible. Too cold and wet and miserable to even joke about sleeping-bag buddies.

Sleep was not an option, even as exhausted as they were. This extreme misery wouldn't allow sleep, even when sleep was as necessary as breath. Sometimes you had to hold your breath, and sometimes you just didn't sleep. Neither private could really remember sleeping for almost seven weeks.

He who sleeps—dies.

They were all guarding something, but they couldn't remember what it was, and it didn't matter anyway; it wasn't the responsibility of these two privates until almost daybreak, when they would venture out of the tent into the forest to relieve whatever miserable duo from their platoon had the duty now. The only responsibility at the moment was not to cry and not to drown and not to freeze and not to jump out of the dark, wet tent, screaming a surrender: please, *please* let me go home now, you heartless bastards. Jones could remember his recruiter, a staff sergeant with a spare-tire belly, leaning back in the chair behind his plain metal desk, paging absently through a *Penthouse,* saying without looking up as Jones signed his enlistment, "The key, kiddo, is to not let 'em break you. It's just a mind game, that's all. You've got a few years on the average recruit, that's a plus. Let 'em scream, let it wash over you, you'll be all right." Jones desperately wished he could crawl his physical body back into that memory and slam his fist into that fucker's chubby face.

Misery, Jones had decided, true misery, comes not from the moment. It isn't the inflicted action that causes misery. The fist crushing into a face, for instance, doesn't cause the misery. That could be overcome. Anything in the moment, in the *here* and in the *now,* could be gotten over—one more push of muscle, one more force of will. The misery, he now knew, came from *knowledge*—knowing that the *here* and the *now* was not going to go away, that you could draw on all of what was inside of you for one more push of muscle, one more burst of adrenaline to get you through, but what you would find on the other side was just one more thing to be pushed. That was intolerable, that was where the misery lived, and that was as dark and cold and wet and black as this pup tent in the freezing Kentucky night.

This situation, Jones decided, was a case study in his definition of misery. There would be no relief, as there had been no relief for . . . well, for longer than he could remember now. The last time they had slept, or thought they were about to sleep, had been an unbelievable slipping into bliss with a promise from the drills of a Thanksgiving Day to be spent leisurely polishing boots and cleaning rifles inside, a chance to read a newspaper, a late-afternoon processed-turkey meal at the mess hall. Heaven. They had all slipped into that sleep, slipped hard and deep, so hard and so deep it probably took a record-breaking ten seconds—too long—for the first of their feet to hit the cold tiles next to their racks at zero-four-fucking-hundred in the morning, zero-dark-early, as the drills, *all* of the drills—for the first time since Reception Day—stormed the bay, overturning bunks and lockers and breaking bottles of black shoe dye on the tiles, screaming with a vengeance, all of them fully dressed in starched green BDUs with their campaign hats, pounding and screaming to GET the FUCK outside *NOW!* It had been snowing lightly at 0400 on Thanksgiving morning *(it's downright TROPICAL out here, Privates!).* A snow that would turn to slush and then turn to rain as the day progressed, as they spent the first two hours of the day outside on their backs, then their stomachs, then their backs, then their stomachs, muscles failing and popping, grown men doing everything in their power to not beg for mercy. It had not gotten any better from there, this particular journey in terror finally landing all of them in this forest, unplanned and unexpected—just like war is, *Privates,* Rose screamed at them, this is for your own good-for-nothing good.

But this was not like war is; there was no battle to win, no country to protect. This was Ft. Knox, Kentucky. The only known enemy was in the Iraq desert, and his leash had already been shortened. There was no war here. And there was no relief, and there—right *there*—was where the misery lived.

They would get through this night, live through this, just to be able to march back to the barracks in the morning, through the rain, fifteen miles, return filthy and soaking and no way to stop that filth and soak from spreading across the barracks bay they had slaved to spit clean for two days to get their never-received Thanksgiving holiday, get that bay as filthy as themselves, to clean it again, to return to the field, to return to the range, to shoot more fake bullets at fake enemies because this was like *war,* to go and go again for another week, and would there then be sleep? No, Jones decided. There would not be. Probably never again.

Trevor, who Jones had thought was dozing and out of it, suddenly popped on his red-lens flashlight, directly into Jones's eyes. "Get your hand off my ass," he growled, his breath a frosty cloud. "And stop thinking. I know you're over there thinking. It won't do you any good, so fucking stop it. You're keeping me up."

If it had been even remotely possible for Jones to smile, he would have. He liked this Trevor Alphabet, was glad they had been thrown in together. They could, at least, be miserable together.

And, Jones thought, Trevor was a strong motherfucker—what they both needed now the most was another strong motherfucker to drag them through this to the finish.

The light clicked off, and they listened to the rain and their own teeth chattering.

5

Breakfast was huge, and so was Trevor's mom, Mrs. Alphabet, the author of the feast. Amazing to watch, she moved her bulk like a dancer; from one end of the counter to the other, a very pleasant lady wrapped in a pink housecoat, pouring coffee and refilling plates as Jones and Trevor, joined by the elder Alphabet father and the younger Alphabet brother, ate. The kitchen was filled with packages and Tupperware containers and grocery bags that Jones assumed would shortly be Thanksgiving dinner. A raw, dressed turkey sat in a roasting pan on the far counter, glowing various shades of reflected red and green from the small TV next to it, the volume down to nothing, Bryant Gumbel gabbing away in silence about the holiday parade in New York.

"So," Trevor's dad said to Jones around a piece of bacon, "they got much deer in New Jersey?"

At least he said it with a smile, Jones thought, then answered, "Not like here, I'm sure, sir. But I really wouldn't know. This is my first time hunting."

The old man grunted. "That's what Trevor said. Be careful you don't shoot your own pecker off, fella."

"Peter!" Mrs. Alphabet took a swipe at the old man's head with a pot holder. He ducked it, and grunted again.

"Guess you don't get to shoot much black powder in the army, right?"

Jones looked somewhat beggingly toward Trevor, waiting for him to take over this conversation. But Trevor was buried in his eggs, and made no move to rescue. Jones looked back at the old man.

"Um, nope, never have. Trevor says it's a fifty-cal. That must be a helluva ball. I shot fifty-cal machine gun. But never musket, not once." He grabbed his coffee, leaving an opening that the old man wasn't going to take. "Looking forward to it, though."

The old man finally gave another grunt. "Mess your shoulder up, it will," he said. "If you're not careful, that is. Packs a wallop. But she'll cut a big enough hole for you, if you manage to actually hit something."

The old man turned his head toward his oldest son. "I passed your cousin Ernie's place this morning, right before y'all got here. He got an eight-pointer hung up at the garage."

Trevor looked up, laughing, trying hard to not spray his scrambled eggs from the corners of his mouth. "I talked to that idiot on the phone yesterday before we left Virginia." This drew a swat toward him from Mrs. Alphabet's pot holder; Jones figured "idiot" and "pecker" must fall into similar categories for her.

"He didn't shoot that deer, Pop. He hit it with his truck! Coming home from Overdell's two nights ago. Told me the warden was giving him shit"—another swat with the pot holder, this one connecting—"because he saw it hanging there, and Ernie hadn't registered. Didn't believe him that he hit the damn"—yet another swat, her aim improving—"thing. Ernie said he showed him the broke ribs and all, but the guy was still threatening to write it up."

"That fat cow of a warden wouldn't know a broke rib from a bullet hole from an asshole"—two swats on that one—"if it was up his own nose."

The old man pushed back from the table and lit the cigarette he shook loose from a pack of generics on the table. "Hit it, though, huh?" He shook his head. "I don't know whether to congratulate him, or laugh at him." He sipped his coffee and gave a quick cough behind his hand, smoke spilling out between his fingers. "Hurt the truck at all?"

"No. Dented the grill."

Mrs. Alphabet finally sat down herself, a low *whoosh* escaping from underneath, molecules of air rushing to get out of the way of that mountain of flesh, her hands automatically brushing down her housecoat to smooth the fabric and the fat.

"Overdell's be open tonight, I think," she said, reaching for her coffee. "Trevor, you going to take your friend out there after dinner?" She smiled at Jones, simultaneously dropping her eyes to ensure he still had enough of her food on his plate.

Jones looked at Trevor. He had mentioned something on the way up about a bar in a cornfield, never closed, even on holidays. Trevor, hick that he was—and quite aware of it—had promised Jones they would do all the hick things he could muster up in their week off. This was repayment for Jones suffering through a weekend in Manhattan almost two years before—a weekend of elevators to skyscraper tops, frozen ferry rides around the island, and waiting in line to see David Letterman.

"Yep. Not only does this Jersey idiot"—no swat this time, interesting—"not hunt, he's the only soldier I met who sucks at pool. Gonna take him out tonight and whup him."

"Mind the drunks on the road," she said.

Trevor nodded and went back to his eggs.

6

Thanksgiving night, one year prior, Mombasa, Kenya—four hundred miles south of a Somali city called Mogadishu—American soldiers quietly arriving in this neutral port to form-up and await deployment orders.

There was a pistol pressed into Jones's neck.

His head twisted to the left, like he wanted to use the barrel of the pistol like a bear will use the trunk of a tree, to work out knots and itches.

"Jambo," the pimp whispered from behind him.

Jones didn't know the man was a pimp.

"Jaaambooo!" the pimp whispered again.

Jones could feel the spray of spit that left the man's lips, just inches from his ear; could smell the coffee and pepper-sweet mango breath.

Sitting on the bed in the corner of the tiny room the girl Alysa laughed softly, making no move to cover her dark body. Going about her business she reached for the box of tissues on the floor and began wiping, slowly, the insides of her thighs, moving on to stomach, breasts, and mouth, without ever taking her eyes from Jones's.

Jones was also naked, standing very, very still in the center of the room. A single lightbulb hung from a cord over his head, swaying gently in the sea breeze coming through the window. Naked, save for the cold steel pressed hard into his neck, and the warm cloud of Kenyan ganja buzzing in his head. Jones felt a great and invisible weight pressing down on his shoulders, his ankles and feet bearing the weight, pushing into the cement floor.

Jones was still sticky from his time with her. Their act had been rough and playful, one sneer shy of violent—the strong mulatto girl pawing Jones like a sparring partner, laughing as she pushed him inside her, then pulling him down and rolling on top, her open palms pressing and kneading his chest as she thrust.

The pimp, still unseen to Jones, staying behind his shoulder, snapped the fingers of his left hand, crisp and strong, motioning for the girl to hurry up and leave. A small and pitiful noise came from Jones's throat at the sound of the snap. The pimp started talking with a low growl and Jones's head snapped up at the sound of it, another quick breath leaving his throat.

"*Why* you not pay? *Why* you make me come up here?"

Jones looked at Alysa with a blank face, and she laughed again, wrapping a small towel around her midsection as she stood up from the bed. She was gone then, that quickly, but Jones could still smell her, dark and rich and warm. And bitter. For the brief moment that the door was open he could hear children yelling at the top of the stairs. They were the women's babies, and were left to play on the landing in the evenings, running up and down the long, narrow hall and asking for candy from the men who passed through. Jones had given a root beer barrel to the youngest of the boys he'd seen. An old woman who sat, unmoving, at the top of the stairs had fixed him with a searing gaze as he'd passed. He just shrugged his shoulders and followed Alysa into the room.

With the girl gone, the pistol pressed deeper into his neck.

"*Fuck* you," the pimp spat. "You come to take a whore but don't pay?"

Suddenly, amazingly—stupidly—Jones got it.

"What is that? What is that?" The pimp was almost screaming now. "What's wrong wit you? You a man to take my whore but now not pay? You not a *man*. The man, he pays for what he take. Why you not pay me?"

Jones weakly shrugged his shoulders, not able to make his brain come up with a way to explain this—this *misunderstanding*—to the pimp.

"You don't pay, and you don't talk. You was the man wit the walk and the talk in my door, but you no man now. Can't talk. Scared so you might shit on yourself, standin' naked. Where is the prick you used on my whore? Where? Tryin' to crawl inside you, you so scared. A man who don't pay for what he take, he got no right to a prick, you hear? Fuck *you*, America."

From deep inside his stoned and confused brain, finally, *finally*, there was something for Jones to grab on to . . .

He whispered, "Not . . ."

"What?" The pimp's lips were directly against Jones's ear now.

"Not, not American," he fumbled.

That was standing order number one, the one to remember: no mention of USA, no sign of weapons, no uniforms, leave your D.D. card on the boat, and if asked, claim Canadian.

"Canadian!" Jones yelled. "I'mCanadianyousonofabitchandIdidn'tpay herbecauseIdidn'tfuckingknowIdidn'tknow*youfuck*Ithoughtshewasjustagirl!"

The pimp swung up with the barrel of the pistol and smacked it into the side of Jones's head, just above the ear, the young soldier's head snapping to the left. A warm rush of blood flowed down his neck.

"I don't give a fuck! You ALL American, you think I care? Think? White no-prick not payin' for my whore, you fucking America!"

A wash of red swam before Jones's eyes, floating red ribbon, then black, then red again, swaying on his feet.

"I—I paid for the room—"

"You pay shit!"

"I paid!" Now the black ribbon was back, but Jones had discovered it felt better to yell, it kept the colors down from his eyes. "I paid you for the room and the girl was right there and I handed you the money right out of my fucking wallet fifty shillings for Christ's sake like last time I put it right in your hand you said fifty shillings for the room!"

Jones whipped his head around and came eye to eye with the pimp, looking into that black face and the black eyes and that breath and the scar that ran across his forehead like a crease, pulsing now, slow and steady but almost audible.

"You. Pay. Shit." The pimp whispering now, then rising back in pitch. "You pay the fifty shilling for the room. You pay for the room in tis building, tis building, my cousin Benny tis building and tis room. But the whore, she mine, and you don't pay shit for her, America."

Now it wasn't red or black, but both, a swimming band of radiant dark cutting across Jones's eyesight, the barrel of the pistol two inches from his nose.

"I did this last night, I paid for the room, I didn't give extra."

"Last night she took what you didn't give out of your wallet when you was drunk. She took what you had, what you owed, America. Tonight you drunk again and say you pay no more and she tell me you ain't got no wallet no more."

My wallet? Jones thought, crazily, the red crashing down now. *Where's my fucking wallet?*

The pimp whipped the pistol up, pushing it straight into Jones's forehead, while his left hand came down and grabbed Jones's balls, pulling straight down and squeezing. The black went gray, and all Jones remembered was falling into the pimp, who cursed in disgust, then hitting the floor. He managed two thoughts on his short trip: *Isn't today Thanksgiving?* and *Where's my fucking wallet?*

7

Trevor was leaning against the workbench in the garage, oiling one of the muskets. The old man, Trevor had explained, used to do reenactments and had gotten into black powder as a teenager. He hadn't hunted with anything else since, and expected the same from his boys. It was cold in the garage, and they both had on their parkas.

Laid out on the bench was a whole collection of guns; rifles and muskets and God knew what else—Jones didn't know anything but an M16 and a fifty-cal machine gun. Shining in the middle of the collection was a nondescript pistol, cleaned up, but this one quite recognizable to Jones— he'd used it before, in a village called Jiliri. It was the pistol that had once belonged to a two-bit pimp in Mombasa, a pimp that thought he had died and gone to heaven when a U.S. Army watercraft company had shown up in port in November of 1992 to prepare to move into Somalia—a nation that at the time no one west of Kenya let alone New York had ever heard of—a pimp that dressed his girls in respectable clothes and taught them how to pick wallets, a pimp that had lost his gun to two drunken, crazed American soldiers.

After Jones came-to that Thanksgiving night, now well into the early hours of the next day, he had found his clothes (*oh, thank you God for not letting him think to take my fucking pants*) and stumbled back to the Florida Club next door. He found Trevor and Bob where he had left them, on the second floor balcony, barely holding themselves up against the railing, a sea of empty cans, bottles, and plastic cups at their feet. Trevor was just about sleeping upright, Bob had his arm around a girl that Trevor recognized as a friend of Alysa's. The previous night, as he was leaving the club with Alysa, Jones had yelled to Bob over the noise, holding the girl, "Dude! Next door! They say there's a hotel next door!" Bob was convinced they were whores though, no matter how much Jones and the girls protested, and said he didn't mind conversation but he'd stay in the club. He was married, for Christ's sake—even if his wife didn't remember, Bob remembered. Now, Jones stumbled out onto the balcony, blood dripping from the side of his head where the pistol had whacked him, and fell against Bob, bouncing off him and into Trevor, who woke with a yell.

"Fucking-A! You're bleeding!"

Trevor had watched uncomfortably as Jones and Liz had blown up at each other a few days ago at the port; he'd held his tongue when Jones had started drunkenly flirting with the girls in the bar the next night.

Jones, dazed, let his eyes follow his head to the street below, and saw his pimp standing on the corner, talking to a man that could have been his twin (*Cousin Benny?* Jones thought). "That's him! That's the fuck right there—"

Trevor and Bob followed his hand, then Trevor looked back at Jones's bleeding head. Then, they were gone. Jones slipped to the floor of the balcony and fell asleep. When he woke (*getting a lot of little naps tonight, I am*) he was being hauled up from the floor by Trevor's left hand. The right hand held the pistol, formerly the property of the pimp. Trevor's K-Bar (he called it his *forget-about-it* knife), which had been strapped under his khakis to his left leg all night, was now stuck down into his belt.

"I can't seem to get it together tonight, Alphabet," Jones had moaned quietly. "You know, I'm usually quite a social guy."

Jones blinked.

The garage. The cold. Thanksgiving.

Hunting.

Jones stepped to the workbench and picked up what he thought was a Bowie knife, hefting it absentmindedly.

"Tell me again," he said, smiling, "where the fun will come in? We lay down on the ground, in the cold, with muskets, and wait for Bambi to run by, and when he does, we shoot him. He dies. If he doesn't run by, we just lay there getting colder."

Trevor slipped the trigger mechanism back into place, then flipped Jones the bird. "Yeah, something pretty much like that." He reached over for his mug of coffee, sipped, then grimaced. After only fifteen minutes in the garage the coffee had gone ice cold. He put the cup down, picking up the musket again, keeping his eyes on his hands.

"Liz called while you were in the shower," he said without looking up.

"You're just telling me now?"

Trevor raised his eyebrows. "I didn't know if that was good or bad."

Jones stayed quiet for a moment, then said, "It's good. Very good. She gonna call back?"

"She left a number."

"I'll call her tomorrow. She's taking leave at Christmas. We're—uh—gonna hook up in Ohio."

"It's good to have a girl."

Jones laughed softly. "Is that what she is—my girl?"

Trevor looked at him now—as straight and serious as Jones had ever seen him.

"You're a stupid motherfucker, Jones. You know that?"

"Yes. Yes, I do."

Trevor nodded his head.

"Don't fight it, Jonesy. It's a good thing."

"I'm done fighting." He looked down, and then he smiled. "And, yes, it is a good thing. A very good thing. And I most definitely am done fighting."

Trevor looked back down to his gun. "Wish I could say the same." It wasn't clear if he meant his reenlistment, or something else.

Jones wanted to ask him then—ask him how it was with him, how he was doing, what he was going to do. *How is it with you?* The moment was there, but he couldn't find the words. So he said nothing.

Moment gone.

Trevor laughed then, out of nowhere, loud and shaking his head.

"Jonesy, you're gonna get me a girl tonight, right?" Trevor put the gun down. "Right?" He fluttered his eyelashes.

This was their old game.

"This is *your* town, Alphabet. I don't know the girls, they're *your* friends."

"Yeah, I know . . ." Trevor sighed, mocking himself. Then he laughed, "I couldn't even get a *hooker* in Kenya!"

Jones laughed so hard he slipped the tip of the knife against his hand, drawing a small bead of blood.

"First, you weren't trying. Second, you got a free pistol out of the deal." He squeezed his palm, drawing another bead of red to the surface. "Tell me, honestly, you wouldn't rather have a new pistol than a new girlfriend."

Trevor smiled and looked down on his collection. "You know," he said, and winked, "you're absofuckinglutely right. Let's go get drunk and eat turkey."

8

The turkey was dry, but who was Jones to complain? Mrs. Alphabet was in all her glory, twenty or so relatives piled into the little Michigan ranch house, putting down Stove Top and Budweiser and Mrs. Smith's. Trevor had been home twice before, briefly, since Somalia, so thankfully there were no questions on that subject. When this leave was up Trevor was going back to Virginia only long enough to pack his bags; sergeants were in short supply these days and his new corporal stripes came with orders for drill sergeant training. He would be returning to Ft. Knox for the nine-week school. His Uncle Ralph, a gnarled and wiry farmer, planted the whole day in the La-Z-Boy next to the TV, was a Korea vet, and had no shortage of ribbing to give his nephew about his odds of passing the rigorous drill physical with the extra meat the young man was carrying. Jones knew Alphabet would pass, though. It was, however, amusing to consider his former fellow tormentee as a yelling, screaming tormentor in the very place they had met. Mostly, though, as the day passed, Jones contented himself with sitting on the couch, stuffed, listening to the Alphabet cousins rage on about football.

After everyone went home, Trevor and Jones, with the younger Alphabet brother in tow, went to the bar (planted square in the middle of a cornfield, just like Trevor had promised) and spent the night playing pool with Trevor's high-school friends. Even two hours from Detroit, most of these fellows worked in one way or another for GM. Most of their dads and uncles had been farmers, but there wasn't much of that left anymore.

They bunked together in Trevor's room that night, asleep by 1 A.M. since—like the majority of the county—they'd be getting up before dawn for the hunting. Trevor was almost three years younger than Jones, had joined the army right out of high school, and the walls of his bedroom—the paper a motif of Civil War cannons and eagles entwined in banners—were still papered with posters of Kathy Ireland and Cindy Crawford. Arranged on top of the dresser so precisely that Jones was sure Mrs. Alphabet must have done it were Trevor's graduation certificate from basic training at Ft. Knox, his army watercraft operator's license, and a framed glossy of Trevor and Jones dressed in desert BDUs taken in Kismaayo, all facing slightly in to a green plastic folder that, without looking, Jones knew to be the certificate made out to PFC Trevor M. Anuscewitz that had accompanied his Bronze Star given for action near Jiliri, Somalia.

They had lived together a long time, so Jones was used to Trevor's snoring, and he fell asleep easily, the soft fabric of the sleeping bag pushed up against his face, the pad underneath a million times more comfortable than the torture devices issued by the army.

He woke with a start, the red digital clock on the night table above his head reading 4 A.M. *(zero-four-fucking-hundred, Privates! Get the fuck UP!).* Straining his neck sideways and peering through the dark he saw Trevor, in just his boxers, his wrestler's frame silhouetted in the moonlight through the window, crouched on his bed, eyes wide open but blank, teardrops popping out of the corners of his eyes. He had yelled, or Jones thought so anyway. Jones raised his whole upper body up and was about to say something to him when Trevor dropped his jaw and yelled again, not a holler, really, but a low and loud groan, followed by an unmistakable and helpless-sounding "Oh, fuck." He stayed there a minute, not moving, eyes fixed on something, then sighed, his body shaking. He dropped on his shoulder and—so quickly Jones thought maybe he had imagined the whole thing—he was snoring peacefully again.

When the alarm went off an hour later *(zero-five-hundred! are you pussies still in BED?!)* Jones hushed it quickly, left Trevor to his snoring, and crept through the house to the living room, pulled back the curtains on the front window, and stared blankly at the dark lawn for ten minutes. He heard the coffeepot timer click on in the kitchen, then went back to wake Alphabet.

9

Jones placed his right palm flat on the ground, preparing to push himself up, when two explosions made him drop his arm and face back into the dirt so hard he could taste the frozen Michigan soil on the tip of his tongue.

It was so quick, but it didn't seem like it, really. It played like a slow movie:

To his right, the first explosion wasn't really an explosion at all, but the natural blast of cracking bush limbs and foliage as a deer that had been lying almost right next to him—hidden in a stand of something brown, frozen, thorny, and dead—burst out and crossed the small expanse of clearing in two bounds, then slammed through the wall of brush that started the treeline. Without thinking, Jones's hand moved against the will of his brain—which had secretly decided yesterday he wouldn't actually shoot anything—and he slipped his finger across the trigger, bringing the barrel up and the sight of the musket to his right eye in one clean swoop, the tail of the deer falling neatly into place in the steel groove. As his finger started to pull, the second explosion came, and this one was real.

As Jones's right eye caught the deer in the sights, his left eye—in the process of closing to improve his aim—caught the unmistakable flash of a rifle blast, blowing out of a stand of trees, and even before he heard the *whump* of the black powder shot he saw through his rifle sight what he thought was a most amazing thing: the deer, which had most definitely been moving forward, was suddenly and without breaking stride (or turning in that direction) moving sideways. It was like a hurricane-force wind had happened from nowhere, blowing all of its power directly into the side of the running deer, shoving it to the right as easily as you would push an unaware pedestrian off a curb. It was too late to stop his trigger finger from pulling, but he decided in a split second that he was a bad shot and didn't trust his brain to tell him where Trevor should logically be in the treeline. As his finger pulled the final weight on the trigger, he jerked his left arm up, and as the musket thundered a deep and deafening pulse into his body, the stock slamming painfully into his right shoulder, the barrel of the gun shot the ball not toward the treeline, but up into the air, clearing anything that could have possibly been in its way.

Two seconds to settle, although again it seemed like two years. He dropped the musket straight out of his hands, and pushed himself up. He couldn't see the deer, or Trevor. The woods were silent.

He gathered himself to push the rest of the way up when, from directly in front of him, came another shot, blasting from the treeline to this left, shooting straight across his vision to the right where the deer had been.

It's like Kismaayo, he thought, remembering the tracer play back and forth across the city they had watched on so many nights. And then, on the heels of that, a third shot, and a quick glimpse of Trevor moving furiously across the treeline toward where the deer should be; he saw only a flash of his clothes, his face, then he was gone again, the twilight reducing vision in the brush to next to nothing.

He yelled out, his musket shot still ringing in his ears, "Trev! Got it? Got it?"

The bushes shook, directly in front of him now.

"Where's the deer!" he yelled. "Where are you?"

The "you" was just leaving his lips when a gun blasted again and, still inside the space of that sound, within its roar, Jones felt a spray of something hit his back, felt through the ground the hollow smack of an impact, and he knew the tree directly behind him had been hit by a shot.

He threw his entire body to the ground, eating dirt for the second time in less than a minute, his face connecting with a slap against the earth, his bladder letting go without notice—or him noticing it.

"*ALPHABET!*" he screamed, the slow movie over, this all now playing out so quickly, his right hand unthinkingly wrapping around the stock of his musket and pulling it toward his prone body. He yelled, "*Down range!! I'm right fucking here . . . you see me?!?*"

He looked straight ahead, back to the treeline, in time to see/hear yet another shot, except this one's blast went across again, straight to where the deer should be in the bushes. Jones's mind, wandering helplessly, thinking: *I'm going deaf . . . they didn't sound loud enough.* Immediately followed by: *What is he using? It's too quick for him to reload a musket . . .*

He pushed himself back up again, raising his head just enough to get a better view of the treeline in what was now an almost completely dark purple light. He couldn't see either Trevor or the deer. A moment passed, then another. No noise, not even a rustling of the bushes. Then, small and tiny, maybe he didn't even really hear it, the sound of metal on metal.

"Dude?" he called out, although it sounded like a whisper to him.

He strained his neck farther, and was rewarded with four blasts in quick succession, coming now from just behind where the deer had breached the treeline—*pop pop pop pop.* It wasn't his ears deceiving him; these shots were quieter than a musket, and came much too fast for a gun you had to reload each time. He ducked fast, but not completely; it was quickly clear that the shots, whatever they were from, weren't aimed in his direction this time. *He's got another gun . . . ?*

The pimp's pistol.

Silence again, then a moan, impossible to tell if it was Trevor or a noise from the deer. *Or me,* he thought.

Jones flexed all of his muscles, he'd been lying here prone for hours now, then stretched himself out and began to low-crawl out of the ditch.

The last time he had ever really low-crawled was at Ft. Knox, crossing a muddy field—*one with the dirt!*—to take out 3rd Platoon for the glory of Drill Sergeant Rose. His thought now was to crawl through the grass into the trees. He pulled himself up over the lip of the ditch, then stopped. He listened again. Nothing.

"Fuck this," he said softly. If Trevor meant to shoot him, there wasn't much he could do about it—his friend was a much better shot, and a much better woodsman. He didn't think he *was* trying to shoot him, but not much seemed clear right now. On quick reflection, not much had seemed clear for a long time.

"Fuck," he mumbled again. "Okay, buddy," he whispered under his breath, "I'm coming for you."

There is a time to crawl, a time to eat mud, and then there is a time to stand up and walk. Jones stood, slowly, bringing himself up to his full height, the musket hanging loose from his right hand. He stepped out of the ditch, stood there silently for almost a full minute, then started walking slowly toward the treeline.

10

What did Rose always say? What was even more important than being one with the dirt?

Drill-sergeant campaign hat pulled low over his eyes, storming with index finger out and pointing down the barracks bay toward some unlucky private: "He who *sleeps*—dies!"

Maybe.

Sometimes, he who sleeps just dreams.

One night in Somalia, on the Mike Boat LCM-8593, near a tiny village called Jiliri, Trevor fell asleep by accident, and then Jones followed on purpose. Jones didn't die, he dreamed. And this is what he dreamed:

He is standing in Alysa's room, under the swaying lightbulb, face-to-face with the pimp. The black, scar-drawn face looking at him, vein pulsing, smell of mango and coffee, the pimp's pistol pushed up against his chin. The pimp opens his mouth, yellow teeth, cracked and rotting, and says, "Look at my girl,

*America. Look at her. Look at what you fucked and won't pay for. She's soooooo
beautiful, my girl!" Jones doesn't want to look, doesn't want to at all, but the
pimp will shoot him if he doesn't, he knows that. He turns toward the bed,
moaning to himself at what he knows he will see—he sees it every night. It
won't be Alysa on the bed, but a Belgian soldier. He doesn't know how he knows
it's a Belgian soldier, because the man is naked, no uniform, but he knows—
he just knows. The pimp whispers in his ear from behind him, but his voice is
now that of the Alabama corporal, who said his name was Dale: "I told this
fuck to give you your wallet back, I knew you were missing it. But he wouldn't
budge. Finally I said 'Look, ya better give up the wallet or I'll blow a round in
your ass so it takes off your jimmy when it comes out the other side . . .' " He
shakes, but it's not enough, not enough to wake him up, not yet, and he's stuck.
"But what the hell," the corporal/pimp continues, "I'm back here now, might
as well just blow off YOUR jimmy!" With that the Belgian soldier stands up.
Of course he does. He's got the wallet, and he's holding it out. But he wants to
show something first, something on his back. The soldier turns around, and he's
got a snake tattooed on his back, but you can't see the head of the snake because
it's covered in blood. "Yeah, I think I'm just gonna go ahead and shoot your
jimmy off now . . ."*

    BOOM!

*The Belgian soldier looks back, curious. This isn't how this plays out . . .
The shot doesn't come until . . .*

    BOOM!

Trevor's voice: "Oh you FUCK!"

    Jones, instantly awake in the Mike Boat's wheelhouse, pistol drawn
from his cargo pocket without thinking, yells above his deafness: *"What
am I shooting at?!?"*

    "THAT!" Trevor screams, and they both shoot at once, shoot *as* one,
two hammers slamming down on two guns, two bullets exploding from
their barrels, two screaming straight shots from the unbearable noise, two
slugs that pass in a fraction of a second over the lip of the window, knocking back the face with a wallop.

The face is gone. Trevor is up, steps on Jones, the rifle stock slamming into his ribs, and is gone through the hatch. Jones follows on his hands and knees, hearing (*quick, so quick, oh too fucking quick*) Trevor's M16 shooting on auto, it has to be a full clip, a full clip of ammo being unloaded, and as Jones crawls around the side of the wheelhouse onto the deck he sees him, Trevor standing behind the stanchion line, shooting straight down into a little wooden boat, blasting it apart, one solid scream coming from his throat, smoke pouring from the barrel of the M16, a boat that small it might as well have been hit with a bomb—but there's no one in it.

And that quick, that sudden, like a vacuum of sound, it is silent.

Jones jumps up (*jesus there's no noise or maybe I'm just deaf now maybe that's it*) pistol back in front of him (*don't lock your arms remember what they said don't fucking lock your arms or you won't shoot straight*) and in one step passes Trevor on the port quarter and whips around the front of the wheelhouse, aiming straight down into the welldeck.

"Oh, God no."

Trevor is beside him now, and there is a clunk as he drops the M16, just lets it slide from his fingers.

"Oh no, God no, oh Jonesy . . ."

The water laps the steel hull of the Mike Boat, rocking it ever so slightly. Off the port quarter the wooden sailboat slips easily under the surface, for a moment just the mast still sticking out, then gone completely.

Lying faceup at the foot of the stairs in the welldeck, spread-eagle like a bad gangster movie, the body is splayed out. There is no face; no head to speak of, really. But unmistakably, no question, they are looking down at the body of what has to be a boy. A boy. No more than nine, maybe ten, it's so hard to tell because they're all so small but look there's Bine Sessah himself, hair greased and grinning on the dirty T-shirt, Stray Cats North American Tour, oh sweet Jesus, sweet Jesus and sweet Mary and sweet Bine Sessah please we didn't just kill a little boy . . .

12

Twice while Jones crossed the clearing toward the treeline shots rang out. Both times he winced, but he didn't stop. He entered the brush about where the deer had, pushing back branches from his face, tripping once in the dark on a root.

He pushed back a branch big enough that he couldn't see through it, and as he moved forward he was in a clearing. And here was Trevor, and Trevor had the pimp's pistol in his hand, and Trevor had his arm out straight *(but not locked, don't lock your arm)*, and Trevor was pointing the gun at Jones. He let the branch swing back behind him, and stopped walking.

"Jones," Trevor said, "you've pissed yourself."

Jones felt down with his left hand, the wet spot already cold on the camo overalls.

"Yes," Jones said. "Yes, I think I did."

"Okay then," said Trevor, calmly. "Glad we got that cleared up."

They stood there. A moment passed.

"Alphabet," Jones said finally, "I would really appreciate it if you wouldn't point that pistol at me." He waited a moment, then added, "Shoot me if you must, but pick another weapon." He hoped this had sounded steadier than the words had felt leaving his mouth.

"Oh, this?" Trevor looked at the pistol. Then he turned up his arm and raised the barrel to his temple. "I'm sorry, you walked in on the part where I shoot myse—"

"Trevor!" Jones yelled, cutting him off, his feet moving forward without his permission, but the gun had already dropped, hanging limply from Trevor's fingers, at his side.

"Oh, fucking stop, Jonesy," he said—a sad, sad, horrible smile on his face. "As you said, if I was going to take myself out, I'd pick a more honorable weapon."

Jones let his fingers go loose, and the musket he'd been carrying dropped to the frozen ground. As if in answer, Trevor dropped the pistol. He looked down at something, something at his feet, and through the dark Jones saw a mound of flesh and fur.

"What a goddamn waste," Trevor said, shaking his head. "Never be able to eat from that. Too much lead."

The deer was unrecognizable. Trevor had emptied the pistol into its flank and head, reloaded, and done it again.

Jones looked at Trevor, but he was still staring at the remains of the deer.

"Jonesy," he said finally, "I fear that hunting might be losing its attraction for me."

Jones choked back a tightening in his throat. He started to say, "Trevor—" but stopped when he realized no sound was coming from his mouth. He bit his lip and waited.

Trevor looked back up, took a step toward Jones, then stopped.

"I never thanked you, y'know."

"For what?"

"For lying for me."

Jones shook his head. "Sid did most of that, I just followed his lead. And it wasn't just you, it was both of us."

"Ah, say what you will. I know how it went down after, and I know how you operate, Jones. I have a pretty good goddamn idea of what went down."

Jones was silent a minute, then said simply, "Maybe."

After the questions, after the paperwork, the killing of a small, unarmed, curious Somali boy in the Jiliri region had been registered as a "nonrelevant local contact" in the log of the Kismaayo command center.

Jones reached in his pocket for his cigarettes and, lighting one with shaky fingers, said, "Well—and I'm not just saying this now, I've been thinking about it . . ." He puffed his smoke to life.

"Yes?"

Even in the dark Jones thought he could see those huge Polish eyebrows raise straight up.

Jones did want to say something, he'd wanted to say it for a while. It sometimes kept him up at night, especially through those long months of August and September, sitting alone or with Lou, not saying a word for days at a time, drinking beer, watching TV with no reaction in October as a CNN reporter talked about the deaths of eighteen American soldiers in Mogadishu. He thought that now must be the time he'd been waiting for, and he prepared the words, felt them, moved them around in his head, but they wouldn't come. They still wouldn't come.

What he'd said in his head, what he wanted to say now, was: *Thank you. Thank you, Trevor Alphabet. Thank you for saving my life. Thank you for making sure I didn't die in the wheelhouse of a boat in Somalia . . . No, wait, don't say anything, I know what you're going to say. You're going to say:*

"I didn't save your life, Jonesy. I shot a boy, a little boy, we shot him together, blew his head off—but you only shot because I did, and it was a little boy we killed, a little boy who was SO curious, couldn't contain himself. A little boy who knew nothing about men lined up against a wall in Kismaayo and shot first in the belly and then the head, who knew nothing about the ways of Belgian snipers or Green Berets, who knew nothing about nervous, nothing about scared. Nothing about two privates who went through boot camp together, learned to suffer together, practiced on the fields at night their bayonet drills yelling 'Kill! Kill!' with each thrust. He was a little boy and when Americans came around in the daylight they were so tall and different but so friendly and happy and joking with each other and snapping pictures with their plastic cameras, and sometimes you could do tricks for them—handstands, cartwheels—and they might reach into their big pockets and pull out candy bars or root beer barrels and laugh as they threw them at you. Americans, so friendly in the daylight, and their boat sitting RIGHT THERE within eyesight of his uncle's little hut in the village, so friendly and happy these big American men in the daylight—why would they be any different at night? This is who I shot, Jones, this boy . . ."

You'll say that, Trevor, I know, but it's not real, it's not real, just like nothing over there was real. It's all Octopussy Garden. What was real was what COULD have been, just as real as anything, just as real as a pistol in my neck, just as real as blood on my hands, my chest, my face, just as real as watching your own blood flow from a tube in your arm into a bag, a plastic bag, because someone else didn't have enough yet, someone was going to die with my blood in their veins. THAT'S what is real, Trevor, and in that reality you woke up in time, saw the danger, and acted, because you're a strong motherfucker, I've always thought so, you're a strong motherfucker—and in acting so quickly, so assuredly, you made sure I wasn't shot in my sleep, slumped in the corner of a wheelhouse in a boat in Africa, my blood leaking from a hole in my chest, left to become a minor skirmish in Somalia on CNN, and thank you my friend, oh thank you . . .

Instead, what came out of Jones's mouth was:

"Thanks for taking me hunting, Trevor."

Jones smiled, and killed his cigarette under his boot. "Who knew we could have so much fun?"

Trevor smiled back at him—small but real. He opened his mouth, but closed it back up again without saying a word. He bent to pick up the pimp's pistol from the frozen ground. Before his hand touched it, though, he changed his mind, stood up straight, and looked at Jones.

"I'm cold, man," he finally said. "It's really fucking cold out here. I never realized it before, took an idiot from New Jersey to point it out to me, but it's really fucking cold up here in the winter. I've been outside, lying on the ground, all day, in November, and I'm just really, really cold. And I'm starting to think there's no need for that."

He wiped his open palm across his face, looked back down at the pistol, then put both his hands in his pockets.

"I'm cold, Jonesy. Wanna go inside?"

Jones nodded and bent down to pick up the musket, but found Trevor's arm holding his wrist.

"Jones, just leave that there."

"All right," Jones whispered. "Yes, all right."

AFTER

JONES: One Soldier

Yorktown, Virginia—1995

1

Don't mind me, I'm a soldier.
But no one knows what that means anymore.
Not even me.

2

Trevor, the strongest motherfucker I have ever known, briefly returned to Ft. Knox—the place where we had met—right after New Year's.

Following the orders in his hand, he reported for nine weeks of instruction at the drill section of the Ft. Knox NCO Academy.

The irony was not lost on me, or him, but so buried was I in who I was now, and what my life was like, that I didn't dwell on it very long. I was in Ohio when he went, Liz and I staying for two weeks in a spare bedroom at the house of one of her high-school friends. When her leave ended in mid-January we were going back to Virginia together. And after that? Who knows. Liz would be in front of the sergeant's promotion board by February. And I figured I could always find work—the commercial fishermen and tug captains in Yorktown and Hampton Roads aren't set against ex-military like they are in Washington. I could do the work, and I have no problem being uncomfortable for long periods of time.

Liz—she was, and is, a soldier. As it turns out, the last of us. As it turns out, maybe the best of us.

Trevor Alphabet Anuscewitz got selected for drill duty because, like most drill candidates, he was squared away in what he did, in his own little field of soldiering. He also had the right tickets punched: education, good physical fitness, and a tour in Somalia. Nothing spectacular, mostly boring—even with a Bronze Star, according to his official record Trevor had never pulled a trigger in Somalia—but the army doesn't look for spectacular: it looks for stable. I don't know if Trevor felt stable, but you can't see that on a piece of paper.

He told me later that, of course—because how could you not—his first weekend back at Ft. Knox he walked the places we had walked before: the barracks area of Delta Company 2/46, the ranges, the small stand of woods where we held field exercises.

And he said he felt . . . not much, really.

A lot had happened since then.

Mostly, he said—and he was drunk when he said it, not a bitter drunk, but a relieved drunk—he was feeling ambivalent about his new job. My words not his, but I know that's it.

He had reenlisted on a whim two days before his window closed and he would have been a free man, like me. At the last minute they'd offered him hard stripes to sweeten the deal, and he took them.

Two days later, the army fucked him with drill-duty orders.

The last step in the drill school is spending a few weeks with a real basic-training platoon, acting as a drill sergeant, having the real ones grade you and evaluate you. On his first day of this last part of the school—which had begun with him waking recruits by banging on a steel garbage can at 0400—he tripped while on the platoon run, fell wrong, and heard a pop as his knee went.

End of drill status, and the army.

He told me when the ambulance carried him away to the TMC he felt no pain, just a surprising and overwhelming relief: it was done. And it was okay.

The only pleasant thing about his experience at Ft. Knox the second time was the identity of one of his instructors: Staff Sergeant Johnson—a buck sergeant when we met him, fan of Freddie Mercury; a drill sergeant of 2nd Platoon, Delta Company, under SFC Rose. Now Johnson was an instructor at the NCO Academy.

Trevor said Johnson had no idea who he was, had no memory of him as a recruit at all, but was pumped to have one of his former recruits as a student at the drill school. They got along fine, made fast friends, and Trevor spent more than a few evenings at Johnson's post apartment, drinking beer, watching the snow fall through the window in the December twilight of northern Kentucky.

Johnson had some answers about Rose.

When Trevor told me the story, I was not entirely surprised to learn that Rose had spent only one more month as a drill sergeant after we graduated: he was relieved early. There was no mark against him, nothing ever official, he had really done nothing wrong, but somehow he just didn't fit in with the other drills. Things like attacking other platoons before you were supposed to—before the *plan* called for it—did not ingratiate him with the sergeant major. He was quietly called to the carpet, turned in his campaign hat, and flew back to Ft. Bragg. Where he belonged.

Johnson—being a tanker, not a grunt—had no idea what happened to him after that.

What I was surprised to learn was that our platoon was only the third Rose had taught. I had assumed this man had somehow always been a drill sergeant. That's the impression they try to make, and usually it works.

Turns out, no.

He was senior drill of our platoon not because of experience, but because as an SFC he outranked all the other drills, who were either staff sergeants or buck sergeants—like Johnson, at the time.

This didn't sit well with them, either. But that's how the army works: it all comes down to rank.

I've often wondered—especially as I stood at the sink in Louie's kitchen, a place wide open for big questions—what a graph of Rose's graduates would look like, especially put against an army average. Would there be a difference? If you could look at their military careers over the next three or four years after basic training, and then on from there for some of them, how would it look against the army average?

And what about after? If you could measure honor, or even something as simple as willingness to cooperate, in a man, how would Rose's graduates measure up against their fellow men?

And would it even matter?

A week after I got home from Somalia, that rushed and barely remembered week of outprocessing and paperwork for my discharge, I saw one of Rose's platoon—Todd, one of the six of us who had learned firsthand how to eat mud—kicked out of the army for the crime of being homosexual. He was given a dishonorable discharge, after being humiliated in front of everyone he knew and everything he loved. In the few weeks it took to get him out of uniform they reduced him from specialist back to buck private, removed him from his unit, and had him spending his days picking up litter on the sides of the road. I would drive home to post from the Crystal Inn, usually drunk, and see him on the median leading to the Ft. Eustis gates: not looking at any of the cars, but head high, eyes straight ahead.

And in Somalia, in Mogadishu, another one of Rose's boys—Romig, our former house mouse, now a tubby but tough PFC—died in front of his squad's eyes. I heard he tripped running to the chow tent and fell in front of a deuce-and-a-half rolling at ten or so miles an hour; slow, but not enough room to stop. From where I stand, he didn't die honorably or dishonorably—he just died.

And what about me? What do I know about being a soldier? What do I know about honor? What does Trevor know? What do any of us know, really?

I engaged the enemy by taking the life of a little boy. When the enemy engaged me I allowed my comrade to fall while I cried over a dead woman.

I know everyone needs to sleep, and that he who sleeps doesn't always die—sometimes they dream. That can be good or bad, but who cares? These days I often have trouble falling asleep, but once I get there, once my mind loosens and falls into the slipstream of slumber, I sleep without dreaming, and when I wake it is gradual, the awakening of someone who has simply had enough sleep.

I know I am not the best, and I am not the worst.

But I also know I can eat mud, and not many can—our numbers are few. No one may know what being a soldier means anymore, but I have a pretty good idea of what it takes.

I know how to immerse myself in misery, if that's what is required to get the job done.

Is there honor in that?

And does it matter?

AUTHOR'S NOTE

Although some items mentioned herein are based on reality—including names of some military units, some larger cities, etc.—it should be pointed out that dates and times (among other things) have been made to suit the needs of the story. Jiliri and Huley are fictional towns, and this novel is a work of fiction.

Kismaayo (also spelled Chismayo) is a very real place, and there was a time when those caught sneaking across the marsh flats toward the port faced the possibility of a sniper's rifle aimed at their groin. Mogadishu is also a very real place. Those who had served there in late 1992 and early 1993 were sickened but not completely surprised when eighteen members of Task Force Ranger were killed during the Battle of Mogadishu in October; the Marines and U.S. Army grunts who had been navigating those tight and winding streets for almost a year had warned not to underestimate the hidden, sharp teeth of Somalia.

For the record, the Octopussy Garden is also quite real, but no one has been able to pin down its exact location; they say you'll know it when you get there.

For her wisdom, wit, and patience, I am indebted to Diana Finch, and to the efforts of all at the Ellen Levine Literary Agency. Many thanks to Matthew Walker, my talented and fearless editor at Simon & Schuster. And thank you to Trish Todd, Tory Klose, Larry and Gimone Hall, Nick DiGiovanni, Otto Bost, Hope Wesley Harrison, and Gregg Cagno.

—C.B.

SOLEBURY, PENNSYLVANIA

THE ICE BENEATH YOU

DISCUSSION POINTS

1. Benjamin Jones joins the U.S. Army at the end of the Gulf War. What was the motivation for this action? One life-altering event or a series of decisions? How does his original motivation match or contrast with his actual experiences as a soldier?

2. Jones briefly discusses what it is to be a soldier in a time of peace, in a generation that has never seen war up close. How do members of Jones's generation view war differently than members of the Vietnam generation? Compare the similarities between the return to the United States of soldiers who served in Vietnam and those in Somalia. Do you think the soldiers who served in Somalia would feel more of a kinship with Vietnam vets than with Gulf War vets?

3. Jones and Trevor Alphabet share a deep bond. What experiences strengthen that bond? Which threaten to tear it apart? At one point, Bauman explains that the soldiers tended to travel in packs of two. Discuss this with regard to Jones's and Trevor's relationship to the buck sergeants, Bob and Sid.

4. The narrative splices together Jones's pre- and post-army life in the United States and his life as a soldier overseas. How does this technique change your sense of the story's development? How would a straight chronological telling have shaped the book's themes differently?

5. Discuss the novel's central incident onboard the Mike Boat in Jiliri. How did it change the relationship between Trevor and Jones? How does Bauman portray the military's official treatment of the incident? Did you find the troops' reaction to be reasonable or ethical? Are such horrific accidents a necessary by-product of war, and if so, are they understandable under any circumstances?

6. It is rare that Jones and his fellow troops are directly engaged in fighting. How does this change the character of violence in the few scenes where violence does erupt? Do you think the characters would have reacted differently if direct combat was more prevalent? If so, how?

7. What does Jones see in Drill Sergeant Rose—a demon, a savior, or both? How do Jones's ideas about him change? What do these changes say about Jones's development as a character? Compare Rose's place in Jones's mind as a perfect soldier to the real-world realities of the confused, scared Lieutenant Klover, or the spit-shined, incompetent Sergeant Cowens. Do you think Jones starts equating his friend Trevor with Rose as a security measure? Is this trust dangerous?

8. In their own ways, Jones and Trevor are both disciplined, committed soldiers, who live to "outsoldier anything that moves." Why, then, on one specific night, did they break their own code and allow themselves to fall asleep? Was this true dereliction of duty, or simply sheer exhaustion combined with false comfort? Does it matter? How do they view their own failings?

9. Is Jones's degrading experience in San Francisco important? Is it coincidence and largely a product of time, place, and economics, or is it a self-imposed punishment? What does he mean when he says "I have a need to be uncomfortable for a long period of time"?

10. In George's house in Huley, Washington, Jones plans a confrontation that never happens. Did he want to use the gun simply to perform his "rescue," or did he truly want to injure or kill the two men? Compare this to Jones's second major break with his soldiers' code, when he abandoned Sergeant Cowens to pull a Somali woman to safety.

11. What obstacles does Jones face in his love for Liz? His own personality? The fact that they both serve in the military? Does she play a role in his decision to stay overseas a few extra days, rather than going home? If they had met in civilian life, do you think the same spark would have existed between them?

12. The U.S. media's coverage of the military comes into play several times through the course of the book. How does the media's coverage of the deployment affect the characters? Why? As the situation gets more dangerous, the soldiers feel that "no one knows we're here." Do they blame the media for this? How does the nature of "peacekeeping," as opposed to traditional forms of warfare, play a role in the story's development?

13. Which scene most powerfully reinforced your preconceptions about military life? Which scene most effectively challenged those preconceptions? Why?

14. Compare and contrast this book—its story, characters, and lessons—to previous novels about war. How does it differ from the ironic, dark humor of *Catch-22*, or the brutally antiwar sentiments of *All Quiet on the Western Front*? How is it similar? In what ways does Jones stand as a witness to the larger events